C000262022

SASHA KNIGHT

SASHA KNIGHT

SASHA KNIGHT

BY SEAN GODFREY

First published in the United Kingdom by:

OWN IT! Entertainment Ltd

Company Registration Number: 09154978

Cover design: James Nunn

Paperback ISBN: 9781916052376

WWW.OWNIT.LONDON

For the one I lost;
there's so much I wish I could have told you.

Chapter 1

There is a canal that steeps by the back of the yard beyond the fence. There are days when I think she's still there, her bare feet wading through the water, worms boring their way into the crevices of her toes. 'Yuh going to get ringworm,' I'd say. We used to play in that canal, throwing pebbles and empty mackerel tins in. She told me that one time she caught three perch just by interlocking her fingers and sifting through the water. It didn't work for me and she called me stupid and *fuh-fool*.

'Gih mi yuh han', mek mi show yuh,' she said. It's the last time I remember her touching me, the slight tickle when her fingers grazed mine, the roughness of her palms when she positioned the underside of my hands to make the net.

She has been missing an hour. She has been missing a day. She has been missing twenty-four years. I see her now in the lost bits and pieces of a jigsaw puzzle I have been working on for millennia – a dirty fingernail, the edge of her left yellow hair ribbon, the heels of her black patent leather pumps. I hold these memories with spread fingers, watching them seep through into ether. I am losing her, not because it has been an hour, or a day, or twenty-four years; I am losing her because I must live.

Today I am standing on the playing field of Horizon Park All Age School and the digger is ready. Black smoke pushes out of the vertical muffler. There is a woman just beyond my rental car. She is old and thin; not frail, though. Her hair is wrapped with a blue and red floral *tie-head*. She shifts her left hand to the wooden cane she's leaning on then raises her right. She may have waved at me or said goodbye; I cannot tell. Or maybe it isn't for me after all. The digger operator slides one of the gear levers. More black smoke. It is time.

Chapter 2

I do not know when it was I became so attached to her; in the beginning we despised each other. No, that's not entirely the case; it was she who despised me first. I was nine years old when she came into my life and she was eleven. That two-year difference is worlds apart when you're that age, isn't it? Eleven means Common Entrance exams and first form in high school and trying to pretend you are fourteen. And nine? Well, you still appreciate the joy of playing marbles and it's okay for us boys to walk down Brunswick Avenue with our arms around each other because we're best friends and football buddies and not that other thing people will kill you for when your voice finally cracks.

She was taller than me, too, that awkward lanky tall when your mummy can't keep up with your growth spurt so your clothes are too big or too short and you better not complain. In those first few weeks I used to stand on tip toes to match her before I realised she didn't care and before I understood that it didn't matter. As it is with children, we never officially met. No handshake to mark the beginning of whatever it was we supposed we were. Not friends, certainly. Not yet.

And I remember the first words I said to her too.

'May I help you with that?'

She was struggling with her grip, bracing it with her right thigh, both hands on deck, knuckles determined.

'Nuh touch mi sup'n,' she said, snatching the grip away from me, her unabashed *patwah* an affront to my middle-class sensibilities. No attempt to be civilised, Mummy would later say.

'I was just trying to help,' I said.

'*I was just trying to help*,' she aped me in that schoolgirl sort of way, head rocking side to side in rhythm with each word, mouth full of air like a balloon. I wanted to shove her, but she already had two wet streaks rolling down her cheeks because of what happened only a minute earlier. But I'm getting ahead of myself. I must start at the beginning and get the whole thing out because I need to make sense of it all.

Before she came I want to say my life was fulfilled. Fulfilled as it could be for a nine-year-old boy. I had my Hergé comics, my plastic soldiers and a dwindling collection of rubber bands I used as payment when I played marbles with my friends. Then June 1979 came and Mummy turned into an entrepreneurial miser after my father left us, large house in St. Jago Heights and all. *Because he needed to be free, Mummy was choking him, holding him back from greatness, only greatness meant being free to explore what lay between the legs of every teenage girl he could find before, during and after the marriage*, so Mummy had to make it on her own. Today we provide any number of explanations, excuses we'd call them back then, for why he left. He'd had to grow up at too young an age, taking care of his three younger siblings so he had no time to be a child; he had to find himself; Mummy wasn't meeting his

4

emotional needs; he needed to see a therapist et cetera, et cetera. Of course I loved him more than my mother.

Mummy used the chunk of money from the divorce as down payment for our new place and we moved to Cheshire Hills which, despite its name, was as flat as roti. And she went to work for the telephone company as an operator. It is the thing I like most about my mother, her voice.

'Jamaica Telecom, how can I help?' She answered each call with the same script. Sometimes during summer holidays she'd take my brother and me to work with her. I'd sit on a small stool with my Enid Blyton and Hardy Boys books in my lap, and every time she answered the phone I could feel the resonance of her voice like the beginning of a full and deep bedtime story. Her upper St. Andrew accent slightly nasal. *I'm not of it*, it said. It spoke of goodness and plenty, an easy life. But all that was no longer. We downsized to three bedrooms and two bathrooms because telephone operator money does not buy you a house in Stony Hill or St. Jago Heights, places with actual hills, neighbourhoods that matched an upper St. Andrew telephone voice.

Cheshire Hills was a perfectly planned suburb of pre-cast concrete, flat-roofed, carbon copy houses all painted white, off-white or beige, thanks to the National Housing Trust. One road led in and out of our neighbourhood, Grover Boulevard, and ours was the first house you'd see on the left. The road flooded every summer when the afternoon rains came and the government ignored all calls to fix it.

Across the street from our house marked the southern border of the neighbourhood and the beginning of an unincorporated sliver of land that a few surrounding communities claimed belonged within their limits. Mr. Long, its owner, avoided paying taxes for years because of this dispute. He was the lone hold-out when the government was on a land grab, paying owners a premium so they eventually gave up. He had several girlfriends and every Saturday morning his wife went on a marathon cursing that started before we left for church, and four hours later when we returned she was still going. I overheard Mummy's best friend Judy say he was called Mr. Long for more than one reason and the two of them sniggered.

It was a large house with his bar-cum-social-hall-cum-nightclub next to it. Every Friday night, just after the start of Sabbath, we could set our watches to his ten-foot-tall speakers facing the street blaring the latest dance hall reggae, soca and Motown tunes. The people from Sydenham came in their weekend best to party all night. Men in platform shoes and bell bottoms and women in hoop earrings, *halter backs* and tight white trousers, danced, ate and drank. The parties spilled into the street, blocking traffic trying to get into Cheshire Hills. Mummy and the entire suburb raised their objections at a neighbourhood meeting at the freemason hall on Old Harbour Road. Mr. Long listened to them present their complaints one by one and when they were all done he said, loud enough for the entire room to hear, children and all, 'All ah unu have a stick up unu batty,' before he walked out. Although Cheshire Hills children did not speak *patwah*, we all knew what *having a stick up your arse* meant. And yes, we giggled despite the pinches our parents laid on us.

So when Mr. Long was murdered by one of the party goers a month before the girl and her family came, no one pretended they were unhappy because Mummy could finally add 'quiet neighbourhood' to the rental advert. I had a week to adjust to their coming after she said, 'Guess what? We're getting tenants.

Pack up your things,' without so much as a pause for me to explain the unfairness of her decision. As if I would. 1979 Jamaica was neither the age nor place of children expressing their feelings and desires with lengthy commentaries on parental slights. *Mummy, let's discuss. Mummy, why do we have to*? No. Mummy said and you did. And so I huffed and puffed and cursed God and cursed Daddy for leaving and cursed Mummy for pushing him away. All silently of course. I took one last look at my empty bed in the corner before moving the rest of my things to my brother's room.

They were three, the mother, brother and her. *Her.* I have to say her name, I know. I need time, though, just a little more time. They arrived on a Sunday morning because Saturday was Sabbath. All their belongings fitted in a rusted white pickup truck with ATSUN chiselled on the back, a gaping hole replacing the leading D. I didn't see the girl at first; it was her brother who strode past me as if he owned the place, dragging his grip behind him. Mummy had a cross look on her face because this was her first time being a landlady and the terrazzo floor had only been waxed and polished two days before. The boy's mother took a giant step over to him and slapped his head.

'Lif' it up. Nuh bodda gih mi nuh problem todeh,' she said. I rehearsed the 'right' way to say it in my head, stifling the urge to correct her; *Lift it up. Do not give me any problems today.* I wanted to tell her it wasn't that hard, you simply had to commit yourself to speaking 'properly'. And her show of violence? It was no surprise because I believed it was the way those people disciplined their children: loudly and in public. He righted the grip with no lack of immediacy, treating each step thereafter as if God was in the building.

The girl followed next. Her mother introduced her to Mummy as she approached the front door.

'Lovely to meet you, Marsha,' Mummy said, and she reached out to fix the girl's hair ribbon. It had come undone, streaming like a kite's tail.

'Sasha,' the girl said without so much as a smile on her. 'Mi nuh name Marsha. Mi name Sasha Knight.' And she folded her arms, lips pursed, head cocked to the side. Mummy withdrew her hand mid-way and looked at Sasha's mother. The box came so fast I heard it before I saw it. Mummy's eyes smiled; Sasha's boldness would only have been charming had she been five years old.

Her brother's name was Stephen Williams, and her mother was Ms. Sheldon. I'd never met a family in which everyone had different surnames and suddenly they were interesting, mysterious, a puzzle. I wanted a different last name too. There was this famous prime minister, one of our national heroes, Alexander Bustamante, and I used to fancy myself with that surname. *Matthew Bustamante*, I'd sound it out over and over. I would imagine I moved to Spain and claimed my long-lost inheritance and there'd be horses and lots of olive trees.

Sasha Knight bit her bottom lip and cried without crying. I watched her cross the threshold of the front door, eyes red, two tiny waterfalls perfectly straight, one on either side of her cheeks and that's when I made my offer to help. She bested me that morning, that's the truth. *I was just trying to help*, her voice echoed over and over. And I tried to say something clever but nothing was coming and time tick tocked away, her tear-streaked face all victorious. I don't understand that. So I did what every boy does when a girl is taller than you and has the last word. I pronounced her ugly.

And when I was done, I mentally compared her to my next-door neighbour Andrene Carpenter and I was sure that Sasha Knight was more than just ugly, she was the ugliest girl I had ever seen. She was black – blacker than me. That was how we judged ugliness on our island back then. *Shi black eee! Him black eee! How come yuh suh black?* I remember one time in Integrated Science class Ian Patterson, alias Blacky, walked by the blackboard and Winston McIntyre said, 'Miss, a khaki uniform moving towards yuh.' The entire class was in stitches; we laughed so hard.

I wasn't finished. She was a checklist of *no's* when she stood side by side with Andrene Carpenter. No long brown hair. No straight aquiline nose. No fair skin – that was another thing we said back then: not light skin, but fair. I had none of these things either because the truth is she looked like me, just poorer. She didn't have pretty clothes like Andrene. On this last point, she insisted on wearing yellow all the time; her single dress, one pair of shorts, her two *gyanzis*, slippers and ribbons; it was quite a spectacle.

That morning she stood there in her yellow halter top that covered two small bumps on her chest, while a pair of yellow terry cloth shorts with a single white stripe down each side, completed her ensemble. Yellow. Yellow. Yellow. Ackee, mangoes, ripe bananas, pine, cornmeal porridge, curry chicken, ripe plantains, jack fruit, ripe June plums, macaroni and cheese; had it not been for her mother's weekly beatings I'm sure she would have only eaten yellow food. I watched her walking away, her back to me, her grip barely hovering off the ground and I could see the part down the middle of her head, its definition already frizzy, making two short pigtails held together at the tips with bright yellow 'bubbles'.

I imagined her eyes rolling back in their sockets, kissing her teeth, her slippers spanking the bottoms of her feet with a high-pitched smack. I still couldn't find the right words and the distance lengthened, the moments clicking away and me standing in the living room by the plastic-covered settee, my thin arms dangling empty seeking some new task; she was already down the hall. Into my room she went – *no hesitation, no concentration* – remember that game? She claimed it for God and family, flag firmly planted.

Chapter 3

I used to believe that time healed all wounds. These words are lies. They are the musings of a people who conquer and take. And there's the rub for me because I am neither conqueror nor taker. I am one who stands still because I think that time will bring her back to me. The air is heavy in this parking lot; thick, weighted, pressing me down. A woman shouts, 'Mi see it, mi see it, Jesas Chrise.' I want to slap her. 'Shut up,' I mumble to myself. 'Shut up. Shut up. Shut up.'

There are things I know now that will change me forever, but I cannot stand still an eternity. There's a world, a life, that's waiting for me when I leave this place. I do not belong. I must get back to it. It is expected.

But she's here with me. Quiet but here. People are gathering at the fence. Blue and white police tape cordon off, keeping the unsanctioned away. People here don't respect such iconography. Like everywhere, they want to know, to gawk, to *susu susu*. I feel them breaking through, their inertia crowding the sacred. I think I want to pee.

'Tell me what to do now,' I say but she's silent. I call out to her again. Over and over I ask, 'Tell me what to do. Tell me what to do.' There's more that I need to fill in the picture.

Someone else has said something, revealed what was meant to be a secret. I should have known this would happen. What makes me think we will be the exceptions? We're nothing to these people; scraps, bits of bacon deposited on the floor by a sloppy eater. I want to be here alone without her, if only for a moment. I must prepare. For what I'm not exactly sure.

'Why have you brought me here?' I say to the quiet. She still doesn't answer. I'm afraid to say her name now and in the present because I will be consumed, eaten, changed.

One of the detectives I worked with said something to his wife who passed it on to a cousin and said, *don't tell nuhbody, yuh hear mi?* And now the whole world is looking on. They aren't supposed to know. God, I hate this place. God, I love this place. I close my eyes and wonder. I close my eyes and wander. It's early morning and the schoolchildren will be here soon. 'Let them come,' I say to *her*. 'If you will not speak then let them come.'

Chapter 4

In the days following their move Sasha settled in quickly and quietly and before long we developed an unspoken routine. She always rose before me and I'd crack open my room door to watch her every morning, waiting for her to drag her slippers on the floor or leave the pipe running so Mummy would get her in trouble. I knew that Sasha knew I watched her, because one morning she turned round and looked me dead in the eyes before I could slam the door. I slammed it anyway because I was stupid and I must have thought she was stupid too. So she would rise and I'd hear tiny movements, clicks, clacks, thuds, and I'd shove my brother's right foot off my tummy and watch.

She wore the same thing every morning: the halter top and those yellow terry cloth shorts with the white stripe down the sides. Once or twice I didn't wake in time and I heard her tapping on my room door. If I didn't get up straight away, she scraped the wood with her fingernails, not too loud, though, we didn't want to wake our mothers. One time Sasha started to open the door, slowly; I was right behind it and she stopped when it was wide enough for her to see me and we just stared, daring each other to be the first to look away. That's how it was for days on end. No words between us, just me timing her waking and her trying to catch me watching her and me trying to catch her watching me.

One morning I didn't hear her at my door and I waited. The minutes passed, my chest heaving, my breathing steady. I put my ear to the door as always. I was annoyed that she'd suddenly stopped playing without telling me. Those weren't the rules. At least as I understood them. I opened the door, slow, sure she was standing there. I don't know what it was I expected as we'd never discussed the terms of this duel, but if I could catch her before she caught me I would win. I swung the door wide and she was standing in the hall, and Ms. Sheldon's boyfriend was walking away all hurried.

He smelled liked my father used to right before he left the house on Friday nights and I was thinking that it was too early in the morning for that.

'Bobby smells like Daddy,' I said.

'Nuhbody ask yuh?' Sasha said and kissed her teeth. I thought she was angry with me because I called him Bobby. I wasn't supposed to do that because Mummy introduced him to me and Donovan as Mr. Bentley, but I overheard Ms. Sheldon and Mummy call him Bobby. Mummy wasn't standing there so I thought it would be me and Sasha's secret. This was only the second time we'd spoken.

We held each other's stare for a minute before she *long out har* tongue and said, 'Why yuh suh faas, mine yuh business,' her cheeks all full of air as always.

'You're stupid,' I said.

'Yuh fool like, yuh nuh know nutten.' She pinched me hard and twisted, and I shoved her.

Mummy must have heard. 'Matthew, is that you out there?' she said. 'Go and put on the tea.'

I used to sneak out of bed on Friday nights after worship and stand by the concrete fence, watching all the people dancing and getting drunk at Mr. Long's. I relished how the bass started from my belly and undulated down to my toes. I could feel my body moving without my permission, first my hips, then my feet. Right foot, left foot. Step. Step. Right foot, left foot. Step. Step. Freeze. Repeat.

I liked how the party's aroma clouded the air, like a million people spraying the same perfume all at once. It must have been a couple of weeks later when Sasha joined me the first time; Mrs. Long had kept the tradition even though Mummy wasn't happy. I didn't see Sasha as she approached. I heard her wheezing, though, a soft whistling train, because she had asthma. And she said what I was thinking, 'It smell nice.' She stopped wheezing then, like it was a holy time.

'Yes,' I said.

The DJ was in the middle of playing *Uptown Top Rankin* and we were right near the end at the part *gimme likkle bass mek mi wine up mi wais'*, and she started dancing. I wanted to tell her we shouldn't since we'd get in trouble because I was Adventist and Adventists don't dance, and she was Pentecostal and Pentecostals only danced at church. But she grabbed my hand, swayed it back and forth, and I could feel her elbow on my arm. I didn't stop her because it was nice to have music flow through me.

The next week she taught me how to tell if our mothers were sleeping because, 'Wi cyan guh earlier.'

'We should wait till later,' I said, because I had to have my way.

'No. Yuh have fi listen fi sih if dem a breathe deep.'

'I can't hear Mummy breathing from my room.'

'Because yuh talk too much.'

We whispered even though we were outside and the music was louder than a jet engine. And so the next Friday night she came to my room when Donovan was in dream land, his right leg on my tummy because he didn't know how to sleep any other way. She stood over me and flicked my ear and I got up all groggy because I hadn't heard her come in. She held my hand and we stood in the hallway; I could hear it then, Mummy and Ms. Sheldon breathing deep and snoring. It was only ten o'clock.

'Dem naa get up till tomorrow mawnin, trust mi,' she said. We'd go watch and dance barefoot, dance for forever. I liked how the zoysia grass felt under my feet, like carpet. Later, when we were right proper friends, we'd lie down there, the same grass like soft prickles in our backs. And on the nights when there wasn't a party we watched the black empty sky, hoping we'd see one twinkle because the lights from Spanish Town washed out the stars.

We did it for several weeks, I can't remember how many. Then Mummy caught us. We never accounted for her going to the fridge to munch on leftover chicken foot soup, that she'd always done so, only she didn't realise we were outside. Didn't count on her seeing the crack I left in the door because I hadn't closed it tight behind me and the light from the party streamed through.

'It's my fault,' I told Ms. Sheldon. 'I asked her to help me find my pencil.' But Ms. Sheldon flogged Sasha anyway. And Mummy beat me too for lying but mostly for listening to dancehall *tegareg* music.

'Matthew, yuh bringing down shame on mi head with this behaviour,' she said when she was finished.

After that night Ms. Sheldon would beat Sasha regular, just because. The kind that you grow up and brag about. *Yuh think you get beat'n, man, I remembah dih time when Daddy had a piece of iron...* Although Sasha got it worse, Stephen wasn't immune and, unlike his sister, he was a talented screamer. *Ai yai yai, ai yai yai, ai yai yai* over and over. And he wouldn't stop even when Ms. Sheldon told him, 'Yuh bettah quiet or ah give yuh more where dat come from.'

She had two boyfriends, Ms. Sheldon; one fair and the other dark like me. Mummy only met Mr. Bentley not the one Ms. Sheldon snuck in on Thursday mornings when she thought I wasn't around and Mummy was off at work. The room door was always closed. One time Sasha and I put our ears real close to the wall because we wanted to hear what they were saying but we couldn't. We went outside and took turns hoisting each other up on our shoulders and peeked in the window. We could see the fair one, not Mr. Bentley, on top of Ms. Sheldon and he bared his teeth grunting like he was chasing away predators, as if he could sniff Mr. Bentley on her.

He'd go on and on for minutes at a time and Ms. Sheldon would slap his chest over and over and say, 'lawd, lawd, lawd.'

The first time we looked I said, 'He's hurting her.'

'Trust mi, shi like it,' Sasha said flatly. 'Yuh nuh know nutten? How come yuh suh fool? My turn now.'

We switched places. Her feet sat on my shoulders and I could feel her arches perfectly locking onto my shoulder blades; I remember she was lighter than I expected, like she was ready to fly.

'Are you sure?' I said, 'I thought it was supposed to be different. On TV…'

'TV?' she said too loudly and then the fair one stopped grunting and Sasha ducked really quickly because getting caught was worse than death.

Of course things ramped up as they do with children. She opened her mouth to show me her chewed up food. I flicked her ear. She punched my arm. I tripped her. She hid my knapsack. I put lizards in her hair. She hawked and spat in my porridge. We punched. We scratched. We pinched. We fell out. We made up.

One day she went too far. The week before Vacation Bible School, my favourite Puma sneakers Daddy gave me the previous Christmas went missing. I searched everywhere because I couldn't bring myself to tell Mummy. Then one afternoon, not long after, in the middle of dandy shandy, Sasha crouched low to duck the ball, almost to the ground, because Andrene Carpenter threw it too far down like she wanted to hit dirt. There on the back of Sasha's yellow halter top I saw perfectly straight thin strips of orange suede weaved into the terry cloth. I had to look twice to be certain. I imagined the state of my shoes, butchered for its hide to satisfy the fashion imperative of Sasha Knight. Yes, I wanted to hit her and no I didn't because had I tried she would have clobbered me. I scowled at her but she refused to give in.

And so I plotted my revenge; I'd take one of her *gyanzis* or a foot of the black patent leather pumps she wore to church every Sunday and douse it with pee water. Or I'd hide her exercise book or snap her pencil in two. I had so many ideas.

Summer came to a close and the new school year began. Sasha's school ended an hour later than mine so I had sixty minutes to pour out my vengeance before she came home. One weekend I stole the keys to their room from Mummy's purse and bided my time. I found my opportunity one Thursday when I caught an early taxi. I grabbed the key from under my white briefs and tiptoed to their door. The key sluiced into the lock and with a quick turn the door opened.

The darkness of the room surprised me as it was still bright out. I reached to switch on the light before a paralysing fear seized me. I waited a moment then my eyes adjusted. A lumpy double bed sat in the far-left corner, a pink blanket slung over it. On the floor, inches from what used to be my bed, rested a small cot. I guessed Stephen slept there. A sheer beige curtain dressed up the closed red wooden windows. Below the windows stood a dark brown chest of drawers crowned with a white crocheted runner, displaying several porcelain-like ballerina figurines. *Hurry up. Hurry up. Hurry up*, I told myself. My eyes searched the room for Sasha's things. It should have been easy going since her possessions were colour coded. A dresser stained the same dark brown as the chest filled up the opposite corner from the bed. On top was a treasure trove of items available for my taking: three combs, a few hair pins, a bottle of Vaseline lotion, a tub of hair oil, a can of Right Guard deodorant, a peach powder case and two empty perfume bottles.

I could have easily removed her comb but I wanted something less conspicuous. As I opened the top left drawer of the dresser my heart stopped dead. Behind me the bed creaked and someone breathed out hard. I stood stationary, my fingers about to rip a pair of her yellow panties. An unrelenting urge to pee weighed me down. Another voice moaned. I ran out of there, the drawer open, my stolen key still in the door. I slumped by the wall outside their room and tried to think of a good lie.

'A who dat?' a man's voice called out.

'Nuhbody not here,' Ms. Sheldon said. 'Gwaan back ah sleep.'

I waited on the man to come after me but he only said, 'Awright,' before the voices faded. I locked the door and walked away, Sasha Knight's panties still in my hand.

I wish we had ended right there, two kids in an unending duel, the silliness of childhood captured in a series of revenge plots and counterplots. She'd win some and other times I'd just manage to reach a stalemate.

'Bet yuh cyaaan seh bloodclaat,' she said one evening. She had her hands on her waist, leaning slightly forward, her lips all twisted up. It was just the two of us in the house. She knew I couldn't say a curse word.

'That's stupid,' I said.

'Yuh cyaaan say it,' she laughed.

'Bet yuh can't spell Mississippi.' I tried misdirecting her.

'EM, I, ESSESS, I, ESSESS, I, PEEPEE, I,' she sung it out. 'Your turn, fuh-fool bwoy.'

'M-I-S-S-I-S-S-I-P-P-I,' I staccatoed.

'Yuh cyaaan say it. Yuh cyaaan say it. Woooyeeeee.' She laughed and laughed.

I tried to trick her and went with *blood cloth*, a pause between each word. Everyone knows it's not the same. Everyone. *Claat. Claat.* You have to say *bloodclaat.* I can say it now, though, but that doesn't help anything.

There are times when I wonder if I ever hugged her, told her that she was pretty, that I liked looking at her shiny wet saliva-soaked thumb when she dislodged it from her mouth after sucking it all day. Or how she ate *blacky* mango in one go, even the skin, and Ms. Sheldon had to tell her to, 'Stop eat like bwoy pickney.' Or just screaming at Sasha, 'If you flick my ear one more time…'

The evening I stole her panties I hid them among my precious things, my first Hergé comic, the green plastic soldier with the rucksack on his back and an M16 in his hands, and my replenished collection of coloured rubber bands. I liked how they felt on my hands. They were soft like warm sea water at Puerto Seco Beach on a Sunday afternoon. I meant to get back to them, eventually cutting them into strips just like she did to my shoes, only I'd glue them to one of Mummy's crotons as part of my great reveal. But I forgot about them because there was football and Christmas and friends and life.

The days and weeks passed, and Sasha and I were made up friends again. Every free minute we played dandy shandy, jacks and marbles. Only the dying sun and our mums calling after us drew our unwilling bodies back into the house. She beat me at marbles and I beat her at jacks. We needed Andrene, Donovan and Stephen to play dandy shandy. Although we played together Sasha never liked Andrene. Sasha said Andrene ate her *nose naught* and I called Sasha a liar because no one as pretty as Andrene Carpenter would rummage around in her nose and eat her own boogers.

Sasha said, 'Awright, yuh nuh have fi believe mi.' So I told her she was lying again and she said, 'Yuh cyan duh dis wid yuh finga?' She bent her left index finger so far back I thought it was going to fall off. That is how it was with her. She told you something one time and if you didn't believe she moved on.

So we were children and happy because we had three hours of daylight left and when Ms. Sheldon came home from church she was always in the best of moods especially if Sasha *did get inna spirit*. I was at the ready with ball and jacks, listening for Sasha's heels on the tile floor right before she scratched at the door. I curled up on the bed, my stomach in a joyful anticipatory knot.

I should have known. Ms. Sheldon had started in on Sasha that morning at breakfast before they went to church. 'Close yuh mouth when yuh ah eat,' she said, and Sasha tried but it wasn't working because she just couldn't. She was going to get hit and I looked deep into my plate and waited for it. Only this time Ms. Sheldon seemed preoccupied, like something was off with the world that day.

Mummy came to the dining table and asked, 'Yuh find it?'

'No Mrs. Archer, but I t'ink I know what di situation is,' Ms. Sheldon said, and her eyes shifted to Sasha like she held the winning cards in a game where everyone was a cheat.

The flogging began in the hallway as soon as they stepped through the front door, as if Ms. Sheldon had been holding her pee for hours and she finally found a clean toilet. It was the switch again and I could tell Sasha was trying to run but Ms. Sheldon had her locked in good and tight. Sasha wasn't moaning yet and Ms. Sheldon hadn't begun to talk so I knew that there was more to come.

The switch broke halfway through and she sent Sasha to get another one. I opened my door and I tried to say *run away and don't come back; I'll find you*, but I couldn't breathe and my mouth wouldn't move. Sasha looked past me, sweat and tears flooding her face.

'Gyal pickney, yuh betta…,' Ms. Sheldon started, then inhaled deep. She walked with purpose into their room and I knew then, in the long pause, the moment God gifted me, I should have said.

I closed my door and sat on the edge of the bed and listened. *I'm sorry, Sasha.*

Ms. Sheldon was back and this time the *snap snap snap* sounded deeper like *thud thud thud*, something that would make good on Sasha's skin.

'Ah weh yuh duh wid it, hmmm? Ah weh it deh?' Ms. Sheldon paced her breath; this would be a long-distance run. And Sasha turned quiet and I wanted her to speak, to cry, to wail at the sky, something. She had already said her piece, though, offered the one and only true answer.

'Ah don't know, Mama; mi nevva touch it, Mama.' And Ms. Sheldon must have been on her the whole walk from church, asking her over and over for who else would have dared.

Then I heard the rush of feet; Sasha took off and I willed her on.

'Run. Run. Run,' I said. I opened my room door to follow her and I barely saw her back and I was thinking it was my turn to grab her hand and we'd be so fast. So fast. But she was already outside and Ms. Sheldon was right behind her. And she was going to tell Mummy that I told Sasha to run so I said it soft. I shouldn't have because this is Jamaica and running from your beating is like fleeing from police. When they catch you, you're going to *feel it* because you made them work. Sasha was young but Ms. Sheldon had longer legs and she caught her outside under my window. The licks were coming quickly now. Back. Arms. Legs.

'Yuh betta find it, yuh hear mi pickney, yuh betta find it.' Five more licks. 'Yuh betta find mi tings. Mi wuck haaad fi di two a unu, an' yuh tek mi tings?' Ten, fifteen, twenty more, *whap*, *whap*, *whap*. And it was over.

The *thing* was in my hand, squeezed into a ball, and I should have said but I couldn't think of a good lie, one that would save both Sasha and me from a flogging. Because even at nine I knew there were no acceptable explanations for why a boy had a girl's underwear in his possession. A part of me must have known all along. It was the size and cut. They were the *delicates* of a woman, not a girl, a lady who had someone to show it off to. Yellow panties against black skin, an even darker spot at the V, a woman with proper hair down there. The things those men must have seen, and I know I should have said. *I'm sorry.* But it was too late. Sasha was on the ground under my window and she wasn't moaning anymore and she wasn't crying either. I know because this time I didn't cover my ears with my pillow. I cracked the louvres open and watched as her yellow ribbons un-bowed into those two kite tails, she could never get those ribbons right; watched as blood blotched the tops of her socks; watched as the world took her.

Today I feel guilty, as if that changes anything, like it would have made her life easier. The truth is that back then I went to bed and fell asleep hard and woke the next day and the day after like nothing happened, because on our island children don't have time to dwell, like closing your eyes wipes the slate clean. I get it now; why Jesus says we must become like little children to follow him. How else can we take his words for real; *I will forgive their iniquities and remember their sins no more.* Jesus, an old man with a shot memory; *I'm sorry, what was it you said you did again?*

There were more floggings that week. One evening Ms.

Sheldon came home and we children were in the living room, playing with her boyfriend. We had all taken rounds sitting in his lap; it was Sasha's turn. Ms. Sheldon dropped the brown paper bag of groceries and pulled Sasha up in one go. We didn't understand, because we were happy that we finished all our chores. And I mean everything, even the tasks that weren't due till the next day.

'Ah weh yuh a duh a sit pon big man lap?' Ms. Sheldon said, because Sasha should have known that Mr. Bentley's cock would harden the moment it rubbed against her bottom, that man *cyaaan help demself, suh yuh mus know*. And her boyfriend just sat there, blank-faced, he the victim of a cruel little girl. We looked on, frightened, because we wondered if Mummy would beat us next and would Andrene's father flog her too when he found out. Because we couldn't have known that this was a girl rule. Then Mummy came in right after and Ms. Sheldon had a second switch because, like always, the first one broke. She told Mummy what Sasha had done and she flogged Sasha again right there in front of us and Mummy looked happy, like someone else had finally caught on that Sasha was already a slut.

Then there were the times when Sasha was flogged because she couldn't keep track of the tiny things a *girl chile* should know: *close yuh foot yuh panty ah show; wash yuh brother clothes; set di table; iron yuh brother clothes; wash yuh panty good; peel di yam; soak di white tings inna bleach watah den spread dem out pon zinc pan. Sweep out di room. Yuh nuh finish yuh homework yet? Stop drag yuh foot. Mi tell yuh fi talk? Mi tell yuh fi stop talk? How much time mi have fi tell yuh fi close yuh foot, yuh panty ah show?*

I should have told Ms. Sheldon off that day she beat Sasha because of me. Tell her to go fuck herself. I should have told Sasha I was sorry right then and there and took my flogging from Mummy and listen to her tell me *something not right with yuh. What yuh doing with big woman things?* Her eyes large as breadfruit and her mind calculating how much of my father ran through my veins; it couldn't be her, just couldn't. I should have grabbed Sasha's hand and run into the bright sunshine and we'd pick mangoes and June plums and we'd never ever stop. That was what I should have done, but I was nine and Jamaican and Adventist.

Chapter 5

I remember many things about that time but I can't recall trees. Yes, we had an Ackee tree in our yard and we used to climb it on those long summer afternoons after we gorged ourselves on mangoes and pipe water and we went to River when we shouldn't. I mean I don't remember trees in the neighbourhood, random-like, in the median, front yards or on pavements. I can only see sky and dirt and marl, a snowy field of white gravel, those large concrete construction pipes the National Housing Trust was still using to build houses and cut new roads, and pools of water on empty lots with mosquito larvae ready to bloom and bite. We should have had trees, lush green things because it rained heavy every summer afternoon, massive drops like cartoon water, but I can't recall it or why that even matters now but it should. It's as if I'm missing the things that anchored our lives, without which we are a dream.

We found a dead boy once. I didn't know what death should look like but it sure didn't look like him. He was smiling, a big wide grin, like somebody told him to say cheese and forgot to tell him they'd already taken the picture. I threw up when the minutes passed and he wouldn't move. He was floating in the canal behind the house and must have gotten stuck on something. I opened and closed my eyes. For an instant I wished the boy had never lived, felt, played marbles. He looked my age with dark skin and burnt orange hair, one of those strange phenomena in people of colour.

Sasha and I could see down the banks of the canal on either side. Sloping backyard fences reached towards the water in a futile attempt to connect. There was a long white gash down the middle of his forehead as if it had been split open and re-stitched like a poorly crafted doll. The water wasn't streaming along as it hadn't rained. A bald tyre edged alongside him and behind it, like a tailgating car, an old brown grip. There was a traffic jam.

So I was watching him not move and I wondered what that felt like, to be still for all eternity.

'Do you want to be dead?' I asked. As soon as I said it I knew it was stupid but she didn't call me *fuh-fool*.

'Sometimes,' Sasha said, like she'd thought about it for ages, considered the ramifications, weighed its impact.

'Me too,' I said, and she put her left arm around me and pinched my shoulder with her right hand. I shoved her and we laughed. We lay in the dirt on the banks of the canal and watched the boy and the backyard fences and the sky changing for rain.

'Kirk,' she said after several minutes.

'No, I think his name is Delroy.'

'Dat name stupid.'

'No stupider than Kirk. Do you know anybody named Kirk? That's a surname.' Of course there were plenty of Kirks and I'd known one but I couldn't give in.

She didn't say anything for a long time and I waited for her to speak. Even then I sensed she had more to say than me.

'Delroy Kirk,' she said finally.

And I said, 'Yes.'

Then we just kept laying in the dirt even though we knew we'd get a beating for messing up our clothes.

I don't know when I became so odd. It never occurred to me that we should call the police, tell a friend or alert our parents. We just watched, our arms around each other, both of us silent.

Chapter 6

Sasha called me one evening out of the blue while I was at Andrene's. It must have been months after blackheart man took her into that cold dark place because I was beginning to forget. And I was starting to feel happy again, the way children are supposed to. We were playing monopoly, Andrene and I, and the phone rang. Old fashioned fire alarm ringing like you don't hear these days. We didn't have a telephone in our house back then and when I asked Mummy why, she said, 'I work all day talking on that thing. I don't want it in my house.' And that was that.

The phone rang three times and stopped and then another three times. It was a Saturday night and the ten-foot speakers were beginning to fire up at Mr. Long's. I looked at the olive green thing and waited. By then I had moved next to it.

Andrene warned, 'Don't answer it. Daddy will be upset with you.' It was the only time I didn't listen to her.

When the phone rang once more I picked up on the second ring.

'Hello,' I said. 'This is Matthew. What's your name?' The speakers were in full swing and I had to use my index finger to close my left ear. Andrene Carpenter tugged on my shirt and motioned for me to give her the phone.

' *'Ello?*' the static-filled voice of a girl came back.

'Hello?' I said. 'Hello? Are you a friend of Andrene's?' I had been working on my formal telephone voice, mimicking Mummy's accent.

' *'Ello?*'

'Hello? You have to speak louder. I can hardly hear you.'

'*How come yuh suh fool?*' And I began to breathe hard like when Daddy was going to come by the house and I wished he would stay this time because *I have to show you my new book and, look Daddy, look what I can do, and see, I still have the shoes you sent me last Christmas.* A smile rumbled from the depths of my stomach.

'Matthew, give me the phone,' Andrene said, her right hand over mine, pulling the receiver from me.

'Andrene, wait nuh.' I may have had a bit of a snip to my voice. 'Sasha?' I shouted into the receiver. 'Sasha, is that you? Just tell me where you are. I'll come.' Silence. I glanced at Andrene then whispered into the talking end, 'Are you at River? I won't tell. I promise.' More static and air. And I realised then I didn't need to hear her speak another word. We could sit there, each of us breathing into the phones, and I knew she was trying to say but she couldn't, that the words weren't ready yet, that even if she said them, it would all be jumbled like the 1000-piece jigsaw puzzle we didn't finish.

I felt myself floating down and I wasn't sure if I was ready to go into the darkness because I was afraid and I couldn't see. Then Andrene stepped in front of me, her brow knitted. The static was gone and I came back to earth. I should have kept talking, *I'm sorry*, shoved Andrene Carpenter away and talked and talked, but I liked her and I was hoping there was still time for her to be my girlfriend or me to be her boyfriend – there is a difference. I didn't know that it would be another three years before I heard from Sasha again and by then I couldn't remember that day. I looked up at Andrene for help but her index fingers rested firmly on the two white pillars that ended a call and started another. Sasha was gone.

Chapter 7

She caught me. Four weeks after her beating. They were half way up my arm on the third go round. I was beginning to keep secrets from the world then, thoughts that belonged in the creases of my mind, pleasures I reserved for myself. I want to think that I don't know why I took them out that afternoon or why I failed to destroy them as I'd promised. I can only say that the knowledge that the panties belonged to Ms. Sheldon changed them somehow; now I had to own, hold, touch them. So I do know why. They were a naughty and guilty gift to myself, the box of chocolates slipped under the sofa by a chronic dieter, an unreliable car you simply can't get rid of, the girlfriend you know is cheating on you but every time she says, 'Hey baby,' you melt.

Evenings, when Donovan was at Rory's and Mummy at Judy's and no one would interrupt me, only then did I retrieve them. It was a Sunday and Sasha should have been at church speaking in tongues, rolling on the ground and crying out for God's mercy or a miracle. I was invited once, on the sly of course since Mummy could never know.

Sasha said, 'Yuh waan sih sup'n?'

And I said, 'Yes,' because no other answer would do. I sat

beside her and she danced like everyone else and rammed her knees into mine. Then a woman near the altar did something, I couldn't see over the hats, that made Sasha stand and walk all the way to the front. She stepped over me like I was a plastic bag and was in the aisle before I could get my question out: *where yuh goin?* I slid to the end of the pew. In a minute, Sasha's body twitched and flailed on the floor and Ms. Sheldon looked really happy, sunshine on her face, as if this was all she ever wanted for her only daughter.

Sasha hugged me when she returned. Her face and back were wet.

'Your time next. Mi show yuh how fi do it,' she said.

And so that Sunday afternoon in my room, my bottom on the edge of the desk chair, my breath growing shorter, the panties closing in on my nose – on that day I would finally give in and smell them – she burst in. We had recently begun a new challenge: who could scare the other the most and I was winning since I was quite crafty. Once, I took the dropper from an empty medicine bottle, filled it with water and dripped it on her one drop at a time, but slowly so she wouldn't look up immediately. A proper scream I got out of that one.

It was her turn now. That's how I was found out; caught in the middle of the day at my and Donovan's desk. When I was six, Mummy spent an entire summer teaching me the principle of sacrifice and reward. She made me water the crotons on the veranda and when I was finished she gave me a tiny bowl of Cheese Trix. When I asked for more, she said, 'Water the roses then I'll see.' I remember I pouted a while before giving in. It worked, all that training, because I did my homework first, diligent, methodical, thoughtful. I spent my time writing out all the long division steps even though I knew the answers.

So here was my reward and I'd take my time because pleasure should be savoured. I gently pinched the right hip of the panties with my left hand and let the soft fabric drape like a curtain over my right arm. I started at the tips of my fingers on the opposite hand then brushed the hairs all the way up. I tried them bunched up, then folded. I'd switch sides every two or three minutes, counting the times I caressed each arm; it had to be even. That day, though, something else took me over. Maybe I'd sensed the end, the way we know the last song is the last song at a concert from our favourite band, that no amount of *encore encore* will bring them back on stage.

And so they were past my shoulder, up my neck and at my chin, just one more inch then heaven. There she was, right in front of me, a big roaring 'raaaahhh' she let out. I didn't even hear the door open. She still had her church dress on and she was sweating as if the spirit had taken her again like that day. And she was grinning, victorious, like she'd brought out the biggest scare of all. It was amazing, her lack of imagination.

She knew, the moment she saw the thing draping my chin. There was nothing to say. But of course I spoke, the way the guilty always do, as if the words will make it whole.

'Sorry,' I managed. 'I think this is your mummy's.' And no, that wasn't enough.

She was on top of me before I could get the next *sorry* out. I didn't think she'd do it. She slapped my face, a good solid open palm box. It was the kind you reserved for grand moments, calling out your cheating husband in the church parking lot, or Marilyn Monroe being grabbed and kissed without her permission in that movie. It stung, so I stood and punched her in the stomach. When she bent over I was full of regret so I reached out to help her up but she clocked me on the chin. I snatched a fistful of her hair and ribbons and pulled as hard as I could. She pushed me into the chest of drawers; the handles dug deep into my back and I let out a soft yelp. I bent my knees and slid underneath her. I made it to the door but she hooked me by the shirt collar and I fell backward to the floor. She sat squat on my belly and I could hardly breathe. She punched and slapped and scratched, and I pulled and pulled on her hair and all the while we said nothing because what else was there to say? Everything that should have been said missed the use-by date. We rumbled and tumbled, wordless and tearless, the cold terrazzo tile bruising us. It ended there, sudden, an undecided round of a boxing match. It was our one and only serious fight.

She left for school that Monday morning after our fight like all of us, her exercise book and a worn-down pencil in her hand. That's what I told myself all those years afterwards and I believed it, baptised myself in the knowing. I sat next to Andrene in Mr. Carpenter's Ford Cortina and Sasha went left, down the road to Horizon Park All Age School. All the other children in our neighbourhood turned right like Andrene and me, snug in their parents' cars, our knapsacks filled with hardcover exercise books and pencil cases, sharpeners and nice smelling pink erasers. So Sasha walked all alone down Grover Boulevard, her thumb in her mouth now that her mother was out of sight.

There was a time, three, maybe four years ago, when I was certain she disappeared the day of our fight, that I was the one who pushed her into the hands of blackheart man. I struggled to fill in the hours afterwards, where I went, what I said. Every detail mattered. Did I follow her at first then give up? The sky, was it sunny or grey? I needed to place all the characters in our neighbourhood, who sat where, who drove what, which women wore trousers and who wore skirts. We would have passed Mr. Miller and his jerk drum just a few feet away from Mr. Long's, plastic bottles of his secret sauce to the right, the smoke warding off mosquitoes and flies, chicken and pork grilling side by side and his assistant lying to the Adventists, 'the pork nevva touch di chicken, trust mi, Miss.' Did we hear Mr. Chapman's 50cc motorcycle, his horn announcing *icicle*, *nutty buddy* and ice cream cake wrapped in translucent white paper, the cloud from the dry ice wafting up when he opened the wooden box? I would have remembered, wouldn't I? I would have remembered all of that.

I know that like all children we saw things we never should have, peeked into the bedroom of Ms. Callahan two houses over and watched her in her bra and slip. Sasha and me, we'd giggle, unable to explain to anyone else what it was we found so deliriously funny. But there were other things, the ones that make you pee or stand still in your shoes and socks, things you never see when your friends are around, things that happen to your best friend only you didn't know she was your best friend yet, and you stand still and watch.

The first time I saw a man hit a woman I was ten and walking home from school. I was at the corner of Young Street and Cumberland Road, the place where they meet to form Brunswick Avenue. On the Young Street side there was a man that sold sugar cane and coconut from a wooden cart on tiny wheels. He took up the entire pavement and he always had a queue. Sometimes I'd stop to watch him use his cutlass to slice the heads off coconuts or strip the skin from sugar cane. I'd grown to love watching this man. He had a blue transistor radio that he'd listen to the cricket on.

I don't know what the woman said to him, but he stood and punched her. She didn't fall or cover up the spot where his fist connected with her face. Instead, she said, 'Sorry,' and then, 'awright, baby.' It was as if the strike marked the end of a long and complex business negotiation. *Okay then, I find your terms reasonable.* Clive Lloyd and his massive bat hit a six and the commentator on the radio was beside himself. Sugar cane man reached behind him then placed a bundle of cash in the woman's hands. She seemed so pleased. I watched him greet his next customer, big laughs as they discussed the game. He picked up a coconut and tossed it around in his right hand. How strong he must have been because green coconuts without the husks removed aren't light. I glanced to the left and the woman was strolling down Young Street like every care in the world had been lifted. I stood there on the pavement looking back and forth between them until the woman turned off and I couldn't see her anymore. I remember I was happy how it all turned out because she walked away satisfied, and the man cheered as West Indies demolished Australia. I was happy even though I peed my trousers.

But then there was a hole and a tree and a wheel. And me and Sasha peeping on Ms. Callahan and something else in the dark only it wasn't dark, it was broad daylight. It was all scattered, pieces of Sasha everywhere and I didn't like how it made my head feel, like Maths I couldn't understand. Later there would be even more bits but for now, at ten, I pressed all of Sasha down like in

Luke 6:38, *pressed down but not running over*. You think it would have grown but it didn't. It stayed there and stewed and cooked and baked then turned cold and hard. The tree and the hole and the wheel and blackheart man in the dark that wasn't dark, and Ms. Callahan, and the punched woman, all of it preserved, frozen in time because I had to live.

This is what happens when your mother tells you to, 'Stop di foolishness and go study for your Common Entrance exam. I don't want to hear another word 'bout that stupid girl.' Or when your eyes play tricks on you one morning and you have to swallow it, all in one gulp, because blackheart man will get you if you remember.

Chapter 8

I go through changing seasons of memory these days, between certainty and doubt and whatever lies in the middle of that spectrum. Here is what's true. Sasha never told on me. Never. And I wished she had. At least I'd have something to show for how I betrayed her.

She didn't speak to me for days afterwards, though. Yes, it's coming back to me a bit now. So it must have been long after our fight that she didn't come home. But I can't remember the day, not the date, but the actual name of the day, Monday or Thursday or Wednesday. It's foolish but I believe it could help me to somehow help her.

I told her once that my favourite day is Tuesday because it sounds like two days. She looked at me for a moment as if trying to work out the permutations of my pronouncement. Then she smiled and said, 'Twodays, Tuesdays.' We sang it together, 'Twodays, Tuesdays, Twodays, Tuesdays,' and we laughed and laughed. I search the grooves in my brain for something, anything else. I almost have it; it'll be the tiniest of things that will make the picture whole.

* * *

Sasha and I said goodbye the morning she never returned. As I said, I went right, and she turned left. Did I look back? Yes, I want to say I did and I could sense a weariness on her. I would have wondered why she was walking so slowly, because if she didn't hurry up she was going to be late and the principal would be at the gate with a big leather belt awaiting all the stragglers. One whack as you passed Mrs. Campbell and you tried to run through so she would miss and you could tell your friends how fast and clever you were.

Sasha always dragged her feet when she walked to school. Her uniform was too short even after Ms. Sheldon had loosened and re-hemmed it. And the torso was too tight, the cloth cutting into her armpits. Mummy bought Sasha a pair of brown shoes, the ones with laces and a low heel. They belonged on the feet of Immaculate Conception High School girls, not hers. She wanted baby dolls, she told me later, but she said thanks without a grateful face and Ms. Sheldon boxed her. Sasha smiled with water running down her cheeks; I couldn't understand it, pain and smiling.

The truth, though, is that I never looked back because when I sat next to Andrene Carpenter I was so happy that my knee was touching hers. I would have been looking at her gold star earrings and the blue and green bubbles and her pretty watch, staring at the hairs on her arms, amazed at how they laid flat and long.

So Sasha was alone, no eyes watching after her, no one missing her because he knew they won't be playing dandy shandy for at least another eight hours and eight hours was a long time then, long and forever. No one missing her because she would cup her hands over his ears to tell him a secret and he liked the feel of her breath, loved when she said words like *fuh-fool* because you have to say fuh fuh to make the f sound, liked when she said all her sentences in one go and he could feel every inhalation and movement of her lips when she told him, 'Mi a guh have a truck and a jeep and two big house inna May Pen,' and he would laugh and ask her to tell him more. No one missing her because he would buy two June plums at lunchtime, the prettiest yellow June plums, and he'd watch her eat them, a part of him wishing she'd offer him some and he'd follow her to River again that Sunday when Mummy was at Judy's a *labrish*.

I prayed and begged God to send her back. I asked Mummy if I could go look for her, 'because I know where she is, Mummy, she told me to meet her at the... the... the place, please Mummy, please.' And Mummy telling me it was time for evening worship. We sang our songs and read our scriptures and prayed our prayers and Sasha wouldn't come home.

Chapter 9

What does it mean to find solace in bones? That's all there is to see here among the asphalt, tar and gravel. I've come here to put *us* to rest, to finally give her peace and I look around at the school car park, empty except for the digger and my rental car right outside the gate. The place is still cordoned off with blue and white plastic cords that read Crime Scene: Do Not Enter, the same ones they use for road closures, and I cannot think. The school looks different from how I remember it, bigger, as if Sasha's swollen body underneath is stretching it to the very ends of the earth. I think now of all the children who have walked, run, played here, of Sasha collecting their laughter, their tears, their skinned knees and spilled sky juice.

I bought the first bottle out of my pocket money a month before my tenth birthday. That's what we used to call it. My new next-door neighbour said, 'Do you mean an allowance?' She'd spent time in America and that's how they say it. I like that. Allowance sounds like you're tapping into your inheritance just a little. Pocket money is a one-off and it may be a week, or never, before you can expect the next instalment. Only I had to earn my allowance;

extra chores around the house or helping Mrs. Anglin water her roses. Other times my father gave me money when he stopped by to see Mummy. He'd say, 'Come here,' and he'd shake my hand then play punch me and I could feel the thick cash pressing into my fingers. He'd wink and nod, sealing the secret bond between us because Mummy couldn't know. I overheard her tell Judy that, 'He thinks he can buy their love.' I told him and he laughed. So I saved it all, obsessively planning my life ahead.

It's lavender, that first bottle, and squat with a crystal cap that has a gold rim at the base. Beside it was a larger version and on the other shelves there must have been a dozen different perfumes. The counter at Ammar's smelled of lemons and spice and scented powder. I hadn't meant to buy it, that much I remember, but I just stood there looking at all the bottles and powder boxes and that spray thing that looks like a ball at the end of a string. Then the woman behind the counter appeared out of nowhere and said, 'What yuh need, sweetheart?'

I think I grinned because she was tall and smelled nice with perfectly formed white teeth from a dentist's waiting room picture.

'That one,' I said and pointed to the squat lavender bottle. I was breathing hard and could sense myself almost laughing.

'Yuh mummy will like it,' she said and handed it to me. She wasn't supposed to do that because people ran off with things all the time, but I believed she liked my face, as if I reminded her of the son she desperately wished to have. The bottle was cool and weighty in my hands and I could feel the smooth edges of the glass caressing my palms. I held it up to the light, spun it round, letting my fingers trace the outline of it.

'It's not for Mummy,' I said, without looking up and I realised then that I didn't even remember why I was in Ammar's in the first place. For an instant I wanted to smash the bottle into bits, the entire lot, burn the store down.

'Oh yuh have a little girlfriend,' she said all smiley and twinkling, and it came back to me then why I had to have it. Just this one; I made Sasha get beat'n, because I didn't say. She was going to come home, and it would be like when we used to watch the party goers after Friday night worship, and if I didn't have it she would be angry and leave again because I keep forgetting. I just keep forgetting.

I didn't like that the woman said *girlfriend* as if she and I shared some special knowledge that required a cypher to unlock. I half expected her to wink.

'No, she's not my girlfriend,' I said all sharp and bristly and the lady cut her eyes at me.

'Facety likkle pickney,' she mumbled and wrapped it in brown paper, shoved it towards me and walked away.

'You didn't cash out the birthday card,' I called after her. At the far end of the counter another woman in fancy jewellery glanced up with serious eyes and the lady with nice teeth returned and made the change without a word.

I wrote my first letter that evening. I say that as if I actually recall doing it. The truth is I would have written the first letter long before then and it would have been waiting on the bottle and the card like they made a set. I know what the letter says, what all of them say. I can see my improving penmanship, the cursive taking on an established flair with each passing year. I curl the tail of the capital S of her name like a snail's shell. I must make it beautiful for her. The paper is all brittle and yellow now. I am afraid to read it all.

Chapter 10

I remember the first time I forgot her. Not a fading memory, the lens becoming unfocused then nothing; no. I fully suddenly forgot. By then she had stopped talking to me for almost a year and our new house hadn't been filled yet. My new next-door neighbour introduced herself as if we were potential business partners.

'Hello, my name is Treesha, but it's spelled T-R-I-C-I-A. See?' She shook my hand with a vigour belying her small frame. I was watering the crotons at the fence and I didn't see her. She was prettier than Andrene Carpenter and I didn't know that was even possible. She had very long black hair, straighter than Andrene's too, so long that Mummy used to call her Crystal Gayle. She had olive skin like Jesus and her little silver earrings sparkled in the sun.

Before I could answer she asked, 'How old are you?'

'Ten,' I said.

'Same age as me.' She smelled of strawberry lollipop and orange rind. 'When did you move?'

'Around three weeks ago.'

'Oh, I was in San Diego then.' She said it just like that, as if

San Diego had been one more inconvenience that stood in the way of her meeting me.

'San Diego? In America?'

'Yes.'

The next day she told me she went to Toronto over the summer too.

'Canada,' I said and she kissed me on the mouth.

'You're a good boyfriend. My other boyfriend doesn't even know where Toronto is. He's stupid but he's pretty.'

'You mean handsome.'

'No,' she said, 'he's pretty.'

'Boys can't be pretty. Boys can only be handsome.' I was affronted. She stopped a moment and licked her candy ring. It looked so strange, this ten-year-old sucking on a pacifier.

'You talk too much but I still like you. This is Sandra.' She produced a blonde-haired doll out of nowhere. 'This one's yours.' A boy doll magically appeared in her other hand. 'His name is Michael.' I played with her even though she was too old for dollies and I'd later dream the little plastic things came alive and hacked off my fingers. I played with her and forgot Sasha in that dark, dark place.

I met Tricia's parents soon after, Mr. and Mrs. Davis. Her father was dark and her mother was pink. Mr. Davis rode his bicycle from one end of North Avenue to the other and I'd watch the tyres roll along as he passed me back and forth. Transfixed, I stood there as if the twirling spokes and black rubber hid the map to Atlantis. There were times when I followed him, running back and forth.

It should have made me happy, giggling like the ten-year-old schoolboy I was. I didn't laugh, though. I ran with him to the Bent Street end, and he'd turn around to avoid me and the cracks in the pavement. He must have thought it a game; he'd slow down to allow me to catch up and without looking, it seemed he sensed me at the rear tyre, he sped up. North Avenue to Bent Street and back and all the while I watched those tyres roll and roll. I saw a picture forming if only I could adjust the antenna. Maybe the tyres weren't right, or the bicycle, the road, the sun. I needed more. A door just beyond called to me, as if trying to say my name and all I had to do was step forward and turn the handle. There were days when the door was too far away, a great chasm standing between us, and I'd stretch my arms all the way but I couldn't reach it. Sometimes it was right in front of me, clear as day and fear gripped me. I knew if I opened it I would be no more.

'This is Matthew. He's my new boyfriend I told you about,' Tricia said when she presented me to her parents. 'He talks a lot but he could make a good second husband.' We were on the veranda, Mr. and Mrs. Davis seated, her leaning on him. I liked how they fit together, spanner and bolt. I wished they'd never move.

'Welcome to the family little man who likes my bicycle.' Mr. Davis rose and squeezed my shoulder. I knew I was supposed to say *thank you, sir* or *the pleasure is all mine*, nice etiquette-y things Mummy taught me but I stood stationary, my mouth partly open.

'He's just joking,' Mrs. Davis said in what I now believe was an attempt to ease my consternation. 'My, you're so serious.'

Every Sunday afternoon I ate dinner with them and afterwards Mr. Davis and I watched Big League Soccer on their colour TV. I was surprised to find that Chelsea wore blue. On my black and white I guessed red. Week after week I became a fixture so much so if I missed a day Tricia came to find me. I was sure I would marry her.

Then my father showed up.

My father. Mr. Archer. It's strange when a boy doesn't know how to address the man that sired him. You call a man *daddy* when you've ridden on his back or he's bought you a patty and cocoa bread after picking you up from school. But to call him Mr. Archer would have been cheeky and everyone can hear resentment in that. And we do not criticise our fathers, regardless of their faults. No matter the twelve or thirteen half brothers and sisters born to the *gyal dem pon di side*, our mothers dutifully playing their roles as patient caretakers, holding out for the slops their husbands and partners handed down.

So when my father stepped out of his shiny black Mercedes that evening, so gleaming no one had to tell Donovan and me not to play next to it, his shoes straight from America or Canada or England, not bought in American flea markets but in the best department stores, not on sale, who was paid in US dollars and smelled like he'd be fucked later that night, stood in front of me and said, 'Where's your mother?' I was so happy he addressed me I used as many words as I could to tell him where Mummy was.

'Mummy? Oh. I think she's in her room, but she was outside earlier grafting the roses and she was using the egg shells from breakfast. And then she went inside. And we have a phone now...'

Mummy came out right then and said, 'Oh Paulie, I didn't know you were here.'

Liar! I wished she had let me finish. She wore tight white jeans and wedge heels and red painted toenails. She wasn't supposed to do that. Her blouse had orange and red and yellow flowers on it. Her perfume was different, like the women at big people parties.

The next evening he showed up again and this time he touched my head and my heart burst out of my chest. Tricia was with me and she held her hand out.

'Nice to meet you, sir.'

When she left, Daddy said, 'You have a nice little girlfriend.' He rubbed my head again and laughed. I loved how his hands covered my entire skull and I just wanted him to touch my head forever. I was happy I never stepped through that door in Mr. Davis's bicycle spokes, so I stopped following him after that because it was still calling, pulling me into the darkness.

Daddy, that was the first time in ages I thought of my father like that. He gave me ten dollars and back then ten dollars could purchase the world, and he said, 'Guh buy your girlfriend some ice cream.'

And I said, 'She's not my girlfriend.'

And he laughed and laughed.

They spoke in whispers, Mummy and Daddy, so no matter how much I eavesdropped I heard nothing. Still, I'd already begun to plan my life with him in it. My world transformed forever into a clone of the Davis's. Mummy, Daddy, Donovan, me; all together again. First on my list he'd teach me how to drive that car. Then we'd move to Stony Hill and live in his big house with upstairs and downstairs. Far away from Cheshire Hills and Horizon Park All Age School and blackheart man. I told Tricia we were going to move.

She said, 'I'm okay with a long-distance relationship.'

Night after night Mummy and Daddy dropped us off at Judy's or the Davis's, and most evenings they wouldn't return till

Donovan and I were fast asleep. It was beginning to happen, my life taking shape. Mummy was all grins and cheer and although I didn't like her coyness when Daddy looked at her, I didn't care because she was with him and we were going to be back together again.

Sometimes Daddy stopped by when Mummy wasn't home, and he'd give us money and send us to play with Tricia and Graeme. More and more Daddy came by earlier and earlier. There were times when Donovan and I came home and he was already there as if he was waiting on us. I didn't want him to leave at nights and more than once I clutched him and begged him to stay. Other times I'd cry or tell him about my day and some new fact I learned, hoping to keep him with me. Then he was back the next day and my heart raced and sometimes he allowed us to sit on his lap or swing from his hard biceps. Afterwards Donovan and I would run off and play with Tricia and her brother and sister.

On special nights we'd return from Tricia's to see Daddy and Mummy dancing.

'In my worldly days,' Mummy once told me, 'I was very light on my feet.' They were fantastic together, his hand on her waist, her arm around his neck. And Mummy allowed me and Tricia, and Monica and Graeme, and Susan and Donovan, to dance along with them even though Pastor said dancing is a sin. I'd never been so happy.

Then a week passed when Daddy never came. We asked after him and Mummy said, 'Time to do your homework,' or, 'Clear the table,' or, 'Have you studied the memory verse for Sabbath School?' And she said the same things every day for a week. One evening, not long after, Tricia met me at the fence.

'Hey,' I said. 'Did I sound like I'm from America when I said that?'

'Leave me alone,' she said. 'Your daddy did something bad to my mummy. I don't want to talk to you again. Your father is a bad man.'

'No he isn't.'

'Yes he is. He—'

'My daddy's the best daddy in the world.' I cut her off. I didn't care that I sounded like a six-year-old. 'He's taking me to Disney World at Christmas and Dunn's River Falls next week, and Montego Bay and Hope Gardens.'

'Oh really! Your daddy's never coming back. My daddy told me. My daddy said your daddy can never show his face round here again if he knows what's good for him.'

'My daddy is coming here tonight. Watch and see.' I couldn't believe she was taking this one thing from me.

'My daddy says your daddy…'

I didn't want to hear another word. I wasn't even boyfriend number one. So I leaned back, opened my right palm and swung. She looked at me like this was some new game but I wasn't smirking like when we played Monopoly and she landed on one of my hotels.

'I'm going to tell Daddy,' she said, then cried. It was as if she had practised her response and somehow messed up the order. I slapped her again and again. And she meant it when she said she'd tell her daddy. Mr. Davis paddled me good and told Mummy and she flogged me proper too.

Of course Tricia was right. Daddy never came back. I was eavesdropping on Mummy and Judy when Judy said, 'Shi get rid of it.'

At first I wasn't sure they were talking about Mrs. Davis because they called her Cynthia. The fence now segregated Tricia and me. Mr. Davis blamed Daddy for the whole business because he couldn't conceive of a world in which his wife chose to sleep with my father. Mummy tried to handle it because none of this was exactly new to her. This time was different, though. All Daddy's other women lived in Rivoli or on French Street. Even when they sent my half brother or sister to come knocking on our gate to ask after him, Mummy could sleep well knowing that she was the one he married, and they all would crawl back to the ghettos where he found them. Mrs. Davis, though, was another thing. She was one of us. It was the kind of mistake you never make. You fuck around on the outside and leave the tribe alone.

No one has the luxury of changing houses when the inconveniences of life reside at 10 North Avenue and you live at 12 North Avenue. So Mummy tried her best to do what all women must: soldier on. Only she couldn't quite do it. It was her hair I noticed first, clumps of it in the garbage. The wigs were next. She stopped cooking, then cleaning, and it took Nana and Dada to finally come help her.

The door began to call for me again, only this time I stood behind the gate and watched Mr. Davis on that bicycle. He stared stern at me day after day, eating up the hours before he left Mrs. Davis. Up and down he went and he couldn't know that I was ready to open the door and I wouldn't come back.

Chapter 11

I say today that I will never forgive my father and even I know that's not true. He couldn't understand what I needed from him then. How much the house, the car, Mummy, Daddy and two little boys living next door to a pretty girl who kissed me on the mouth at the fence, who I might marry one day, meant to me. How much I needed to forget. As I said, I was really happy. But it was a kind of tightly wound joy that you must spend all your time guarding because it took very little to untangle. There was a time I felt like Sasha caused the mess, that she made Daddy disrupt the Davis's life. It was as if she knew that she would be gone from me forever if my father behaved himself.

After Daddy never came back, Sasha made a brief stop in my life. I'd dream about her every other night. There were shadows of her here and there, flash dreams in which she was an ancillary character. She'd pop up as the middle seat passenger in a taxi or one of many friends who possessed the gift of flight. She was an after echo of an after echo, a ray of sunlight refracted through a window then sliced into pieces by horizontal blinds. I'd wake up and recall that I saw someone familiar, a face whose name evaded me, a sense that this person may have been important to me somehow but not in this life, nor on this plane.

The day she went with blackheart man I ate chicken foot soup. I had a single dumpling and whistled down each and every noodle one by one. We tried playing a noodle game once, Sasha and me; whoever found the longest one reserved the right to demand any action of the loser. Our fingers braved the hot liquid. We clenched our teeth to hide our 'ouches'. I found one first and lay it flat on the table next to my spoon.

'I beat you,' I said.

Then she caught one twice the length of her pinky. 'Mine longah dan yours, *abey*,' she said and *long out har* tongue.

I opened my mouth and showed her my chewed up dumpling and we giggled all quiet like no one could ever know. We fished out four or five each before I felt an angry breeze flow over my head.

'Yuh a waste food?' Ms. Sheldon said. I evaded her face, my eyes fixed on my bowl as I'd become used to what I'd see. Afterwards I gave Sasha my noodles and I swung my feet and tickled her knees with my big toes, and she swung her feet back and rested them on my thighs. We sat there and ate our soup and I watched her wet cheeks dry, leaving white streaks, and we tried not to laugh but we did anyway, but much quieter this time.

So the night she didn't come home, the one I used to think I remembered, I had been waiting for her while we were having evening devotions. It was the last thing we did every night before going to bed. At seven o'clock on the dot we gathered in the living room and I asked Ms. Sheldon, 'Where is Sasha?'

I spoke out of turn so Mummy said, 'Yuh bright.' I knew what she meant so I turned quiet. But there was more.

Chapter 12

Time sped up and slowed as it always does. I cannot recall eleven or twelve. It was as if I'd slept an entire two years and woke to find thin black hairs invading my crotch. There must have been birthday parties, cakes, gifts, trips to the beach and Mother's Patty and Cremo Ice Cream. I passed my Common Entrance exam. I would have been eleven then, my name printed in *The Gleaner*: *Matthew Archer: Calabar High School.* Mummy proud and beaming, her big son on to high school. New khaki uniforms, unbroken-in black leather shoes, knapsack, pens and pencils and a protractor set. But all of it has escaped me.

And Sasha silent.

I turned thirteen. There were four bottles by then. Four bottles, four cards and four letters. There they were spreading in the bottom drawer of my dresser, gentrifying the real estate that once belonged to my Hergé comics. So I lulled my life away, numbing my mind, my head, my breath. Maybe it wasn't that she was quiet after all, only that I had become used to carrying her.

That summer Mummy was at her end because Daddy finally did her in. His women stopped sending their children to look for him and they showed up to *trace off* Mummy. They parked themselves at the gate standing akimbo just like Sasha used to, their voices rising with each passing second that Mummy refused to face them. All of them young; late teens to early twenties at most. In another life they could have passed for my big sister or first cousin. In the beginning Donovan and I were not allowed to hear what they said, then gradually Mummy stopped covering our ears or sending us to our rooms. She spent those evenings with her face to the TV, her crochet needle gripping and tying as the next handbag took shape. We'd hear the dull ping of the knock on the gate as stone hit iron.

'Where yuh going?' she'd say.

'The gate, Mummy.'

'What about the gate?'

They stood there and judged Mummy aged and broken for all the world to hear.

'Yuh favah old crocus bag,' one said.

'Ah me him love,' another said.

'Old John Crow,' the girl who looked like she could not have been more than fifteen barked as she walked away from the gate. I watched them all daring Mummy to come outside and I wondered what they saw in my father.

'Yuh cratches dry up.' This from one with neat cane row hair and a sky juice in her left hand. She wore slippers like Sasha, only hers were pink and white. I wanted to love her, to tell her sorry for what my father did, that she was not alone, he'd left us too. She came several times later with a child slung on her hip and I kept waiting for her, for all of them really, to jump the locked gate, open the front door, and plant themselves on the settee. And what would Mummy have done then? *Dried up cratches*, the girl said every time she came; the reference to a woman no longer able to… I cannot say it. She's my mother, after all.

Our neighbours did what they could to shield us.

'Mrs. Archer isn't home, dear.'

'You have the wrong house, Miss.'

'No Archers live around here. Just go on home now.'

Of course that failed. The women weren't fools. Their numbers grew. The little hair Mummy had left sloughed off and Nana and Dada came for her again. This time Donovan and I were sent away.

Everything that held our family together fell into the sea. The house lay empty. Daddy was gone. Mummy was 'resting'. I needed Sasha then. She used to tell me that if I closed my eyes really tight, 'tight suh yuh cyan sih star,' I could erase the world. She'd help me, hold my hand firm when we sat under the Ackee tree.

'Yuh have fih close yuh eye dem fih one minute,' she said. Both of us at the same time or else it wouldn't work.

'I'm closing them,' I'd say and I used to peek sometimes because I wondered if she was watching, but her eyes were always closed and I'd smile. On the days when her asthma was about to come on I could hear her wheezing. She had warm and dry hands, but coarse and hard from washing her brother's clothes. I liked how I had to fight against her grip or she'd crush my fingers.

'Open dem now,' she'd say between her wheezing and a shower of leaves poured over me. 'Your turn.' And I'd return the favour and we'd dance under the Ackee tree.

Sasha wasn't here now, though. I stopped listening because that is what I was supposed to do. The day after he took her away I was walking through Spanish Town. It's easy to forget that you live on a piece of rock surrounded by water when you're strolling through a city in the middle of an island. Nearby towns that are only a few miles away seem like entirely new worlds, pregnant with joys to dazzle the mind and dangers to tremble your heart. You think of all the places she could be and how you could exhaust several lifetimes of searching and never find her.

So there I was in the middle of Spanish Town. Multiple record stores competed with each other over whose speakers were the loudest. Ammar's clothiers took up an entire block. Jamaica National Building Society, their blue and white signs still lit although it was daylight, sat opposite. The meat market was one store over next to Ammar's. The hardware store, with its addictive smell of construction glue, was further away on the next block. And then there were the light poles, one at every corner. Chunky dark wooden behemoths. Not a square inch left to tack on a piece of paper among all the commercials for dance hall concerts and parties and the occasional advert for the latest evangelistic crusade.

I'd remember those light poles years later. One evening, a few days after my thirteenth birthday, I brought my papers. Crude things. I drew Sasha's face on them, reconstructing it from memory. Once, when Ms. Sheldon was on the veranda *susu susuing* with Mummy Sasha let me follow her to their room. We kept our eyes and ears alert, though, our legs ready to run. The windows were open and the room smelled of lotion. Sasha said, 'yuh waan sih supp'n?' She slowly opened the second drawer of the chest. Layers of clothes stacked neatly according to type: slips, blouses, brassieres. She placed her hand underneath the pile and pulled out a light purple powder case with a glass cover. It was larger and more beautiful than any of Mummy's and I was surprised. I could tell it was rarely used. She removed the cover delicately, her wrist steady, and held the case to my nose. Flecks of scented dust swirled around me, and I meant to tell her we should put it back now because I feared she would drop it. But just then, out of the corner of my eye I saw a picture frame, face down, its cardboard kickstand slightly elevated, squeezed into the left-hand corner of the drawer. Before Sasha could stop me I reached in and turned it over. It was a picture of Sasha, only she looked older, like a proper woman with husband and children, and I was thinking that she had the power to reverse age and I wanted to ask her to teach me how to do that too. We stood together looking at the picture, quiet, while I waited on her to explain. Then I saw the words *To My Beloved Sister* in the bottom right-hand corner and I realised the woman was Sasha's aunt. Sasha put her finger in her mouth, lathered it with spit and shoved it into my ear and I dug my finger in my nose and rubbed it on her face and then we chased each other.

Later that day I peeped in the room because I wanted to see the purple powder case and the picture again but Sasha wasn't there. Ms. Sheldon's back was to me and she held the frame in her left hand and I began to wonder if I had put it back in the right spot. She leaned her head as if studying it, preparing for her own still life rendering. She looked at the picture for minutes, trance-like and I couldn't pull myself away. She kissed her teeth once and just then it looked like she was turning round so I started to walk away real quiet when I caught what must have been the vocal end of a paragraph that began in her head and ended with '…serve yuh right… luv tek weh people man.'

So I drew this picture of Sasha from the recollection of her or maybe that picture of her aunt, I'm not sure now, as if I was seeing her *through a glass darkly*. Each rendition slightly different because a photocopy machine for personal use was a foreign concept back then. I disguised myself with a cap I borrowed from one of my classmates so no one could tell Mummy on me. I wrote at the bottom of the posters in block letters, PLEASE COME HOME. I pasted them over the concert ads. Rain took them that same evening, the kind that ends a winter drought, so I redrew them and pasted her face all through town, but every afternoon the rains came again and soaked them. I caught a break the following week when the storms eased. I'd check in every evening on my way from school half expecting she'd left a message telling me where to find her.

Not long after I was dragging myself along French Street, checking each light pole, and that's when I spotted black markings on one of my posters. It was one of my best renditions and I ran. The closer I came the more the marking favoured an oblong place holder like those used in comics for dialogue. I instinctively glanced from side to side, sure she was watching from the shadows and I was ready to go with her. A smile reached my eyes and I could hear my heart in my ears it was beating so hard. But as I drew close to that oblong it became clear that it was a marking produced by the puerile mind of a pubescent boy whose understanding of sex was informed by the current crop of 'blue' movies. This wasn't the only one desecrated and I tore them down, gathered them all in my knapsack, went home and wept.

Chapter 13

As I said, that summer Donovan and I were sent away while Mummy was off to get her nerves sorted. Judy took Donovan, and Nana and Dada shipped me off to St. Thomas, right outside Morant Bay. The desecration of Sasha's face was too much so I stopped feeling. I say that as if I chose to, like I'd been properly diagnosed and prescribed.

I would be living with the McKenzies, friends of Mummy's who, upon seeing me, rattled off the usual *yuh get suh big; last time I saw yuh, you were just a baby*. I felt a desperation coming on when I stood in front of them, a sense that I'd abandoned my station as the crisis was upon us. I waited for the taxi to pull away before I turned to my new caretakers.

'Mrs. McKenzie,' I said.

'Yes, love.'

'I have to go back home.' I tried to sound as if I may have forgotten something of intellectual import like my Maths or Physics book. Nothing to lose our minds over but the kind of important that only parents of promising Rhodes' scholars understood.

'Don't worry, sweetheart. Your mummy is going to be okay,

alright? She just needs to rest a little bit. Don't you get tired sometimes?'

'Yes Mrs. McKenzie, but I need to do one thing. It won't take long, I promise.' But they weren't hearing me.

'Do you want to see the backyard? We have a nice pool, mon,' Mr. McKenzie said as if that ought to solve my dilemma. I let it alone. He had short grey hair and he'd married into McKenzie money and McKenzie name according to Mummy; at least that's what I gathered from the bit I eavesdropped. He was an Indian from Guyana and Mummy and Judy said that no one can pronounce his real name. He had very dark skin, almost purple, and it was strange to see that; Indian people who were darker than Black people so I couldn't understand why we were designated Black and them Indian.

I wondered if I should have told them the truth, that I worried I'd lose my precious bottles and letters and cards; anything could happen to an empty house. The collection was beginning to unsettle me, like carrying a glass of water for an aunt you can never please. *Matthew, turn off the light, yuh wasting electricity. Matthew, slow down, yuh eating too fast. Matthew, why are you always on the road like yaga yaga people?*

The first six weeks were uneventful, with trips to the beach and the parish library every day except Sunday and Sabbaths and I gradually forgot about my precious things. Then their daughter returned. When Mr. McKenzie introduced us he said, 'Marlena just spent the summer in Switzerland, didn't you *doux-doux*?' He looked at me when he said 'Switzerland' and the whole business felt like a geography quiz. I was about to ask him if he was really Guyanese as he sounded Trinidadian to me, but Mrs. McKenzie whispered something to him in a language I didn't understand so I left it.

Marlena was sixteen. When I asked her how old she was Mrs. McKenzie laughed and said, 'This one's precocious, eh?'

Marlena said nothing to me for a few days and that was fine with me. The beach was a five-minute walk away and I'd met a girl, Simone, only a couple of houses down, who had taken to me. We were holding hands at that point, each week graduating to the next rung on the couples' ladder. Kissing was the next and final level and we planned on doing it on a Saturday night after church.

One afternoon two of Marlena's friends came round to visit. I conveniently needed a drink of water, so I made my way to the kitchen where they stood in various girl poses. Her friends, like Marlena, ignored me, even after I said, 'Good afternoon.' I overheard her telling them about Basel and Geneva, the boyfriends she had, and the projects she worked on. I closed the fridge and turned to face them. The girls seemed interested in Marlena at first, but every other sentence she would say, 'Good governance, that's what Jamaica needs.'

'I was in Gothenburg...' she said.

'Where?' the skinny friend said.

'Sweden,' Marlena said with a hint of impatience.

'Oh.'

'And they have a mass transit system that just works. Now why can't Jamaica do it like that? Trains that run regularly and on time, can you imagine? Good governance, that's what Jamaica needs.' Her friends, though, wanted to know more about the boyfriends.

'What do white guys' cockeys look like?' the short one said.

'Charlene, stop it,' the skinny one said.

'Okay Miss Hypocrite, yuh know yuh want to know too.'

Charlene smacked her lips and turned to Marlena. 'Alright Marly, I was talking to Cheryl the other day and she said that they like going down there, yuh know, with dem mout'?' Charlene and the skinny one were all snorts. I am ashamed to say that I, too, found good governance less enlightening than the boyfriends, so I shared the girls' disappointment when Marlena stood and said, 'I don't have time for this foolishness. I have to study. I'll talk to you later.'

'Awright,' the skinny one said.

'Wi know yuh busy chile,' Charlene said like they were off to plot Marlena's downfall.

Marlena took no notice and escorted them to the door. I hoped she would change her mind and let them stay but she closed it and immediately asked me, 'Did you lose something?'

'No.'

'Then what yuh staring at?'

That same afternoon Marlena opened my room door without knocking. She had been so quiet around the house that I initially thought she'd left. She looked at my books for a second before grabbing my Hergé. She laughed then said, 'A bit generic, isn't it?' It sounded like a nice word, *generic*, but I could tell she meant to shame me. *Definition through context, Mr. Archer*, I recalled Mr. Foster's English class. She wasn't done. She ignored my Agatha Christie and went straight to *Emil and the Detectives*.

'Matthew, Matthew, Matthew, come on now, I know you can do better.'

'What do you read?' I asked, defensive.

She smiled as if she saw my soul. 'You should embrace your Caribbean heritage. Come.' She led me to her room. Her fingers danced along the bookcase. 'So which one should I pick, which one for the clever boy?'

I liked how she said clever. I could see her tongue caressing the roof of her mouth when she sounded out the 'cluh' of the 'cl'. I was clever because earlier she asked me if I knew who the president of West Germany was and I said, 'The head of state is called chancellor and his name is Helmut Schmidt.' She didn't call me clever then. She called me bright.

Her room was more than twice the size of mine with a bookcase that covered an entire wall floor to ceiling. The stained mahogany wood spoke of a time of women in sheer nightgowns at their desks penning letters to their lovers in faraway places. Her dresser, in the same finish as the bookcase, held myriad perfumes and powders. She showed me a silver case and inside was a peach-coloured cushion with hair pins stuck in it.

I said, 'You have a box just for pins?'

She smiled. Her brushes and combs were immaculate and placed in descending order of size. Next to her dresser was a small table, the legs an elongated S shape whose tips looked like claws biting into the carpet. A matching stool sat in front. I opened my mouth to ask her what she used the table for but then I saw the thin brushes and nail polish. Her bed was stacked high with white pillows on top of thick sheets. I fought the impulse to roll in it.

She turned back to her bookcase.

'It's in order,' she said. 'I bet you can't figure it out.' Her eyes glowed and I set myself to the task. 'You have one minute.' I was taking too long so she said, 'Yuh know what? This one's too hard for you.' I was offended. 'Over here is my trash collection, Mills and Boon and Harlequin.' My mouth must have been open because she said without a pause, 'Don't look so surprised. You'll learn soon enough that every woman needs a little trash.' She winked and I smiled but I didn't know why. I cocked my head and stooped to look at the shelf below her 'trash' collection. I barely made out the name Anaïs Nin. I wondered if her friends knew this side of her.

'Oh what else… what else… Over to the right…' I fell in love with her then. The movements of her arms, dancing fingers like a pianist's, the white cotton dress. It was formulaic, I know, boy falls in love with girls in white dresses; I had seen the movies and read the books. She handed me a copy of *Green Days by the River*, shoved it into my hands really. We stood there a few moments before she said, 'What yuh waiting for? That's it. Go back to yuh reading now.' I didn't know I was staring again.

The next day she took my hand and I let her drag me to her room. It's something I still like, a woman's hand in mine, or is it the other way around, taking me someplace secret and new. She asked me to help her with questions for her A levels. I can't recall which subject. I perfected my diction so I'd seem even cleverer than the day before. I planned to use the word *sonorous* in some way, as in, 'Mtume have sonorous voices don't you think?' She didn't notice. After an hour she said, 'Run along.'

On the third day, her parents took the neighbour's son to the Baptist Church vacation bible school. We were in the kitchen finishing up the dishes and when we could no longer hear the car's engine Marlena turned to me.

'Finally!' She studied my face for a minute before she grabbed my hand like the day before and up the stairs we went. We were at the door to her room when she stopped, barely out of breath, faced me, narrowed her brow and asked, 'Yuh want to see something interesting?' Yes, yes, I did. I was happy to be able to feel again.

I was so far away from my life, from Daddy's women and my bastard sisters and brothers, from Mummy's madness, from… I could feel there was something else but it was shapeless and cold and I didn't want to think its name.

Marlena could have taken me any place that day. Still, I had my pride and didn't want to seem too eager so I considered my response. But as always I was too slow.

'Yuh nuh serious.' She let my hand go and disappeared in her room. I followed her.

'I *am* serious,' I said. The words came out like a five-year-old begging Mummy for chocolate cake, so I lowered my head to make my voice sound deeper and repeated my defence. 'I'm very serious. What do you want to show mi?'

'Close yuh eyes.' She paused. 'I said close your eyes.'

'Okay,' I said.

One time Sasha made me wait a full two minutes with my eyes shut before she unclenched my fingers and placed a cool hard round thing in my hand: a marble. I played with it for days on end, mesmerised by its yellow and blue filament. A bigger boy than me stole it one day at school. At knife point because I wouldn't give it up. His friends held me down, elbows and hands on my belly, chest and legs. He pressed his knee into my wrist and my fingers weakened. It was gone. Sasha said, 'Whappen to yuh?' when she caught me crying.

'Nothing.' We stood there looking at each other for minutes until she figured it out. No questions.

'Blackheart man tek it. Mi wih get it back fih yuh.'

The boys were waiting for her when she followed me to school the next morning as if they knew I'd return with reinforcements. She didn't drag her feet then. She marched to school, didn't care that she missed the first hour of classes, her right arm around my shoulder, my left around hers. I thought she'd back down when she saw them and I was ready to run the other way if we had to. They towered over her, all five of them.

'Which one?' she asked, but I was afraid to tell her. No matter, she walked up to the biggest boy.

'Mi mark yuh face,' she said and walked away. That evening I had my marble.

Standing in Marlena's room I expected some touristy trinket from Switzerland. Secretly I hoped for a bottle opener with a picture of Zurich in the background and a magnet on the back. One day, when I was old enough, I'd use it to open my first beer, watching the froth rise, and I'd drink it in a single gulp. The wait was unbearable, but I held myself together.

'Yuh sure yuh ready?' Marlena said.

'Yes.'

'Hold on, take one step to your right.'

'Like this?'

'Good. Now.' She ordered me to open my eyes.

My breath stopped. I fought the instinct to flee because I shouldn't have been there and I understood why that cold shapeless thing was coming. I tried to look at Marlena's long black half Indian hair laying there in full perfect curly strands on the pillow, movie-like. I really tried. But she had breasts, real breasts, firm and doughy at the same time. I don't understand that combination but that's how they looked to me. They were smooth and black, and her nipples were blacker, almost purple, and I stared. She began to massage her left one and said, 'Watch this.' A whitish liquid seeped out. 'Come taste it!' I stepped back but an agonising thirst threatened to overcome me. A stone rested in my groin and it grew heavier the longer I stared at her. I took another step back.

And then a whisper from behind me, *Run*. It had been so long since she'd spoken that I had to think to be sure. It was nice to hear her voice without the telephone static and I wanted to ask her how she got there. *Did you take the bus? Who gave you a ride?* And how did she know which house? I began to turn round to face Sasha. But I couldn't do it because of Marlena's breasts and I asked Sasha to just *wait, give me five minutes*, that's all, then Marlena held my hand tight in place on her left breast. She looked me dead in the eyes and I could feel her left hand manipulating my right, guiding my fingers and palm, moulding my hand to mimic hers.

I couldn't recall how I came to be seated on her bed right next to her, the sheets cool on the backs of my knees, because I was certain I'd taken several steps back, so far back I was at her door.

I liked it, my hands on her breasts. And I know I wasn't supposed to, not yet. There was plenty of time ahead. I was breathing hard and had so many questions and couldn't Sasha give me just one more second because she was screaming now. *RUN, RUN, RUN, RUN* and I kept trying to turn round but my head was stuck like a rusted screw. I didn't want her to leave me again but I'd earned this one thing that took the numb away after Daddy left.

'Run where?' I finally said out loud because maybe she would stop screaming for a minute.

Marlena said, 'What?'

It was enough to break Marlena's spell, so I spoke into the darkness.

Sasha, where are you? And Sasha said, *RUN RUN RUN*. Her

voice was everywhere now so I asked her again, *Where are you?* But she kept screaming, *RUN RUN RUN* and a part of me wanted to grab hold of her voice with my empty hand and pull her out. So I stood, dragged my hand away from Marlena's breast, and gawked, my mouth dry because I was beginning to think I could do both, look at Marlena and find Sasha. But Marlena started on her other breast and now I was looking at left and right and I was under. So I couldn't stop staring at Marlena because I wanted to live again. And I couldn't stop looking because I just wanted to see breasts.

Marlena said, 'This is special, only for you. Nobody else has ever seen this.' I knew she was lying because of those Swiss and German boyfriends, all older and taller than me, but I didn't care. She loved me and I loved her.

She was different from the little girls of my pre-teen days. Andrene and I did something like it once. Correction. Faith, Donovan, Andrene and I did something like it. Under the bed, where else would it be? Donovan had said, 'Come see.' I was in the middle of flying my kite. 'You have to see,' he insisted. And when I looked, Andrene and Faith had nothing on and my mouth was wide open because Andrene said, 'Close your mouth. Flies will get in.' I wanted to tell Donovan, *Mummy going to beat you*, but nothing came out. Instead I knelt there looking back and forth between my brother and Andrene before she grabbed my hand, pulled me under, and positioned me on top of her.

We were play acting, copycatting what we'd heard second and third hand that adults did. Only touching parts, scrounging around in each other's privates.

Marlena, though, had curvy places and soft places. She made me touch her down there. Not that same day but the next. She said since I was so bright, smart and intelligent; she said it just like that; bright, smart and intelligent with all the commas in the right places, she would show me more things. She asked, 'Yuh like what ah showed yuh yesterday?' She was stone-faced, like she was testing me, attempting to determine if I was worth the effort, if I could be trusted with the priceless things she held.

'It's alright,' I said, but I could tell she knew that I liked it a lot because she smirked. That time she didn't ask me to close my eyes. She seized my forearm and I couldn't believe how such softs hands could grip me so tightly. I stopped breathing when she slid my hand lower and it was passing her navel on a slow motion downhill glide. And Sasha came back. *Run, run, run,* but her voice was so much softer than the day before. Why didn't she talk to me when I went back to my room to read or on my walk to the beach? Was that too much to ask? And where was she all those years? So I told her *No, you left me, so no I want to stay here and watch*. I could feel her trying to say more but I hummed *show mi yuh motion trah la la la laaa* to drown her out because I thought I'd have more time later.

I let Marlena take my right hand and put it in her panties and it felt like tangled string. She was sitting up in bed, her fluffy pillows supporting her back. The cushy thing wrapped around my fingers and tickled me. She moved my hand lower and she felt soft and warm and sticky. I looked at her. And she looked at me. I didn't know my penis could get so hard.

Her mother interrupted us.

'Marlena come help with the groceries,' Mrs. McKenzie said.

'Be there in a minute, Mummy,' Marlena said with my hand still on her soft part. She winked and I was ready to hear Sasha then, but it was too late.

The next day Marlena opened the bathroom door while I was showering and inspected me.

'Yuh growing,' she said when she held my penis. 'Good for you.' Her hands felt like it had no mass and she left just as suddenly as she burst in.

On my last day some of her friends from school, not the ones from before, picked her up. She wore white shorts and a white blouse over her bathing suit. She told them to, 'Hold on, ah soon come,' and she made me touch her down there again, but it was smooth this time. I drew my hand back. The change alarmed me. 'I think you've had enough,' she said, 'wish me luck on my exams.' And I stood there in the shower with cold water raining on me.

I ran into my father at a football match at Prison Oval stadium a couple of weeks after I returned home. The Oval isn't like the ones on Big League Soccer; it's an open grassy area where all the fans stand around the perimeter of the field. The prison is on the west side, rings of barbed wire and broken bottles with the sharp edges up, submerged in concrete at the top of the wall. I shouldn't have been there because Mummy despised the place. I was still reeling from Marlena because I hadn't heard from her after that last day; she couldn't understand what I gave up to be with her. So I nursed my hurt by looking at other girls and wondering what lay beneath.

In the northeast corner of the field a DJ spun soca and dancehall reggae, all the new songs of the time. Right in the middle of his set he started playing *Shine Eye Gyal is a Trouble to a Man* and I missed Sasha then. The song seemed so out of place. Sasha and I used to love the part *Rastafari know shi cyaan tek it* but we didn't know the words so we'd say *Rastafari know shi cyaan mek it*, and we'd listen to RJR-FM all day in the summer hoping they'd play it and then we'd sing really loud dragging out the *knoooooww* and fall down laughing afterwards. Now that I was older, I understood the lyrics and was thinking Marlena was my *shine eye gyal* because *the things I've done shi don't appreciate.* The bass rumbled through my stomach and I closed my eyes and the DJ said, 'wheel' right at the beginning of the second chorus. I hate when they do that just when the song is getting good. Out of nowhere I felt a stab in the middle of my back.

'Gih mi yuh money bwoy!' Deep laughter. A hand gripped my shoulder tight and spun me round.

'Daddyyyy.' My voice gushed with childish glee. I caught myself before I hugged him. We boxed for a minute before he pretended I clocked him with a right uppercut. He held onto me like he was trying to get the referee to pull us apart and it tickled.

'This my big son right here,' he said to the girl beside him. My heart was all thunder.

'Di bright one?' she said in a Belizean accent. Daddy nodded with twinkling eyes and I wanted to take a picture right then, freeze him in effigy.

'Hello, honey,' she said then scratched my chin and kissed me on the cheek. She used her right thumb to remove the lipstick stain she left behind. I'm sure we exchanged names but I can't remember hers.

'Goin' be a doctor one day, right big man?' Daddy said and punched my chest.

'Yes Daddy.' I was slightly out of breath and trying to think of other things to say but I hadn't time to prepare so I just looked at him.

'How yuh mother? Shi back yet?'

It hadn't occurred to me he would have heard of her hospitalisation, that he even cared.

'She's fine,' I said, willing myself to be angry for her because he was so happy and light, but then he touched my head and I didn't care anymore. I started to shadow box and I waited for him to spar with me again only this time I'd let him knock me out and I'd hug him then. He didn't see me, though. The two teams took the field.

'Gih mi two minutes,' he said to the girl.

'Yuh like har?' he said when he caught my eyes following the rhythm of her backside as she walked away.

'Sorry,' I said and looked down. His chuckle made me smile. I began formalising the words I'd tell him, the five-paragraph structure when you first learn to write essays. The referee blew the opening whistle and I felt Daddy slipping away. It was as if he and I lived in two different universes where time didn't sync, and the Prison Oval was a rift in space that allowed us only seconds with each other every few years. Only my seconds were millennia for him so I had to tell him everything in headlines, being careful not to bury the lead. The roasted peanut man drew close and Daddy bought me a packet. The smell of pickled carrots, scotch bonnet pepper and fried fish soaked the air.

The home team fans erupted in anger when the defender scored an own goal. The woman in front of us shouted, 'Dah bwoy deh ah guh dead.' I was standing to Daddy's left and I glanced down at his hand; he was still wearing his wedding ring. I must have looked confused.

'That?' He turned his left hand right side up. 'Yuh mother and me complicated.' I knew the next set of words by heart: *when yuh get older you'll understand.* 'Hope,' he said after that. 'Not a thing wrong with that; yuh know what ah mean, big man?' His eyes glassed over while he spoke and I sensed he wasn't talking to me anymore. Except for our occasional sideline coaching, we watched the game in silence. I turned to him when the referee called for an injury break.

'I was at Mr. and Mrs. McKenzie's when Mummy was getting better.' I began my first headline and launched into the next without thinking. 'And I saw Marlena naked and Sasha was trying to tell me not to look but I didn't care. I looked anyway. And then I touched Marlena down there but Sasha said I shouldn't but I told her shi cyaan tell mi what to do. It did nice, Daddy.' It came out in a single breath. His eyes were smiling but not like when you're proud of your big son. More like *that's nice but maybe next time you should...* I inhaled but he shook his head and squeezed my shoulder to stop me before I went on.

'Who Sasha? Never mind. Look Matthew, a real man doesn't kiss and tell, alright big man?'

'I just wanted to...' My eyes flooded and I couldn't hold back the tears. 'Sorry,' I was saying to Sasha because I couldn't believe how easily I downplayed her to impress my father.

'Listen to mi good. Some things are for you only,' he said. I couldn't answer because I was bawling quietly with my head down. 'Yuh listening?' He pulled my chin up to face him, squeezed my shoulder once more and smiled. 'Awright, man. Awright.' His thumbs wiped my tears in one swipe. 'Look, if yuh quiet then nobody can ever tek it from yuh. Awright? Always remember that.' I said okay but I didn't understand, I wanted him to be proud of me. We watched the home team concede four more goals on the way to a five–love rout in the first half.

The DJ was at it again and the girl waved and shimmied

her shoulders motioning for us to come dance with her. Only the die-hard football heads showed any interest in the game at that point. Daddy mouthed something to her and she blew us a kiss and continued dancing. I couldn't think of what else to tell him. I know I should have made a fuss about an A in Maths and Integrated Science last term or trying out for the table tennis team next month. But I thought I was using up all his years with me in silence, that I was selfish because I could have shared some of this with Donovan.

We stood silent once more and I watched all the girls and women dancing, and I was thinking of Marlena's soft part and maybe Daddy could tell me how to get her to talk to me. I wondered if he'd let me hold his hand even though I was too old for that; or maybe he'd take me with him because I didn't want to face my sojourn. There was so much in my head. But at that moment, out of the corner of my eye, I glimpsed his girlfriend call him over, her face full of meaning and this time he was by her side. I watched them both, the ease with which her arm looped his neck like Mummy's, his big hands on her waist. He and Mummy looked better but I still wanted to know what that felt like, my hand on a woman's waist, me standing behind her, those hips swaying in front of me.

Daddy must have told me goodbye, *tek care of yuh mother, you the man of the house now*, all the things parting fathers say to their big sons, but I can't remember. I only knew that his girlfriend and all the other women looked so good and I wanted Marlena's breasts and the other soft part and I wanted to find Sasha. But I couldn't do both, so I let Sasha leave me again and I didn't stop her.

Chapter 14

It's drizzling but no one is leaving. There are more and more bodies outside the gate: noisier ones. They pour in by the dozen out of thin air. It's as if they have come by bus, completing the second leg of a pre-arranged all-inclusive holiday package deal. A small van with a mural of a plate of oxtail and white rice painted on the side has appeared. The driver, a muscular woman, pushes out the side of the van like a window and hooks a metal rod under one of the edges to keep it open. I smell Ackee and salt fish and callaloo and fried bammy. Within seconds there's a queue. I will it to rain harder and it does. This is not my doing and I thank Sasha for listening to me.

I tell her I want them to go. I hate these people but this isn't the time for such feelings. The operator turns the digger off. When I demand to know why, he says, 'Rain, my bredrin.'

'This not so bad, man,' I say.

He looks at me for a moment then makes his way to the food van. I glare at the police and one by one they join the line. Someone has turned on music, a tune I don't recognise. Bass is thumping and the people are laughing.

There's no point in being angry. It will be done in their time, not mine. I ask her again to tell me where she is. I can feel her working up a whisper and I listen.

Chapter 15

I began third form by rote: knapsack, pen, pencil, T-square in hand, Sasha a blip, mind clear. I had Physics, Chem, Bio, Technical Drawing, Maths, English, P.E. I was still taking French and like everyone else in class I spent my summer on the beach, (and in my case a couple of weeks with my hands on Marlena) my vocabulary atrophying in the heat of the sun. I forgot the most basic of conjugations.

'*Être, Monsieur Archer.*' Madame Estefan pointed the metre stick in my direction on the first day of class. I didn't catch all she said because my head was swimming in black nipples. Instinctively I looked behind me hoping that another Archer was taking up French, sitting in one of the empty chairs along the wall. Madame Estefan, though, did not allow back benchers.

'Me, Miss?' I asked, my brow knitted, giving the thing between my legs enough time to recede.

'*Oui, Monsieur Archer.* You are the only one with that name.' Ruffles of apprehensive laughter flowed across the room. '*Maintenant, Monsieur Archer. Vite, vite*! In time now.' The stick struck her table for the usual start of the conjugation rhythm.

'*Je suis,*' I said. And before the next strike I rattled off, '*Tu es, il est, nous sommes, vous êtes, ils sont, elles sont.'* I couldn't believe my luck; it came back to me so quickly.

'*Non! Non, non, non, Monsieur Archer.* You're not listening. I said *l'imparfait. L'imparfait*! *Commencer*!' The rhythm restarted.

'*Je... Je serai?*' I began, my rising pitch at the end hopeful I had the imperfect tense.

'*Est-ce une question Monsieur Archer?*'

'I...' More laughter.

'*Je serai, Monsieur Archer? C'est le futur*! *Mon dieu.* Who can help him out?' All heads and eyes found much interest in the books in their hands. '*Monsieur Moncrief.*' He too mumbled and fumbled, making up conjugations and pronunciations that could have passed for Russian, Spanish or German. Peter Rollins had his hand up, but he always did and Madame Estefan looked through him.

'*Mauvais élèves*! Quiz on Wednesday. Read chapters one to four,' she said. If it had been allowed she would have caned us all.

By quiz Madame Estefan meant a full-blown test. I studied, but not as much as I should have, and when I was shoved onto the sardine-packed *jolly* bus that morning it dawned on me that I'd also failed to do the homework she had assigned.

I was back on morning shift and the quiz was right after devotions. It was the same routine on the bus every day since first form; the fruitless search to find the perfect position, hoping the boy behind you knew better than to wedge his elbow at the base of your skull, or trying to avoid inadvertently rubbing up against the backside of the Alpha girl or the St. Hugh's girl or the Queen's girl in front of you. That morning it was a St. Hugh's girl and she had twice been the recipient of my inability to reliably control my erections.

So every time the driver pressed the clutch we swooned forward and when he changed gears we swayed back. Seesawing we went all the way from Spanish Town to Kingston, my penis begging for relief. At that point I just wanted to avoid any part of the St. Hugh's girl's body getting remotely close to my crotch. The last time I pricked her I said, 'Sorry, the gear change…' Then she stabbed her heel into my toes.

When the driver pulled out of the bus stop at Pembroke Hall I managed to shift left to avoid the girl's buttocks. I could see the floral arrangement of school uniforms we were leaving behind; Immaculate Conception High girls wore white skirts and blouses and light blue ties with brown shoes and socks. Holy Childhood girls donned royal blue pleated skirts, beige blouses and a mini royal blue tie that started at the neck and ended halfway down their chests. St. Andrew High girls wore yellow or blue straight dresses. St. Hugh's girls green, Wolmer's girls light blue straight tunics and a white blouse, Queen's High a grey tunic, white shirt and a burgundy tie, Merlgrove girls a straight blue dress with a pleat on each side of the skirt section, and Alpha girls navy blue tunic with white belt and white shirt. Yes, these are the things you notice when you're thirteen and you go to a boys' school.

Everyone agreed that Queen's girls were easy and Immaculate girls were pretty and rich. Under their uniforms Holy Childhood girls fought a sexual craving so strong they had to pray before Mother Superior every afternoon before they went home or they'd become whores. The dresses and skirts on every girl, I concluded, were too long, so I had to make do with the smoothness of their calves, praying for a stiff breeze to lift those hems over their knees.

There I was thinking about calves and legs, white slips, white panties, white bras, and the erection was coming again. It took time to deflate and the gear was readying to change once more. The weight of the boy behind me pushed me back into St. Hugh's girl. I pictured her taking hold of my thing and snapping it, first in two, then four. I mentally ran through the verb *avoir*. *J'ai, tu as, il a*.

The clutch sent us leaning forward, *vous avez, nous avons, ils ont, elles ont*. Another gear change and I was unwittingly aiming for St. Hugh's girl and there was no time to move my pelvis out of the way. I worked on the *passé simple*: *J'eus, tu eus*. We were at the intersection of Molynes Road and Washington Boulevard and I had to shift because the conjugations stopped working. I bent my knees slightly, hoping that I'd at least not assault her with the full force. And just then, through the window, I saw her.

I blinked and blinked again and again. She was still there. Four years had passed. Four. And it was like the week before she left; all of us, Andrene and Donovan and her and me playing dandy shandy in the carport and our parents calling us in to have a bath. She was walking down Molynes Road, strolling really. It couldn't be. Then I saw that bobbing head drifting away as the bus passed through the light. It was her. And she was still wearing them, bubbles and ribbons, but it didn't look right, a girl with proper breasts and certainly hair down there and the hair on her head should have been pressed by now.

'STOP. STOP. STOP,' I screamed.

'Why yuh have to bih suh loud?' St. Hugh's girl said.

'STOP.' I didn't care if she was pretty and she would tell her friends about the *tegareg bwoy* on the bus this morning. I felt the place closing in, all the passengers an ocean drowning me. I cried out to Sasha.

'Wait for me. Wait for me.'

I began to shove St. Hugh's girl out of the way when the woman at the window seat said, 'Yuh have fi ring di bell.' She sat underneath it but refused to press it for me. She shook her head and returned to her Mills and Boon novel. I stretched over the man beside her and rang. St. Hugh's girl punched my arm. I was closer to the front but she wouldn't let me pass so I headed for the back door.

'STOP. STOP.' My throat burned. 'STOP,' my voice now at its loudest point. I could feel my words as a soundwave hopping over cars and bicycles, squeezing through the pedestrians, overpowering transistor radios and boom boxes, crying babies and children playing on their way to school. Sasha was at The Open Bible Church now and I began to drill my way through the bodies.

I'm coming. I'm coming. I closed my eyes for a moment to concentrate on Sasha's mind. It was she who started it. We would stare at each other for minutes on end, our mouths shut. Initially we saw each other's images in our heads, then we felt our exhalations and inhalations, and sometimes when we really focused the thumpity thump of our hearts.

I was the first to hear. We never knew when blackheart man would come and so we'd be quiet, still as ever as we practised.

'Wha' mi a t'ink?' she'd say, two of us barely breathing, our bodies flat against the ground. I used to watch her chest rise and fall and I'd think of a bicycle pump. Me and her breathing and looking up into the evening sky, the zoysia grass tickling our backs. And it just happened one day, sudden. All I know is that I could hear her shouting, so loud I wanted to tell her *shhh*. So I answered with my mouth, my voice cracked and happy, 'I like

Horlicks too,' and she hugged me and said, 'don't forget.' She turned her head sideways, our chests still facing the sky, and said, 'My turn,' but she didn't hear me that time. She heard me later, though, and when she did she was sad and I couldn't understand because I was thinking about heaven and a cloud and me and her flying.

So that morning on the bus my knapsack hooked itself on an arm, slowing me down even more. I took occasional glances through the window as I pushed on. Shove, crane my neck, look, repeat. And she was still there only she was getting away from me really fast. 'Stop, driver, stop.' I was almost at the back door. 'Stop.'

'Ring di bell,' another woman shouted, 'im fool eeee?'

I stepped on legs and toes. More than once I felt a fist in my back. So many bodies. It was as if the closer I got to the exit, the thicker the crowd became.

'Get out of the way. Get out,' I demanded.

'Him facety and renk,' a woman said. There was no time for apologies. I took one more look through the window and I could see Sasha's head beyond the Esso petrol station. The driver had to stop now or I'd miss her.

'Stop di bus! Please!' I was ready to throw myself through the window but someone shoved me and I fell off the steps and on to the gravel.

Several yards stood between me and Molynes Road.

I ran.

'Sasha. Sasha,' I called after her but it was rush hour and the blaring horns and bad mufflers scattered her name. A couple of yards from Molynes Road I crossed the first two lanes. I stopped in the middle on the median and waited for traffic to ease. And then the light turned red. I adjusted my knapsack and switched my T-square to my right hand. I was off again. I turned down Molynes Road and she was nowhere. Then it hit me; what if, like me, she too turned? How would I know which road? And even if I picked the right street, did she go left or right?

I was running aimlessly now and I had to stop. Then I began to convince myself that it couldn't have been her and I was thinking about the French test and the fat round zero I'd receive and how do I explain that to Mummy.

'Come out a di road,' a woman shouted as she passed me, her hand still leaning on the horn, 'yuh stupid or something?'

I hopped on the pavement and there, just beyond the bar, was Sasha's head.

She was quick.

'Yuh have fi move faas cause blackheart man wi tek yuh weh,' she used to say. 'Come, hole mi han'.' Off we'd go but it's hard to run when someone's holding your hand, like they're pulling you along and you have to keep up, not because you're afraid of blackheart man and not because you want to be faster than her as your nine-year-old self used to believe; you have to keep up because you don't want her to leave you ever.

This time I was catching up but there were cars everywhere, stopping right in time and honking. 'Watch weh yuh a guh eediot bwoy.' 'Come out a di road, yuh nuh si big man waaan drive.' The noises confused me and I lost her for a few moments. I saw the ribbons again at the entrance of some school. I couldn't make out the name.

Someone was following close, a step or two behind her. Who was that? It had to be Stephen, I thought, but this man looked older and purposeless like he was trying his luck: *What's up, beautiful*? I imagined he said. She would have ignored him and he would have said, *guh weh gyal, mi si yuh pon video*, and she'd say, *just like yuh mumma*. No, he wasn't her brother. He gave up by the time she crossed Headley Avenue.

She wasn't in her school uniform. It was seven thirty in the morning and she was simply walking, not like going somewhere, more like it was a constitutional or something. She should have had her books and a knapsack or just the one book and pencil like she used to.

'Sasha. Sasha.' I'm not sure if anything was coming out at that point, my voice box had already passed its limits.

I was at Seaward Drive, a little past the gully, when a car slowed beside her. He turned down his music. A nice car, something Daddy would drive. He kept creeping along, *chanting har down*, and I hoped she was telling him what *im cyan guh duh with himself*. Instead she leaned in and her head fully disappeared through the passenger side window.

'Leave her alone,' I shouted.

'Run my yute,' a man on a bicycle mocked.

'Him mussi deh pon sup'n,' someone else said.

'Sasha.' I was losing my breath once more. The man was still with her and the drivers kept blaring their horns because I was on and off the pavement dashing around slow pedestrians.

'Leave her alone. Yuh betta leave har alone.'

'Ah yuh girlfrien' dat my yute?' a young girl selling bags of coconut drops, grater cake and peppa shrimp said as I ran by her. She slapped her thigh with her free hand and laughed. 'Yuh cyaaan handle dat likkle man.' She laughed even harder, and all the pedestrians laughed too and I wanted to punch them in the face for thinking of us like that.

I ran. The French and Physics books in my knapsack slowed me down. I should dump it or I'd never catch up, I thought.

'Sasha. Sasha.' I was begging now and I didn't blame her for ignoring me because I betrayed her with Marlena and Daddy. She crossed Brettford Avenue and she was so fast, as if one step equalled twenty of mine, like I was running in place in an unending dream. My shoes were too fancy for this race, first-day-of-the-school-year shoes, but I had to keep them on because this is Jamaica. She crossed another street and another.

The car following her stopped once more and she leaned in again for a moment and then her head was back out of the window and I was happy she left him. But he was still with her, his car crawling, ignoring the blasting horns and cussing. She stopped a third time. She looked taller than I had remembered, rounder too, with hips like a woman and for a moment I wondered if I had been foolish because why would she want to be seen with a boy like me. By now she would have been fifteen, and that was woman territory, courting big man with big man car and big man cock and big man job and big man house and big man wife and big man daughter her age.

He had a car that smelled like almond mixed with lemons, the breeze carried the scent that far. It had a good sound system, playing Marvin Gaye, and I could tell that inside was clean and had air conditioning. So she was stopping to talk to him once more and I was still shouting, 'Leave her alone!' And it was her like I remembered but different, good different, full of joy. I thought I should leave her be in the happy place she found; that maybe Mummy was right after all, that Sasha was just fine, a wilful child who couldn't care less about me.

And she still liked yellow. Yellow skirt and a white *gyanzi*. And it wasn't ribbons she was wearing but some fancy clips and beads. Sasha Knight was getting in the car and I couldn't catch up and when the door opened the music was louder and it wasn't Marvin Gaye but Teddy Pendergrass; a soul song, smooth and nice and she wouldn't have to take the bus, and she wouldn't have to walk, and someone was paying attention this time.

'Sasha!'

I was laughing and crying and I realised then, as my breath was leaving me, my chest heaving and hoeing, that I hadn't laughed in four years. Not even a proper smile. And I was cracking up as if I had finally gotten all the jokes I'd heard in my life, all of them at once setting my body on fire.

The man must have said something wrong, or he changed his mind, because she pulled back and started to turn my way. So maybe she wasn't that happy after all, perhaps she still needed me. My heart was deafening. I was nearly beside her now and I couldn't call her name I was so tired. Ten more steps, that's all I needed and then from somewhere I found one last strong wind and I said her name, 'Sasha.'

She was turning round because she knew that voice, like she understood that if she didn't listen it would be over. Everything: dandy shandy, marbles, getting inna spirit, River, the sky, June plums and mangoes, existence. Love. Five more steps.

Then she began to fade. She was turning around, and I could see her ears and the corner of her mouth and her thick lips, like a hundred sets of lips cross-laminated to make one, but it was becoming night, and I was flying, flying, flying into that darkness. I felt a rush of wind on my right ear, that breeze when your friend leans in to tell you a big juicy secret and it's going to tickle and I was ready to hear. *Tell me what you want to say. Hurry up*, I said, and I was still laughing because life wasn't cruel after all. God brought her back to me and I was going to tell her sorry that I made her get beat'n and sorry I didn't listen when she told me to run from Marlena and sorry that I told Daddy that I didn't care what she said and I was going to promise to listen from now on.

'Lawd, him a guh fall ovah. Ketch him quick, ketch him.' Was that Sasha's voice? I couldn't tell. No, it sounded older and full of the anticipation of a story to share that night: *Yuh shoulda sih dis bwoy, run like him is mad man.* One more step, two at most. Sasha must have been facing me, or I was facing her, and I couldn't see, and then it was a cloud, nice and soft taking me away.

'I have to go,' I said to the cloud, 'please let me go. She's going to tell me something. She's going to whisper it right here.' I tried to point to my left ear but I couldn't feel my hands. 'Please,' I begged the cloud, 'just one more minute.' But I was already there, right on top of it, and I flew headfirst into the darkness.

Chapter 16

I go back to that place where I lost her. It isn't anchored by walls and roads and trees and sky and Puerto Seco beach. It's a place of emptiness where I wait to be filled, only it will not happen. It's the space in between.

She takes me somewhere different now. We're on the way to River, walking the back way through Ensom City, her hand in mine and my hand in hers. River is not the kind of place where you carry a separate bag for your towels and lotions and slippers. You go to River because at one o'clock on a Thursday summer afternoon you just feel like it. And we strip down to our briefs and panties and somersault in. There are others there, *tegareg* children, the same ones that beat you up way back, called you *batty bwoy*, but they're afraid of you now because Sasha has her arm around you and she cut one of them three weeks before and everybody knows to just leave it.

It's clear that I've learned to swim at Mr. Patterson's four p.m. camp three or four summers ago. *Remember to kick, Mr. Archer, kick.* I cannot perform the sea licks the *tegareg* children can but Sasha shows me how; 'just duh dis,' she says and she hurls above the water, her body twists and her right leg slices the air and whacks the river. Twin waterfalls rise as her leg disappears under the green liquid. I try and everyone laughs but she looks at them and they all stop. Bad gyal Sasha. No one will laugh at Matthew today.

Later I'll watch her get baptised here. She in all white, her whole body under the Rio Cobre, the gown blown up like a balloon on top of the water and when she comes out, barefooted, the women cover her with a big sheet. They surround her while she changes. She still looks cold when she's all dressed up in her yellow frock with the yellow sequins in the front and the fairy tale skirt section. I'm not supposed to be here early on a Sunday morning. I tell Mummy I'm going to Gary's to study for Common Entrance. I watch all these people sing *Fiyah, fiyah, fiyah, fiyah fall on me* and *Take me to the Water* and *The Water is Troubled My Friend, step right in.* I wonder if the river has changed, all these bodies dipped in the blood of Jesus, wiped clean. Red blood and white clothes over black bodies. That's all there is here, black bodies. Five more baptised by a man who at most finished the sixth grade. He speaks of giving your life to Jesus. 'Di door ah close right now, breddahs and sistahs. Di... door... ah... close.' He's waiting for someone or something. He doesn't look at me. It's as if he knows I don't belong, that I cannot love God like they do, because theirs is a love borne from day's work and maid service, a love only the invisible can know. I have black skin also but he knows, because I live in Cheshire Hills and I have a lawn and a garage and the same last name as my mother. He knows because all Black people just do. It's not true of course. He sees nothing of what I will face, of how I must love God because I cannot make this journey without Him.

* * *

'Remember dis,' Sasha says on the way home after our swim.

'Yes,' I say, and she's off weaving between the Macca trees. The dirt under our feet is light brown and dusty. We're barefoot. I'm not supposed to be. Mummy will be cross if I don't get home on time to wash it off.

'Arrggghhh,' I scream out. A *macca* catches me on the arm, right above my elbow. Bloody welts are forming. She grabs me by the biceps, pulls several leaves from a plant nearby, and rubs them in my cuts. It burns. She puts her arm around me and I lean my head on her. When I pull away I see that dark yellow spots have formed on her halter top. I didn't know I was crying.

'Come,' she says. We're not done running. We can never stop for too long anywhere except in our fort, two crocus bags that lay under the Ackee tree facing the canal. My summer reading sits unfinished in my room because of all the running. Four books. Poor Anne of Green Gables will have to wait, there are important things Sasha and I must do.

'I can't,' I say.

'*I can't*,' she says. 'Yuh too sawf.'

'No, I'm not soft.' I pout.

'Yuh sawf like ratten ahrinj. Wooyyyeeeee.' She throws her head back and holds her belly. I try to erase the crying from earlier so I stand, my arm scorching in pain. I won't show Mummy the welts because there will be questions I cannot answer.

'Him a come,' she says. 'Run.' And we're off, practising for that day when we know we will face him. I can see the bottoms of her feet, her heels skimming the hem of her skirt. This is a sprint now. Knees up, fists balled, arms swing vigorous. Up Ensom Avenue and the last hill before we leave Ensom City. The bar on the right is open even though it's early afternoon. Out of the corner of my eyes I glance a group of boys surrounding a girl who looks to be clobbering them at Ms. Pacman. Sasha and I can see Mr. Chin's shop directly ahead. On the left we're passing the massive breadfruit tree, so big its branches cover an entire lot. I'm about to catch her this time. *I am not soft. I am not soft. I am not soft.* I say it over and over as I run. We reach Brunswick Avenue and I'm just about beside her. Two more strides at most and we'll be side by side and from there I'm away. We step into the road. We know we should look but we both have to win. She's half a step ahead and in the street first.

'Mih soon ketch yuh.' I breathe out. I like that I can talk like her now, use her language to taunt her. She's trying to answer but she needs everything to beat me. We're halfway across. We know we're halfway because we just do, there are no white or yellow lines that tell you. Government has long given up on that level of maintenance. If you don't know then you shouldn't have a licence. If you don't know you shouldn't cross the road. My arm is touching her now. One more step and I'll be in front. And then I can't feel her arm next to me anymore. No, not her arm but her. I look back because she loves to change the route midway. She likes to turn and twist. She makes mazes even in wide open spaces, dodging invisible trees and holes and rocks.

'Not fair,' I say but she's on the ground, in the middle of the road, splayed flat and something is coming fast. Big. It will chew her up. I go back for her.

'Come on!' I scream. I don't have time to say it her way. *Patwah* is work for me. I have to think about what I have to say first. I kneel and grab her arm. I pull on her but she doesn't speak. She doesn't move. I pull and pull.

'Stop playing,' I shout. 'Stop playing.' The big thing is blowing its horn. It has time to swerve but this is Jamaica and *likkle pickney must know fi nuh play*, so if you are in the way, you'll get it. I pull and pull. I manage to get her head on the edge of the concrete lip of the pavement. The big thing with the big horn looks like it's aiming at us, the radiator grill like a whale's mouth. Headlight eyes the size of oil drums. It has changed gears, not downshifting to engine brake, but cruising.

'Please, please, please.' I close my eyes and make one last tug, but I fall backward. Roaring laughter, another belly kind. We're sitting on the pavement, her out-of-breath cracking up, and me... Me. *I am not soft.*

'Yuh a cry?' she asks, and for an instant she looks sorry but then she laughs some more. She's correct. I am crying. Right there on the pavement on Brunswick Avenue. Five blocks from where I'd later live when she is gone.

'You're not nice,' I say.

Her laugh dies a little. 'Come nuh? Ah weh yuh a wait pon?' she says. 'Wi cyaaan stay too long.' We stand and she grabs my hand. We don't run this time. We walk hand in hand, she's a half step ahead and I let her drag me. I look down the road at the bus shrinking in the distance.

'Yuh waaan tek a bus?' she says.

'No. I want to walk,' I say, angry. I do not like her like this.

That morning in hospital I opened my eyes to the girl in the corner, only she wasn't. Women look different from girls. It's the forehead. It laughs and giggles when a woman is a girl. It sharpens and hardens when she becomes a woman. It loses wonder; it understands that you ask questions before you run off. You don't go to River with your arm around a boy and show him how to do sea licks. And so this woman, not a girl, in the light of the streaming sun, leaning on a table in the corner, in a room full of the gun shot wounded and the machete chopped and the stabbed and the dead body two beds down, asks me, 'Yuh alright, sweetheart?'

I know it's not *her* because my Sasha would have called me *fuh-fool. Yuh faint, wooooyyyeeee!* And we would have laughed together. But it had to be her, Sasha all grown up. Sasha, woman-not-a-girl.

'Sasha,' I said, my voice crackly, 'I was just remembering that one time when we were coming home from River and you pretended to faint on Brunswick Avenue. Remembah?' I tried to get up but my head felt like water vapour and two nurses pressed me down. The woman-not-a-girl wore a pink blanket over her shoulders as if the sun suddenly made her cold.

'No,' I was saying, 'no.' She wasn't wrapped up enough, her arms and legs still bare, like the blanket was a superhero cape. She should have been bundled up in it, covered from head to toe in a shroud.

'I don't understand, sweetheart,' the woman-not-a-girl said. She placed her hand on my forehead.

'It's not right. Don't you see? You're going to be cold,' I said to Sasha. 'You can't be cold.' And then I laughed and pointed to the room and the air and the woman-not-a-girl in the white *gyanzi* and yellow skirt and the pink blanket that was supposed to be making her warm, with her left hip cotching the table.

'I told you,' I said, my voice dim and raspy. 'Yuh believe me now, Mummy? I told you she didn't run away.'

Chapter 17

I feel a raindrop on my right ear. It's like warm feather. I wait for the next one but it never comes. I look up and the clouds are moving quickly as if running from a fast and clever predator. I want them to stay for a minute, to wash and cleanse this place before the digger begins. She deserves at least that.

She's restless, I can tell. There's not enough light here. It's like dawn everywhere else, the moment when you think it will be overcast all day then the sun squeezes through. It's been night for too long, dark and wet. I ask Graeme for a flashlight.

He says, 'I don't want to waste battery.'

'Okay,' I say. I don't really want one; I only need to get closer to her and he won't let me.

'Evidence,' he says. 'We have to make sure it's a clean chain.' This isn't the time to fight, to draw lines. All that's been done before. I've proved my point. I will prove my point.

Chapter 18

It did me in, that morning I fainted. I wanted to rid Sasha from me, make her a stone once more. Instead, there were resonances of her everywhere, faces I'd bump into on the street, on the bus, random visitors at church, cousins of cousins. Once I thought I saw her on a Sunday afternoon at Hellshire Beach, only this girl couldn't have been more than six years old. I almost called after her, *Sasha, it's me*, but she was off to her daddy before I could say a word. Even the tiniest of body parts and functions, an overgrown dirty finger nail, an elbow, a pimple, breathing, a cleared throat, filled me with frantic expectancy.

For weeks I took the most circuitous routes to and from school. I stopped the bus at Dunrobin Road, Liguanea, Cross Roads or New Kingston. I'd transfer to buses going to Papine or Edge Water. I'd sit by the window seat, head cocked, eyes alert, for any moment I'd see her walking, running, laughing on the side of the street in front of Pete's Patties, or sitting on a stoop between her mother's legs, getting *har hair plait up*. More than once a driver asked, 'Yuh not going to school, big man?' And I'd tell him I'm supposed to meet a friend, or I'd say I was on evening shift. I sounded too bookish to be a liar, so they believed me. I went as far as Clarendon one day before I realised I didn't have enough fare to make it back home. I dodged the conductress that time.

I tapped so many shoulders only to have a puzzled and, often, angry face stare back at me. Twice I was slapped. She was everywhere. I had to go further. I saved my lunch money for two weeks, skipped school one Wednesday and took three buses to Montego Bay. I slipped into Walter Fletcher Beach without paying and patrolled the white sand end to end. I saw her under the coconut trees, in the shallow end of the water and way out in the sea. I rubbed my eyes over and over. I was going slowly and quietly mad.

Mummy said it couldn't go on, that, 'Yuh better shape up or else.'

'Mummy, you don't understand. I saw her at...' We were in the living room and she wanted to know why I missed two weeks of Maths class.

'Her who? Yuh too young for that kind of thing.' I couldn't answer fast enough so she said, 'Yuh picking up this woman thing from yuh father. Matthew, we need to have a serious talk.'

'It's not like that, Mummy. Yuh don't understand.'

'Oh really, Mister Man? Please enlighten me, sir.'

'Sasha, Mummy. I saw Sasha. She's still out there.'

'Sasha? I haven't heard you talking about her before. Who is she?' She knitted her brow, a concerned mother worried that her boy was mixed up with a *leggo* girl. I looked at my mother, through and through, my heart in my lap, my head on fire. She'd forgotten her too and it hadn't been long, not long at all.

'Sasha, Mummy! It was you and Ms. Sheldon that said shi ran away. You said that! Remember?' I was screaming and crying and demanding answers and Mummy was looking at me all calm.

That was my cue that I'd better rein this in, but I didn't. 'I hate you. I hate Ms. Sheldon. She's a damn liar and a...' And Mummy boxed me.

'Anything else? Huh? Anything?' Her eyes ice. I was taller than Mummy by then but she dwarfed me. I stood there holding my cheek. 'The sacrifices I made for you boys. The sacrifices and look what yuh come to. Talking to me like me and yuh ah size.'

'Sorry,' I mumbled.

'Sorry?! Sorry?! We are not done yet, mister. We. Are. Not. Done.' And she boxed me again. I swallowed hard because I'd crossed a wide bright line and words wouldn't cut it this time. Then she opened an envelope. 'Oh, we are not done.' She kept on and on. 'Starting up with dis foolishness. I won't have it, yuh hear mi? I won't.' She slid a piece of paper out of the envelope, the kind that you write serious letters on, and I recognised it as soon as she unfolded it and smoothed out the creases.

'Imagine my surprise when I was in Lane's picking up sardines to make fritters for you and your brother. No help from your father. Not one drop. I have to do it all by myself.' She paused for it to sink in and I was really sorry then because she looked ready to cry. I knew she was going to tell her best friend Judy as that's how things are done on our island, *it takes a village*, and Judy was going to corner me one day and tell me *you're a disappointment to your mother*, that *yuh know she does everything for you boys*.

'And Mr. Blair asks me how is Matthew doing? *Just let me know if there is anything I can do to help him catch up with his studies.*' Mummy really wasn't done. 'First, yuh miss yuh French test that crazy morning. I still don't understand that whole business. And now yuh skipping school, jeopardising your future for some stupid girl, Sasha whatever-her-name-is. Is that what you are telling me, Matthew Archer?' I was quiet, head down, no longer full of righteous anger. 'I'm waiting.'

'Sorry, Mummy.'

'That's all you have to say? Because this letter has plenty more. Apparently you had to go to Miami for a... let me see what it says here.' She began reading my words back to me. '*A complex surgery. Matthew will be out of school for three weeks. Please excuse his absence.* Oh and look at this, my signature at the bottom.' Her eyes watering and this time a tear fell. 'Is this how it's going to be, Matthew? Is that what you want to become? A forger? A liar? A thief? A common criminal?' *Every liar is a thief and every thief is a liar.* We'd all heard it.

I tried to be good, threw myself into church, for what other way was there? I joined the youth choir, Pathfinders and bible class. I stopped listening to Prince and Madonna and even though my body itched to move when I passed the record stores blasting Yellowman and The Outlaw Josey Wales, I resisted. I'd hum *It only takes a spark to get a fire going* and *He brought us to the banqueting table, His banner over us is love.* I was clean.

But that only lasted an afternoon or two and I needed to be purified again because it wasn't enough. Never enough. Sasha everywhere. Sasha at the bus terminal, Sasha at church, Sasha behind the man in the white merino and striped *lengths trousers*, three gold rings on his left hand. I had to go deeper, find God elsewhere.

I took up with a fringe group of Adventists who said they were returning to primitive godliness; their words not mine. And I liked how that sounded, a godliness stripped bare, one of consuming fire. We were vegans, for the body is the temple of the Lord. The women wore dresses down to their ankles with sleeves all the way to their wrists. They said things like *latter rain* and *sanctification by faith* and *investigative judgement*. We existed in a permanent state of preparation for the Second Coming.

Still not enough, though. Their piety lacked joy, so I abandoned the fringe group after a few months when I found the under sixteen drama club at church. I vowed no longer to sin and I was there, at the gates of complete and entire goodness. Sasha quiet, forgotten, hidden. Mummy happy. I felt still.

And then it came back. It always comes back.

Chapter 19

There are mistakes you make, errors in judgement that we lay at the feet of childhood. We dismiss them as immaturity and inexperience, and when we grow older we laugh at our folly. But what if there are some mistakes you don't walk away from? What if you see the results distending far beyond the boundaries of your small life?

I had five bottles then. Fourteenth birthday. I bought the fifth one in Montego Bay at the tourist market.

The lady smiled wide and said, 'How come yuh suh handsome? Yuh sure yuh not goin' break her heart?' She wore a red, black and white plaid head wrap with a skirt that matched and a white blouse. She was a caricature of Miss Lou. She stuffed the bag with tissue paper, handed it to me, and cracked up, the kind where you throw your head back and slap your thighs. Why is it I can't do that anymore, real bellyful laughing like that lady? I gave her a smile and she said, 'Definitely breaking her heart.'

'It's...,' and I paused, '...for my friend,' I finally said. I wanted to share if even for a moment.

'Yeah? That's what all the great lady slayers say.' And we

chuckled together. I looked out on the rest of the market, its wood carvings for sale, the coconut shell jewellery, the men and women joshing each other; I heard good music that you can wine to but I didn't because I was still being pure. I felt Sasha beside me, our hands in each other's swinging away. Then I gazed out on the sea and the sunshine and I was thinking about all the progress I'd made, how my grades returned and how Mummy was happy again. I told Sasha, *Yuh cyan talk if yuh want to but yuh have to be careful. Mummy can't find out.* She didn't answer at first. And I repeated it.

Then she said, *Why? Yuh 'fraid ah har?* Sasha kissed her teeth and I grinned to myself.

The lady selling me the bottle said, 'Such a deep smile. This girl must really have yuh heart eee?' I almost didn't like her after she said it, just like everyone else, but then she saved it. 'Ah just joking with yuh, Mistah Handsome. Lawd yuh serious eee?'

I had one ever present problem, however. I was growing up quickly and eyeing girls differently, like how a teenage boy is supposed to look at girls he isn't related to. Sasha couldn't stand it when I was like that. She'd say, *why yuh heart a beat suh faas?* Or *yuh nevva si girl before? Whaappen to yuh?* And then she would go silent. Like I said, I just couldn't do both, liking girls and keeping Sasha with me. And I was liking girls more and more day by day and eventually I couldn't hear her at all.

And that is when I fell. Hard.

I was to be baptised in two weeks. I attended all the bible classes, understood the texts, the fundamental doctrines: the mortality of the soul, the Trinity, the Investigative Judgement, the Beast of Revelation. I took on church with extra vigour. I joined the young people's missionary society. I visited shut-ins and collected ingathering. But it was the under sixteen drama club that exhausted all my free time.

We were all fourteen and fifteen and we thought ourselves regular Sidney Poitiers and Kim Fields. We over-pronounced and over-projected and our director, Sister Peart, would have it no other way. Of the several plays we staged, I had yet to draw any large roles. I was an unremarkable gang member in *Jesus in the Streets*, a court reporter in *God on Trial*, and a stock boy in a shop in *The Grocer and the Deaconess*; all of them non-speaking parts.

Then one Sabbath afternoon Sister Peart called me aside and said, 'Yuh think yuh could be a pastor?'

'Yes,' I said, barely hiding my enthusiasm.

I copied my lines. Twice. I read them on the way to school. I rehearsed in the bathroom so nobody could hear me. June Taylor played Colette, a girl who had strayed, gotten herself 'in trouble', and I was the pastor offering her guidance. Two or three years younger and we would have giggled and sniggered at the word 'strayed' because even the youngest child among us knew that that meant she was pregnant out of wedlock. At fourteen and fifteen, though, the word sobered us because at our church at least one girl per year had made the same mistake.

It was always someone who was barely a year older than us, and we wondered what she could have been doing and with whom. After the news ran through the church we'd usually never hear from her again; at least not at our branch. If she was sincere and came crawling back she was 'forgiven' and re-baptised. She would have been better off trying another congregation, however, one far away in another parish like Westmoreland, because forgiveness didn't include people not talking behind your back or staring week after week. Jamaican Adventists don't forget such things. The gift of the church's pardon, the privilege to walk once more among God's chosen people, came with shame and the *susu susu* of the brethren.

In this play I worried that June Taylor would eclipse me because, except for her, there was not one solid actor among us. In the Christmas play the audience was there in the manger with her and the baby Jesus. When she sat at the desk we felt her penning all those hymns as Fanny J Crosby. And so I watched Pastor Meadows as he preached earlier that Sabbath for Youth Day. I mimicked how he gathered the fingers of his left hand as if holding a cricket ball ready to make his opening bowl, whenever he was making a point. I even duplicated his pauses and his smirk the moment he looked like he had you convinced.

A deacons' meeting forced us to hold the last practice before curtain call that Sabbath afternoon at my house. We rearranged the furniture and I provided drinks like Mummy taught me. Sister Peart took one sweeping look at the living room full of figurines and crystals and warned the group to take extreme care in handling Mummy's things. As usual we ran through the play at first reading our lines. Next without looking at our papers. All twelve of us bunched up in my living room; some on the settee, others on the floor, two or three at the dining table, June Taylor and I by the hallway to the kitchen. I offered them more drinks and *toto*. I didn't want them to leave.

Barrington Bailey played Carlton, the man who impregnated her. He wore dark glasses and a shirt with the sleeves ripped off. He said things like 'whaappen, baby,' 'look at yuh pretty girl, let mi tek yuh to dance tonight, nuh?' We laughed but June Taylor played coquettish and nervous. 'I don't think I should,' she said, and we became serious again. He moved in closer to her. 'Come nuh baby?' he said while pulling her along with him. She paused, filling that one last moment to change her mind with tension. The next scene was in the pastor's office. My hand rested on her shoulder. 'Young Sister June,' I began, 'I mean Colette...' They all laughed. 'Okay, Matthew,' Sister Peart said, 'just do it again.'

Then June Taylor was with Barrington and she was wearing clip on earrings to show she had not listened to the pastor. The stuffed pillowcase would be next but she was in her nice church dress so we all pretended she was big.

We took a break and it was like one long pause in my life. I felt Sasha coming on, not a whisper but a loud clang, as if she was trying to give me a good scare, and I was happy she was awake again even though I kept looking at Denise Butler because I planned to ask her out for ice cream the next day. Sasha was singing low, out of tune, *Take it easy, take it easy better slow down 'bwoy', That's no way to go, does your mother know?* I smiled and remembered that first time she was in my room, self-invited, touching everything, when she paused, mouth open, in front of my poster of the four blonde singers in light blue bell bottoms.

'Ah who dat?' she said, pointing with her thumb-sucking hand.

'That's ABBA,' I said, even though the name was scrawled in capital letters at the bottom.

I thought she couldn't read and was about to ask her if she wanted me to help her but she said, 'Ah wan mirror image AB.' I didn't know she could talk like that. My mouth must have been wide open for she told me to, 'Close yuh mout' else fly a guh guh in.' All those years listening to their music I hadn't noticed that ABBA was spelled that way.

'Really?' I said.

'*That's the name of the game*,' she started singing wildly off key. She stopped suddenly and said, 'mi nevva know seh a suh dem look.'

So I was listening to her sing and I was joining her although it was Sabbath. I wanted to move on to the next verse but Sasha kept with those lines *Take it easy, take it easy better slow down bwoy...* and I didn't mind at all. I closed my eyes and rested.

'May I use your bathroom?' June Taylor said. Before then I could not recall ever speaking to her outside of our lines in the play. Her regular voice sounded flat and serious like a teacher's, as if she couldn't wait to scold you.

I paused before answering; her interruption annoyed me.

'Yes, this way.' I led her into my room and pointed to the toilet beyond the closet. Immediately I began searching for Sasha's voice in the emptiness.

'Yuh alright?' Camille Peart touched my shoulder.

'Yes, I'm just... I thought... Never mind.'

'Awright, crazy Matthew.' She punched my arm and sauntered off to Carolyn Peralto. She stood in the corner next to the TV and Camille leaned against the wall to her left. Camille said something that made Carolyn laugh, full-throated and deep in her alto voice. I watched them, willing their joy to bring Sasha back. Then it occurred to me that several minutes had passed since June Taylor disappeared in my bathroom. I opened the bedroom door a crack and called after her without looking in.

'June.' I wondered if she ran into trouble with the toilet. I forgot to tell her that she had to jiggle the handle then wait for the tank to fill then flush again. I paused but there was no answer.

'June.' I said a little louder. Nothing. 'June.' This time I said her name so loudly that a couple of people turned round for an instant before returning to their conversations. I opened the door and walked in.

Dead ahead was the sole window in my room with sheer white curtains Mummy hung two days after we moved in. To the left, the door to the bathroom. It was open so I knew June Taylor couldn't have been in it. To the right was my bed. I peeked behind the door and there she was standing near the head, a yellow envelope in her hand. Next to her, the fully extended bottom drawer of my dresser. Sasha started to talk then stopped, like she was just as shocked as me. I looked at the drawer and back at June Taylor. All my precious, precious things were ruffled up.

And Sasha said, *Weh yuh a guh duh*?

I told her, *Not now. You have to leave.*

She kissed her teeth and said, *Why? Dis girl fool like. All yuh have fi duh is…*

It's not time yet, I screamed. And then she was quiet because I shouted at her for no reason even though I had explained it all before, that Mummy couldn't know. I had to control myself. Sasha overtook my life when she spoke and if June Taylor knew she'd tell the whole world.

June Taylor smirked and I swallowed. I needed to forget and I had to remember. I can't explain it all. I just know that she brought me back to the beginning and the wheel and the hole and the tree. And I could see it, the Macca tree and my brown socks and shoes and I was still wearing short trousers and I wanted to know why and I could almost see the hole, and then it was gone. For a moment I was happy that the vision escaped me, but June Taylor was still smirking, standing there like an overlord. This girl whom I had not spoken to in any real way before that day, her hands defiling the things she knew nothing about. She looked at me as if I was keeping secrets from her. *Mr. Archer you need to explain yourself.*

'Who is…' she began.

'Give it to me,' I said.

'No.' She hid the envelope behind her.

'Please. Give me my things.'

'Not before you tell me.' She laughed like I was a stupid little boy in his khaki trousers with pee streaking down his legs, pooling at the top of his brown socks. I lunged at her but she was quick. Her body squeezed itself against the wall. I walked away and breathed out hard.

'Okay,' I said when I faced her. I would tell her anything to get my envelope back. I looked closer into the open drawer. She'd gone through all my envelopes, opened, closed and reopened them. The soft yellow panties I'd taken such pains to hide had been unfolded and re-folded improperly. That day of our fight, Sasha was so angry she forgot to take them with her and I was waiting to return them. There was no explaining that one to sneering June Taylor. She read everything. I smelled the room, and it was a concoction of each of the five bottles; she had sprayed them on herself! This time I grabbed each of her arms. The truth is I wanted to punch her but hitting a girl when you're fourteen is different from ten. At ten you liked her. At fourteen you're a wife beater in the making, so I let her go and asked, begged, pleaded.

Mi try fi tell yuh, Sasha whispered, *too late now. Weh yuh a guh duh bout har?* And she was right. She tried to warn me but I wanted to be normal Matthew, chatting-up-pretty-girl-Matthew, get-married-at-twenty-four-years-old-Matthew.

'It's not what you think,' I said. 'Please June, I'm on my knees. Can I have it back?' My eyes watered.

'Well *can* you?' She was all snarky faced.

'Okay. *May* I have it back?'

'May I have it back, what?'

'Jesus!'

'Don't use the Lord's name in vain.' She knew she had me on the ropes.

Now Sasha was asking me over and over nonstop, *A weh yuh a guh duh bout har? A weh yuh a guh duh bout har? A weh yuh a guh duh bout har?* I couldn't concentrate anymore.

'What yuh saying?' June Taylor said.

'Nothing,' I said, but Sasha wouldn't stop, *a weh yuh a guh duh bout har?* And I wished she was singing instead.

Say it properly, I screamed back, *what are you going to do about her? That's how it should be said. For once just say it right.* She wouldn't let me go and I was happy she didn't and I was angry she didn't. I don't understand it, the war inside, this dialectic ripping me apart.

Okay, what will you do about her? She said and was quiet again.

Nothing, I said. *You need to leave now. Please. Leave me now, Sasha.*

'Alright, alright. May I have it back, please?' I said to June Taylor. The bottles were everywhere: on top of the dresser, the bed, the floor. She spent time here, rolled around in it, colonised my room.

'You haven't told me yet. Start with this one first.' She waved the envelope side to side, fan-like, in front of her face.

'No,' I said. I knew Sasha was still with me and I didn't want her seeing all this; they were the first inelegant lines of a portrait. So not yet. Not now.

'Well, you're not getting it back. I wonder what your little girlfriend Camille would say if she ever read this. Let me see...' June Taylor opened the envelope, her eyes shifting between me and the paper.

'Don't. Please. I'll do anything. I'll pay you. What would you like?' I popped the top off my savings tin, a holdover from my ten-year-old self, and bills and coins spilled out. 'Take it, take the whole thing.' If June Taylor said her name I would die.

'*It has been two years since...*' She looked straight at me, reciting my words from eidetic memory. I shut the door and leaned against it in defeat.

'So what do you think you're going to do, *Mister* Archer, hmmm? What?' She cocked her head then resumed reading what I recognised as the second paragraph: *I went to River but you were not there. Why do you like to hide so?*

I leapt at June Taylor. The envelope and letter disappeared down the front of her dress. She braced herself against the wall, her crisscrossed hands adding a second layer of armour over my words. We were toe to toe and head to head. '*How near you are, how near you are, how near you are, how near,*' she began taunting me with that childish song. I reached for her hands but she ran to the bathroom and locked herself in. '*How far you are, how far you are, how far you are, how far,*' her voice muffled by the closed door.

'You're being very mature, June.' I tried insults.

'You just have to tell me who she is and you'll have your letter. Easy peasy, pudding and pie.' She sung that last bit and I imagined her head rocking in tune. 'You're the one that's making this difficult,' she said. I picked up the two bottles on the floor, the one on the bed, the fourth on the dresser, and the last one, capless, resting on top of my pillow, and walked them over to the open bottom drawer. The envelopes, letters, bottles that were in perfect order by year were in a jumbled mess. I closed the drawer and sat on the bed facing the bedroom door. I couldn't imagine my life beyond that moment, all revealed for the world to see. And when Mummy found out I hadn't left the *foolishness* alone... I'd be sent away for good. Off to some boarding school in the country like Munro College and I couldn't leave, and I'd be too far away to hear Sasha because certainly she couldn't travel that far, right? Mummy would distribute my bottles to all her friends, Judy and the rest, and they'd never understand the care they needed to show.

As I said I didn't want Sasha to see these things yet, and I was thinking I'm going to lose her for good this time so I couldn't allow June Taylor to leave but she wouldn't give me the letter.

Peals of laughter bled through the door. Barrington and the boys must have done something stupid. Just then I felt a ticklish finger graze the back of my neck. I turned round and June Taylor jumped back and sat on the opposite end of the bed.

'So, are you ready to tell me?' Her face full of that stupid girly grin. I saw my moment and grabbed the top of her dress but once more she was too fast, dropping backward on the bed, and I only caught the very edges of the neck. She turned over and lay face down, still giggling and I tried to find it all funny like she did, to play along in the hope that she'd give up. But she just kept on. I searched for a weak point, any place where there was space between her body and the mattress. I would simply outwit her.

But every time I found a spot she shifted her weight to trap my hands. I'd remove them and try again but each time she pinned me and I laughed in that 'oh you got me again' sort of way, but I was getting tired of this game.

Then she trapped my hands under her belly once more only this time I didn't remove them. I sat on her back. She wriggled and writhed in futility. She swung her legs violently, trying to dislodge me. It worked for a second as first my buttocks and lower back took some licks. I redoubled my efforts. I moved my hands higher, just below her ribcage, and flipped her over. I held both her wrists with my right hand and sat on top of her belly; her legs couldn't get to me now. I tried to work out how I'd retrieve my letter. She'd read the contents but it didn't matter. No one would believe her without the papers to prove it.

She fought to find her breath and I told her, 'Yuh give mi the letter and I'll get up.'

She grinned and breathed hard. 'Tell me who first. How near you are, how near you are, how near you are, how near,' she sang in hiccups. She just wouldn't stop with that blasted song. And something turned. It was the way she squirmed and fought underneath me. Before then I couldn't imagine the level of physical strength I possessed, how little she could do to get away. It was like holding a piece of paper in place.

It was my time to laugh. I reached in her bosom with my left hand and took what belonged to me. Her dress had no buttons in front and it went all the way up to her neck so I almost ripped it when the crumpled paper and envelope popped out. I felt the hard edges of her small bra and looked at my dishevelled letter and envelope again, and I laughed and laughed. I held her there, my breath shortening.

'You almost tore my dress!'

Everyone in the living room must have heard but no one bothered to find out what was happening.

'That's not my problem. Next time leave my stuff alone,' I said. 'Just leave it.'

I was still on top and she tried to push me off one more time. The game was over for her, but I was in the middle of it.

'Get off me,' she said.

I smirked.

'Mi seh get offa mi.'

I hate myself today, I do, but that afternoon with me on top, her body twisting and turning to get free, I enjoyed it. I would raise myself slightly, and she must have been thinking she'd gotten away, but as soon as she moved I placed my weight on top of her again, my legs on either side of her torso. She was out of strength now, her ineffective attempts to flip me off had taken everything she had. Her breathing was slower, as if she was about to give up. My right hand glued her wrists above her head. I looked in her eyes then down the contours of her neck. I moved my body lower, straddling her, my legs on both sides of her pelvis. I could feel her chest moving up and down and I matched her breathing. It was as if our bodies were joining at the end point of each of her exhalations.

I felt her become pliant under my weight. I kissed her on the mouth and she turned her head away. She was playing coy. I'd seen this on the Sunday matinees. Marilyn Monroe would give in. I simply needed to keep going. So I kissed her again and again. And I was thinking *yes, yes, that's it, she wants me now*. I gave her wrists to my left hand while my right hand explored her private parts, touching and feeling at will all while kissing her.

Then I began to sense that something had gone terribly wrong, like enjoying the best sunset of your life only to feel a knife in your back as you were about to close your eyes and let the moment wash over you. Right about then she should have been returning my kiss. That's how it was in the movies, wasn't it? The guy grabbed the girl and laid one on her. She always pretended she didn't want it in the beginning. There was always some sort of argument, a cover for what they felt for each other. And I was thinking, is that not what happened here? Did she not put the letter in such a private place so that I would come and get it? Wasn't the prize for finding the envelope her body?

But this was different. She was quiet, her body unresponsive. I searched for the right words but her eyes looked through me at that light at the end of a dark tunnel, the one thing she could hold on to, to bring her through this ordeal. And I turned round slow because I knew what she saw and I tried to close my eyes because I didn't want to see it. But I couldn't shut them so I turned round with my eyes wide open, not one blink.

June Taylor stared into Bjorn Ulvaeus's eyes in my ABBA poster, begging him to come get her, although I knew it wasn't him because I looked closer and dark brown eyeballs stared down at me, lids half-closed, hands on her hips and cheeks full. *Fuh-fool*, she said and cut her eyes at me like she used to. I was still on top of June Taylor, but my arms rested limp by my sides. Her wrists were free yet she lay there and didn't try to move even though she could easily have done so and I was sorry. I'm always sorry. I faced Sasha's eyes once more but Bjorn had superimposed himself.

I removed my legs as if it was morning and time to get out of bed. June Taylor rose too, mechanical, her torso bolt straight, arms pasted to her side. She smoothed out her dress, opened the door, and when Sister Peart called us together, June Taylor started where she left off: the lake of fire scene. I didn't need to be there because the good pastor made it to heaven. I sat for several minutes thinking of nothing before I too smoothed out my clothes, placed the letter and envelope in the drawer, put my things back in perfect order, and walked out into the living room; light housekeeping. Right by the hallway to the kitchen, June Taylor stood waiting on the closing scene. I dropped my head below the ground.

'Sorry,' I said. I had an epistle of explanations yet no words.

'Yuh still don't have it right,' she said when we began practising again, 'Start from the part when your hand is on my shoulder.' She turned the page over and showed me my lines before adjusting my hand. 'Ready?'

On stage I thought I'd forget all we'd rehearsed that Sabbath afternoon. June Taylor looked right at me and said her final line in the scene. 'Yes Pastor, I will get baptised again.' I wanted to throw up then, but I said mine without missing a beat either, 'Jesus is always ready to take you back.'

I tried to find her after the play but so many people surrounded her, all of them congratulating: *Your best performance yet. You're setting a good example, young Sister Taylor*. I only needed a few seconds, a minute at most. I'd say I never meant to do it, at least not like that. I just wanted to tell her I was sorry and for her to acknowledge it. I needed her to know she shouldn't have touched my things. That they were not *my* things. I was a curator selecting and preserving them for its rightful and absentee owner. All those envelopes with all those letters, all the pretty bottles stored in my drawer and later in my hall closet. I still have them and I've added more; twenty-four envelopes and twenty-four bottles for twenty-four years.

June Taylor came to church Sabbath after Sabbath, playing her roles. As long as she came she was Jesus's mother, the Woman at the Well, Fanny J Crosby and Ellen White. I settled back to my non-speaking parts. I studied the doctrines at bible class and I got baptised, full immersion. The congregation sang *Oh now I see the crimson wave, the fountain deep and wide* and I peered out over the tiny rectangular glass in front of the baptismal pool at Mummy smiling and Donovan swinging his legs, although he was too big to be doing that. Brother Maynard played the pipe organ. My eyes darted across the congregation, trying to find June Taylor. Of course she was there, two pews behind Mummy and Donovan and she looked straight at me. I mouthed sorry but she held my stare, staid-faced.

Beneath my feet the cold concrete slipped and slid. My white baptismal gown puffed up behind me like Sasha's and I empathised with all the girls who battled the wind every day and promised I'd never sneak a peek again. When Pastor Logan pulled me up from beneath the water I looked left and there she was, Sasha beside June Taylor, her mouth a tightly inflated balloon, her anger on full display. They looked like best friends seated on a too-small bench, their hips jammed into each other's. June Taylor smiled and I thought it was for me, but her big sister was whispering in her ear.

She didn't tell, June Taylor. I wonder when it is that women, no girls, begin to know that they shouldn't say because no one will listen. She was more popular than me, the light and joy of so many, but no one would have believed her for a moment. *No, not one.* They would have said she was taking the whole acting thing too seriously. *You need to watch that in her yuh knuh, Brother and Sister Taylor. Careful. Girl children need to do something with dem hand.* And like that the whole business would have been put to rest.

I used to wonder how anyone can harm another and see them every week, greeting them with a smile, and inviting them home for lunch; well, they do just fine. I did just fine. We keep our wonderful bubble beautiful and clear. And so I held on tight to Pastor Logan's forearm as he dunked me deep into the water, and I stayed there, my eyes closed, hoping it would be long enough to remove the stains.

Like many of us would do over the next couple of years, June Taylor and her family immigrated to America. A few months ago I began searching for her. I sensed I needed to close my life somehow but I know now who made me do it. I thought I may have found her once. June Taylor had moved to New York City. I remember her sister said Queens so I tracked down all twelve June Taylors in the borough. I sent them the same letter, short and to the point: *I am sorry for what I did in April 1983. I should never have assaulted you. I should never have held you down. I hope you can forgive me.* I received a response a month later.

Dear Mr. Archer, it read. *I thank you for taking the time to write me. The years have been very difficult but I've managed. I was so happy to read your letter. I cried for several days. It was what I needed. There is only one problem. You cannot be the Archer that hurt me in 1932. He would be dead by now and that Archer would never have apologised. I hope you find your June Taylor. In the meantime, please know that you have made an old woman happy. Sincerely, June Taylor.*

We still write to each other once in a while and I say the same thing; that I'm sorry and she says thank you.

I eventually found my June Taylor. Even in a big country like America, we are a small community, Jamaican Adventists. Someone will know someone who knows a June Pinnoch who used to be Taylor. I saw her at a General Conference session in Toronto and she looked lovely and thin and beautiful like I remembered her. When I introduced myself she furrowed her brow and said, 'Matthew Archer?' as if trying to recall the scene in which we'd met. Her youngest child fit snug on her hip. He was completely enamoured with a loose pearl on her hat.

'Drama club, the under sixteen, at Spanish Town Church.' I didn't wait for her to answer. 'Would you mind if I spoke with you alone?' People in their Sabbath finest passed her by, saying their *hellos* and *looking goods* and *long time I don't see yous*. She was still the social butterfly she'd always been and for an instant I was annoyed because I hoped that I'd have mattered somehow in her life.

'Oh yeah! Matthew. Yuh went to K.C. or Georges or Calabar, right?'

'Calabar actually,' I said. That's how we Jamaicans have come to reconnect with each other after years apart in this or that new land. *Yuh went to this church, that school, yuh had that teacher?*

'Right. Right,' she said. The baby fussed a bit. 'Hold on for a second. Terra, come stand by Mummy.' Her little girl skipped over, held her hand, and started twirling. June pulled it away to fix something out of place on the baby's face. She wore motherhood as she had acting, perfectly and in time. Without missing a beat Terra took one step over to me and grabbed my hand so I could twirl her.

'Always the charmer, this one.' June Taylor, now Pinnoch, nodded in her daughter's direction. I meant to tell her sorry just then, without all the sordid details so her children's ears would remain safe, but she seemed so right, so good, so whole that I wondered if I would have destroyed her had I said anything, ruined this life she shaped in spite of me.

'I wanted to say,' I began and swallowed. I thought of all the foolish commonplace things we say when we try to catch up. 'I want to say,' I repeated.

'Yuh okay, Matthew? Everything alright?'

'I'm happy for you,' I said and smiled with everything I had. 'God's been good.'

'All the time,' she said and looked into me. Her eyes seemed like she was still trying to place us. For a moment I wondered if she really recognised me after all. Her generic responses could have been made by any Jamaican living abroad. I wanted her to say it, needed her to tell me she forgave me even if she was being gracious, just trying to get rid of me. I was about to tell Terra, *I thank you for this dance young lady*, and go back quietly to my life when I saw it, that recognition of one Sabbath afternoon in a boy's room, a boy you thought you could joke with, a place you could be safe, maybe the one place, and he wrecked the whole world for you. And I understood then that there are some sins for which there is no forgiveness, that I'd have to say sorry for the rest of my life.

So I did. 'I'm sorry. I'm so sorry.' And I stood there and watched her looking at me, silent.

Her little girl held on to my hand and twirled and twirled, and she laughed and said, 'Again, spin me again.'

Chapter 20

The sixth bottle is clear and colourless and the liquid is too. I bought it on my actual birthday. Fifteen years old felt so close to manhood that I couldn't wait to do my O levels later that school year. When I wasn't distracted by girls everything was painfully slow; hours and days seemed to drag on for eternity. I studied and waited. I ate and waited. I dreamed and waited. I lived on the knife edge of pure anticipation.

I spent the summer that year at the beach pretending to teach girls how to swim, my hands, palms up, under their backs and legs as they floated. I enjoyed their faint screams when they felt their bodies were about to sink, back muscles taut with the fear of drowning. And I liked saying, 'I have you; I won't let anything happen. Trus' mi.' And how they said, 'Are you sure?' all the while their arms wrapped tightly around my neck. Every week I had a new girlfriend du jour and that afternoon when I told the girls it was my birthday they showered me with kisses. We understood we'd never see each other after that summer, that this was the last of childhood, and seriousness would become serious business in a matter of weeks when I started fifth form.

I was on my way back from the beach, drunk on all the kisses and hugs I received, it was no wonder I didn't get mono, my head giddy, my mind fully appreciating the practice of polygamy. I came off the bus at Spanish Town terminal, my skin dry and ashy from the fresh water I used to wash off the sea. My eyes itched slightly, the kind you get just before a long and perfect sleep. I turned on to Young Street and there it was on the wooden light pole; one of my posters. A little worse for wear but still legible. It was the only one I'd missed when I gathered them up a couple of years before and it wasn't desecrated like the others.

The face staring back was a hologram. I looked at it for ages, allowing passers-by to bump into me, *cuss mi out*, and keep on their way. I waited for Sasha's face to overcome me. It occurred to me then that I hadn't heard from her since June Taylor and that was months before. I wanted to make it matter, all the work I'd put into drawing the picture, the evenings searching for her, but I couldn't connect to it, not to the drawing, not to all that time. I closed my eyes but I couldn't see her face, recall her voice, her touch, her breath. I removed the poster delicately, careful not to crumple the paper. Not even mould from years of rain disturbed her preserved face. My right hand hovered steadily over the drawing, absorbing energy, as if the picture locked her in somehow. She was gone again, only this time it wasn't that I forgot about her, it was that all the universes had expunged her.

I walked in no particular direction, aimless, my wet trunks and towel sloshing about in my knapsack. I found myself in front of Ammar's. The lady at the counter from the first bottle was still rude.

'What yuh want?' She breathed out hard.

'That one.' I pointed to the middle shelf.

'Twenty,' she said and picked up the wrong bottle.

'Not that one.' I readied myself for the look.

'Suh why yuh nevva seh dat before?'

'I'm sure that I...'

'Twenty-five.' She kissed her teeth before I could finish. I resented Sasha for the hold she had on me. For how I put myself through this humiliation and she wouldn't even talk. And now I couldn't even see her face. I handed the woman a twenty-dollar bill; I hadn't forgotten about the last time when she short-changed me five dollars. I didn't fool her for one minute. She kept her hand open, her head turned to the man a few feet away chatting her up.

I was about to drop another twenty-dollar bill when I said, 'I change my mind.'

She faced me sharply and the man narrowed his brow. I reached over to retrieve my twenty dollars. I was done with giving businesses my money while they treated me like a soiled nappy, my stomach tightening every time I needed to make a basic purchase, as if preparing for hand-to-hand combat. The man straightened up.

'Twenty-five,' the woman repeated, her eyes back to chatting up man. I looked down at the drawing in my left hand and shook my head then released the other twenty.

'Bag please,' I said when she gave me change.

'Fifty cents.'

I held the bottle up to the light and I wanted to sit for a minute, right there on the floor in Ammar's in the women's clothes section, surrounded on one side by jeans, and the other by dresses, and the smell of perfume and powder. I didn't know it yet but my summer ended that evening.

'Yuh can't stand in the middle of the aisle,' the woman shouted.

I must have bought the matching card but I don't remember; it's here with all the others. I know that for days afterwards I stared at the six bottles in my drawer, willing Sasha to start talking to me again, just for a minute. I'm not sure what I wanted her to say. I must have been in some way relieved that she'd finally released me. The timing couldn't have been better, right on the cusp of adulthood, my body coming into its own, and girls beginning to really like me. She finally granted me permission to live but I needed to hear the words from her, to say why she no longer needed me. Did I waste all those years? Maybe all I wanted was to see her face one last time, to confirm that my drawing was close, that I'd remembered.

She said nothing. I resolved to shut away my bottom drawer forever, but I'd already made that promise before and broken it year after year. Moreover, I still ached to search the streets and lanes again, run like a madman into Shadeed's haberdashery. *Have you seen her? She's this tall and her hair plait in three and two yellow ribbons like this, and a yellow dress. She must have come in here. I've looked everywhere. Are you sure you haven't seen her?*

'Yuh have a picture?' the man at the record shop on Hanover Street said.

'No.' I showed him the drawing.

'Dis ting nuh look like nothing.' I could tell he felt sorry for me and he said, 'One second. Wayne, tek a look.'

Wayne said, 'Dis could be anybody, big man. Sorry, my yute.'

She looked like too many Jamaican girls at that age; Sasha, a generic stand-in.

So minute by minute and hour by hour I tried to lock her away once more. I thought it would be easier this time now that her face was gone and her voice muted, everything about her scrambled in the wind.

And then one Sunday afternoon I was in the queue with Camille Peart at the Swirly Cone ice cream shop waiting to order. She had her arm in mine. I turned round and saw the chatting up man with the lady from the Ammar's counter and they were past chatting up, all locked in each other's arms. I was staring and the man looked happy for me but the lady cut her eyes as always and Camille asked me what I'd done.

I said without thinking, 'I want to tell you about Sasha.'

'Who?' Camille said.

'She was my…' My tongue couldn't think of the word.

I was waiting for it to come when she said, 'Remember I was telling you about Carolyn?' I wanted to get it out before she dove into Carolyn and Graeme and the others in our study group as that would be an all-nighter, but I didn't know where to start.

Sasha's face came to me in a dream that night. Not for long. We were on Brunswick Avenue and I was play tripping her with my right foot and we were laughing and she punched my arm then I woke up with wet cheeks.

That's all she gave, a few seconds at most, not even a word, and it angered me, her selfishness, so I started thinking about girls again and I studied for O levels every night: Maths, Add Maths, Physics, Chemistry, Biology. I made the table tennis team at school; practised four evenings a week. When the tournament was over, I took up piano lessons on Tuesdays and Thursdays with Mrs. Dawkins. Every Sunday Camille, Graeme, Patrick, Selena and I group crammed from eight to eight. In my waking hours I stuffed my head with formulas and functions, but at night when I closed my eyes and dropped into dream Sasha came for me.

Not her really, more like a sensation of her, the way you're sure someone's following you yet you refuse to face them. When she finally spoke in my dreams it was as if she came up for air just long enough to accuse me:

Why yuh nevva come fi mi?

Why yuh lef' mi?

Why yuh lef' mi inna di darkness?

And I screamed back, *I didn't leave you. I didn't. I protected you. Look what you made me do to June Taylor? You left me alone and now I'm getting in trouble.*

I'd open my eyes and I was screaming at an empty street; on Cumberland Road right in front of Spanish Town market one Saturday night when all the vendors were already gone. It was so quiet. The place smelled of rotten cabbage and salt fish.

For weeks I pleaded with her, *come back, please tell me where you are; just show mi yuh face.* I needed to move on. But she wouldn't speak and she wouldn't listen.

Of course Mummy found out. My blackouts seeped into my daytime hours. There were evenings I couldn't recall how I got home. Twice I fell asleep on the bus from school and when my friends woke me we were almost at Central Village or the turn-off for Edgewater and I was in the process of opening the back door while the bus moved at speed. I didn't think I needed to tell them *don't tell Mummy.* They said I was going to find Sasha, that *she is right out there in the middle of the cane field.* Mummy told them they were good boys. *Bastards.* They thought I couldn't hear them tattle.

There was serious talk of hospitalisation this time. And as soon as I got better, boarding school in Mandeville because Mummy *tried her best; no help from yuh father, none at all; you boys don't know how good you have it; starving children in Myanmar and Bangladesh and Africa; don't you listen to the mission stories.* More tears and good Jamaican sons don't make their mummies cry.

She called on Pastor Logan several times to pray for me, hand on my shoulder, voice all deep and bass-y. One of those long prayers you were certain God approved of. And Mummy was happy then and she looked like Ms. Sheldon that day Sasha *did get inna spirit.*

I held on for weeks, hopeful I'd keep Mummy satisfied, but Pastor Logan had other parishioners to attend to and I started sliding again, my mind collapsing worlds into each other. I had to change. And that's when Camille became my best friend.

Chapter 21

I want to say that I didn't replace Sasha with Camille, but I would be lying to myself. Camille was the first person in my short fifteen years that made me feel truly rested, like I could finally stop running. In each other's company, life froze in a bubble of teenage dreams and I didn't want it to change. We were barrelling quickly into adulthood, however, and growing up began to reveal the weak points in our insulated world. Because Camille wanted more than I could see. There were things I didn't know about her although she tried to tell me. I listened but this time I couldn't understand.

It started where all important things do when you are Adventist and a teenager: at church. Camille and I teetered on sixteen with its requisite exaggerations and cries of unfairness. All of us thought our parents biased and partial, even complaining incessantly among ourselves about their strict rules, but we *yes Mummyed* and *yes Daddyed* them. On our worst days we rapped to Run DMC and sang along to Sade and Prince, belting out *Smooth Operator* and *When Doves Cry* as if the knowledge of their lyrics made us jaded cosmopolitans. A few bragged about drinking Red Stripe beer or slipping away on a Friday night to see a dance. We *oooed* and *aaahed* as we took in their tales, but the next day we'd cut ties with them because O levels and CXCs and not getting pregnant took up every corner of our lives.

Camille was at Alpha and on school day afternoons we met each other at Cross Roads and bought sky juice and bun and cheese. Sometimes we procrastinated for an hour or two before studying and lazed at the bus stop, matching each other to the ugliest girl or boy; *a your husband dat*; *guh weh a she yuh a guh married.*

On the rare Sundays we didn't study we hung out at the Swirly Cone place at the top of French Street or Pete's Patties across from the jail. I said Pete's patties were better than Mother's and she said, 'Yuh must be smokin' something.' We drank Pepsi and ate peppa shrimp even though we weren't supposed to; *don't touch the unclean, the body is the temple of the Lord.* After my nonstop nagging she relented and followed me to River only for her to conclude, 'never again.' The unofficial church press had us married to each other as soon as we were done with university. She told me not to correct them.

'We'll just pretend for now,' she said. 'When yuh find a girlfriend, we'll tell them we broke up.' We held hands in public and walked home arm in arm. We sat next to each other in church every Sabbath and I'd lean in her nook and Brother Hutchinson used to prod my right shoulder over and over until I acknowledged him.

'Young Brother Archer,' he'd say in his declarative voice. And that should have been enough if I had any sense. I didn't.

My growth spurt edged me three inches over Camille. She was my colour with perfectly creamed hair; *no curly roots showing.* She wore too much baby oil so her skin existed in a permanent shine. I liked her palms; they were light brown with dark brown, almost black, life lines. I asked her once how come her hands were so soft even though she played netball and volleyball for Alpha.

'I didn't tell you?' she said. 'I'm perfect.' We became best friends then because she made me laugh from the depths of my belly and it had been so long. She was the friend you never quite recall meeting, like how you know your brother is your brother because he'd always been. Mummy took notice.

'I like how that friend of yours carries herself,' she said one Sunday afternoon.

I wasn't sure what she wanted me to say so I said, 'Thank you Mummy. I'll tell her.'

'Matthew, yuh getting big now…'

I knew where this was going so I cut it off at the start. 'We're not girlfriend and boyfriend.'

She serious-laughed. 'Alright then. Camille is a nice girl…' The pause right on cue. I didn't fill the silence, though. 'Well people are talking…' I stopped listening so I only caught a few bits. Quite sure she mentioned the words *familiarity*, *circumspect* and *bringing down embarrassment*.

The dreams faded, Sasha a compressed zip file in the documents folder. She was there, just hidden. I fell into Camille's strength; it was as if I gave her my burdens for a while. We went on for months like this until Camille's own problems unravelled before we sat our O levels. There were rumours, at least that's what I thought at first.

Camille wasn't like me. She didn't need or desire the world of imagination to get on with the business of living. She took one deep breath and inhaled the real world whole, embraced and challenged it.

One Sabbath afternoon, filled with this confidence, she took on Brother Francis during a panel discussion at church.

'Spoken like a typical man,' she said without waiting to be acknowledged. As always I was leaning in her nook and I missed what it was he said that set her off.

'Excuse me?' Brother Francis couldn't place the voice.

Camille stood. 'I think you heard me. Women always have to follow a bunch of stupid rules you men lay down for us. Wear this, don't wear that. Obey your husband.' Her hands folded across her chest. She looked at me like we'd discussed this all before and it was my turn to enter stage right. Gasps and stern looks shot our way.

'Well, young Sister Peart, think of it this way. Would you agree that God calls us to love our fellow men?'

'And women.'

'Okay, young Sister Peart, *and* women. You see, when a woman wears something that is revealing she is causing a man to lust. Do you want to cause someone to sin, Sister? I know you don't.' He spoke like a caring father, his voice calm, soft, almost feminine, and for an instant I wanted Daddy.

Camille said, 'So why don't you men learn to control yourselves? Why do we have to be burdened with your problem?'

'Sister...'

'I'm not done yet!' Camille shouted.

'Tek it easy now.' I tugged at her elbow. Multiple adults cut their eyes and thankfully Camille didn't hear Brother Hutchinson say, 'dis one need a strong hand.'

'Okay Sister. Please go ahead.' Brother Francis offered his open palm in peace.

'I believe women should wear whatever we want. This backward thinking is all about meeting men's needs. *A man attaches himself to woman not to enjoy her, but to enjoy himself.* Do you know who said that?'

'No Sister, who?'

'Simone de Beauvoir.' She started to retake her seat like she'd delivered the final blow in a death match.

'I'm not familiar with that person.' Brother Francis looked genuinely puzzled. She straightened up and stood once more.

'She's a brilliant philosopher and feminist. When I was in New York I read her book *The Second Sex*.'

'Alright young Sister Peart, alright,' Brother Francis said.

I tugged at her elbow again. 'I don't know who that is either,' I whispered. I could tell she was losing them and she had lots more where that came from, ready to unload on a church that still had heated debates over whether women should wear make-up.

'I told you about her last week,' she whispered back, annoyed. 'Yuh don't listen.'

Brother Francis wasn't quite done either and without missing a beat he said, 'Well I don't know about this Simone whatever-her-name-is but we have the bible, don't we brethren? It's all in here.' He waved the book above his head. 'Okay brethren, let's turn to First Timothy... that's in the New Testament, young people.' He smiled in our direction. I imagined him leading morning devotions at home, high priest of his household, his wife and children in rapt attention and I wanted that too: wife and good children. And I wondered if it was too late for Daddy to come back and lead our house in worship. 'Alright now; chapter 2. I hear those leaves turning.' Brother Francis waited for the ruffles to die down. 'Good, good. Verses 9 and 10. Yuh want to read it, young Sister Peart? Somebody give her a bible.'

'I'm okay,' Camille said.

'That's alright too, Sister. Do you mind if I read it?' His tone that of a patient teacher tutoring a difficult yet promising student.

'Go ahead.' Camille waved her hand like she'd heard it all before.

'Here readeth the word of the Lord,' he prefaced. '*In like manner also that women adorn themselves in modest apparel.* Yuh hear that, brethren? Alright then: *with shamefacedness and sobriety.*' He looked out on the congregation; believers every one. '*Not with broided hair, or gold, or pearls, or costly array.* Verse 10, *but which becometh women professing godliness with good works.*' He walked over to Camille. 'Here, yuh want to see it for yourself, Sister?'

I knew the next verse and I prayed he wouldn't go on because *let the woman learn in silence with all subjection* would have sent Camille into orbit. He left it there, the bible open, waiting for Camille to acquiesce for God had spoken. I expected her to sit humbly, a little bruised from being handled so thoroughly, but next time she'd learn to bring her own counter scripture. She was still standing, though, arms folded, and before I could pull on her sleeve to say 'just leave it,' she said, 'Well, the bible is wrong.' A tense silence fell upon the congregation before a cacophony of quiet chatter.

'Yuh hear that, brethren?' Brother Francis said, his voice quaking in disbelief. 'Yuh see what is happening in the church?'

Camille sat defeated.

She was silent for a couple of weeks and we were back to meeting at Cross Roads and pairing people off. Then she went on a hearts and minds campaign, only she overlooked the hearts and minds of the church members and went straight to the top of church administration in Maryland. She wrote the president an open letter, her *ninety-nine theses*, in which she highlighted four points to be reconsidered. She demanded an immediate halt to the pronoun 'he' when referring to God, a rejection of scriptural inerrancy, a reinterpretation of the creation story removing blame from Eve, and lastly, the annihilation of male dominance and abuse of power in the church. I wondered if she understood the irony of presenting these demands to a group of middle-aged white men.

She was called to account before Pastor and the church board. When we met at Cross Roads later that week she told me they were all stupid, even Pastor. 'I thought he at least would have some sense, yuh know what ah mean?' I said *yes* but I didn't.

We passed all our O levels and CXCs. We had planned on sixth form and medical school at UWI, married at twenty-three or twenty-four, not to each other, first child at twenty-five, second child at twenty-seven. We'd have gleaming upstairs and downstairs houses in Stony Hill or St. Jago Heights or Mandeville; shiny black cars like Daddy's, every other weekend shopping in Miami or New York; children enrolled at Vaz or St. Cecilia prep.

Camille, though, was on a modified track.

There was a social after church one Saturday night the week after we got our results. All the members met in the front yard, its curved white concrete wall holding the street at bay. In the corner closest to Sherlock Avenue, a campfire roared with breadfruit, corn and yellow yams roasting in the middle. A second fire near the pedestrian gate on Brunswick Avenue roasted Snapper and

Doctor fish. The smoke drove all the mosquitoes away, leaving a still, cool evening. The children ate ice cream and played their tagging games, bumping into adults. Bursts of *slow down* and *behave yuhself* could be heard every two or three minutes.

A ring game was forming. 'Yuh want to play?' I said.

'No,' Camille said. She paused a moment. 'Listen, yuh can do mi a favour?'

'Yes.'

I wasn't looking at her, so she said, 'Yuh not listening.'

'Alright, alright, what do you want me to do?'

'I'm going back here.' She pointed to the rear wall of the church and what looked to me like a black cave.

'Why?'

'Yuh going duh mi di favour or not? It's that thing I told you about. If you see anybody coming call me, alright?' She glanced around as if she'd just withdrawn her life savings.

'Hold on. You're going into that darkness back there?'

'That's the point, stupid. I told you. You don't remember? That thing?' She raised her eyebrows and opened her palms.

'What?' The clapping for the game started and the rhythm made me want to dance.

'Typical man.'

'Alright, Camille, I can't take a lecture right now. What should I do?'

'I don't know. Whistle, sing... think of something. I'll know it's you, alright... Alright?' I was taking too long to answer.

'Yeah. I don't understand why yuh want to go back there. Come play the game nuh man?'

'Matthew, I told yuh all a dis already. I don't have time. Mi gone. Remember, call mi if yuh hear nuhbody.' She vanished.

I ran off to play the ring game *one-and-twenty*. Sister Carter led the rhythm with her clapping and Pauline Spencer carried the tune. *One, two, three, four, five...* We were at twenty in a moment. *One-and-twenty, two-and-twenty,* and I was in the middle of the ring searching all the clapping hands for a partner and someone to replace me in the ring. At the big fire, Brother and Sister Campbell removed the yellow yams and my mouth watered. A few feet to their left Brother Williams guarded the rising stack of roast fish and my belly rumbled.

I skipped along, relaxed, enjoying the cool evening and the ring, and searching for the prettiest girl. Brother Patton, the head deacon, stumbled from behind the wall and I thought about calling after Camille, but I was too far away and it wouldn't have made a difference anyway. He likely just shooed her. We were at *three-and-four-and-five-and-six-and-thirty* when I saw him whispering something in Pastor's ear that stopped him cold. *Thirty-sevennnnnn, thirty-eeeeiiiight, thirty-niiiine, forty.* Karen Kerr said, 'Watch out,' when she almost ran into me. At *one-and-forty* I should have already found a partner. I didn't want to be alone when we got to one hundred but I was looking at the corner of the wall hoping that Camille had already left. *Fifty,* I finally found a partner but I kept looking and my clapping was out of time. *One-and-sixty* I was back in the ring and I'm sure my partner was glad to see me go. *Two-and-sixty, three-and-four-and-five-and-six-and-siiixty,* the adults became increasingly restless.

At *one-and-seventy* Pastor called out in his preaching voice, 'Sorry brethren, we have to end right now.' He sounded so serious not even the children complained.

I tried to find Camille; she would know what happened but Pastor, Brother Patton and some of the church elders took up the space by the wall. I asked anyone I could find if they saw her but no one had. The usual gradual thinning of the crowd didn't happen that night. Pockets of members stood in little atolls in the parking lot, eating their food and whispering.

Donovan found me soon after and said, 'Yuh crazy friend in trouble.'

'What yuh mean?'

'She and Carolyn Peralto…' He locked his fingers together and laughed. 'Dave. Rory…' he ran off to tell his friends. I didn't understand. I stopped Pauline Spencer.

'Yuh know what's going on?'

'Camille still yuh girlfriend?'

'She's not my girlfriend. We're just friends. We just act like…' I began then gave up.

'Well not anymore.' She tiptoed along the side of the building and I followed her. I heard someone say, 'Lawd have mercy.'

Another person said, 'I told yuh 'bout dat chile.'

When we reached the edge of the wall Pauline Spencer and I leaned in to eavesdrop. I couldn't make out anything so I braved it and took a quick look around the corner. Carolyn Peralto buried her face in her mother's bosom, sobbing. And Camille leaned against the concrete fence, her face up, arms folded like in church that Sabbath afternoon. She looked like a scientist interrupted at the moment of a paradigm-shifting discovery that had taken decades of hard work. Now she'd have to start over.

I waved to get her attention but she didn't respond. It was either too dark or she was angry I hadn't warned her. She stood silent as Pastor spoke. I was still too far away to hear. Pastor looked at Brother Patton then Brother Patton brushed past me and put his arm around Brother Williams. They shuffled over to the sweet sop tree and I wasn't far behind. At first I heard a few words; 'reprobate,' 'unnatural,' 'against God.' I inched closer.

'Mi know sup'n nevva did right, yuh knuh. From mi guh back deh, mi jus' know it,' Brother Patton whispered, the kind meant for everyone in earshot to hear.

'Suh weh yuh sih?' Brother Williams asked. Brother Patton shook his head, his face anxious to launch into a story that confirmed all his warnings of a backsliding church.

'Gaawwwd have mercy. Dat likkle girl. Shi pick up dis foolishness from dat antie inna New Yawk,' Brother Patton began. *Dat antie inna New Yawk.* I had to think for a minute. Then it came to me. Even years after Camille's aunt, Antie Merle, left the church without explaining herself, the brethren still spoke ill of her, that she entertained several lovers… at the same time.

'Suh what happen?' Brother Williams couldn't wait to hear.

'Dat likkle girl tongue inna di odda one troat. Jeeeesas Chrise!'

I was certain I misheard him so I turned my ear towards them and concentrated on his voice. And even if I heard him clearly it couldn't have been Camille – nor any of us – this thing they said she'd done. It wasn't real, was it? It just couldn't be. That sort of thing happened in America and England and even so it was something people made up, like rolling calf or illuminati. Girls didn't kiss girls like that.

'Wha!?' Brother Williams seemed equally incredulous.

'And den…'

'And then what?' Brother Williams sounded like he was glad he beat the church sisters to this juicy bit of news.

'Mi bredda.' Brother Patton breathed in hard and I knew this wasn't good because this time the pause wasn't for effect. This one really shook him.

'Mi cyaaan even tell yuh mi bredda, mi cyaan even tell yuh,' he continued. He stopped to gather himself. His Adam's apple slid up and down, wordless. He lowered his shaking head. I told myself to walk away because I couldn't unhear what he was about to say. 'Har han' under di odda one dress and shi...' It looked like he wouldn't be able to say it after all, he just shook his head over and over for a minute. 'Shi a feel har up.'

'What? No. No sir. No. No.' Brother Williams walked away then back again.

'Yes, Elder. Yes.' Brother Patton stopped. 'Jeeeesas, Lawd help mi. Inna di church yaad, mi bredda. In front ah God Almighty.'

I swallowed hard, and I was thinking of Camille's letter and the argument that Sabbath afternoon, that they hated her so much they would make up such a horrendous story. It was one thing for her to kiss another girl but to touch... *Liars*, I wanted to shout, *you are all liars*. And I thought of all the boys that liked her, of how she looked and acted like a girl so she couldn't be.

Pauline Spencer said, 'Yuh did know?' I forgot she was still beside me.

'It's not true.'

'What you going to do? If that was my boyfriend with another...' She stamped her right foot into the ground.

'She's not my girlfriend. I told you that before.'

'Now yuh change yuh mind. Nobody going to blame yuh.'

'I said she's not my girlfriend,' I shouted at Pauline Spencer, so she cut her eyes and walked off.

Pastor held Camille there as if she was waiting on bail and try as I might, I couldn't get her to turn my way. A few minutes later Brother and Sister Peart came for her.

* * *

The next day Mummy gave the official order; no more Camille for me. Whispers turned into soft conversations, then into widespread gossip. Within a day the story leapt the churchyard fence and consumed Ensom City. By the end of the next week all of Spanish Town was discussing *di girl from di Adventist church*. The tales grew more elaborate and bizarre with the telling, each version evolved to reflect the various suburbs of Spanish Town. In Ensom City, the story had Camille in the bathroom with Carolyn and they were completely naked. The residents of Sydenham had Camille's name as Karen and the incident took place in Pastor's vestry. The neighbourhood of Rivoli introduced two other girls to make an orgy.

The trashy papers headlined with *Fifteen-year-old fourth form girl caught in bed...* then the subtitle *...with another girl.* 'She's sixteen and in sixth form,' I shouted at *The Star*. On the radio the advice gurus fielded questions about what to tell your 'girl chile' when you send her off to same sex high schools. The dancehall artists didn't miss a beat. Carlita Mays came out with *Rub-up Rub-up*. Mikey Benz made a hit with,

Shi need it strong,
Shi need it tight,
Fih straighten har up,
Fih live right.

On Brother and Sister Peart's freshly painted concrete fence someone scrawled 'REPROBATE' in life-sized red cursive.

One Monday morning before she headed off to work, Mummy took a look at my face and removed something that wasn't there then said, 'Make sure to tell me if any boy touch you in any funny way.' I didn't bother to ask what that meant.

Only after receiving a letter from Camille blaming then

forgiving me did I realise her parents had sent her away to Portland until the whole thing blew over. But the *thing* was all my friends could talk about. *Yuh did know? What did she tell you? Why did she do it?* They asked with their faces screwed up as if they smelled fresh shit, flies and all. I said it was all lies. I said Carolyn Peralto didn't like Camille, that she was jealous because Camille was head girl at Alpha and she wasn't. I said Carolyn Peralto liked Howard but Howard really liked Camille so Carolyn made up the whole thing. No, they all agreed, not Carolyn Peralto, because who could say such a thing if it wasn't true.

A few weeks later I was leaving sixth form Chemistry when someone covered my eyes.

'Guess who?' Camille seemed so happy. My classmates did the usual *whooooaaaaa, yes Archer, ah you dat*, typical tongue wagging when a girl shows up at a boys' school.

'Camille, you're not taking this thing seriously yuh knuh.' I didn't bother welcoming her back. She stood there smiling, raising and lowering her eyebrows, and biting her bottom lip and I knew she had news.

'Look.' She produced an envelope. I wasn't sure what it was I should be seeing. 'Look closer, crazy... top left corner.'

'Carolyn wrote to yuh?'

'Can yuh believe it? What did I tell you? She said they forced her to say it was me.'

'Forced? Camille, I defended you and you're still talking to her?'

'She didn't mean it.' Camille was full of excuses. I walked away and back. 'We're going to America. Antie Merle says she can get us jobs.' She was over the moon.

'All this time I've been telling everyone that Carolyn...'

'What?'

'Never mind.' I shook my head.

'Listen, none of that matters. Yuh coming, right? I told Antie Merle and she said she always liked you.' She grabbed both my hands and squeezed.

'Camille,' I breathed out hard, 'if Carolyn can do that once, she'll do it again. You're going to risk eternal life for her? This is serious. They're going to read you out. No more church.'

'Mi nuh business 'bout dem church people deh. Yuh t'ink seh mi fraid a dem? Mi don't care, Matthew. Mi don't care. We love each other.' Big big grin. She swung my arms side to side like Sasha used to.

'I love you too but that doesn't mean...'

She pulled away before I could finish. 'Matthew...' She paused and looked at me all horrified. 'Yuh really don't understand, do you? I thought you...' I held her stare because Carolyn was a bad influence and Camille just needed to see it. And none of us would look away first as if we were ready to end it all right then and there.

'She's no good, Camille, and you know it.' I grabbed her hand. 'Me and you, every time. Wi run tings...' I nodded my head and waited for her to complete our mantra. Her face softened.

'Matthew, yuh don't understand.' She shook her head over and over. 'Carolyn's sweet sixteen? Me and her cutting the birthday cake? Remember? I told you she chose me?'

'What? Birthday cake? What are you talking about?'

'I'm a lesbian, Matthew.'

A few boys turned round; their brows knitted as if to confirm they didn't just hear what they thought they did. I paced for a few seconds, ignoring yet another of her *contrarianisms*.

'Okay, we can still fix this. We'll go back to pretending we're boyfriend and girlfriend. Wi give everybody a year or two – I know it's a long time but we'll be at UWI by then. Yes, that will do it. Suh… we run tings…' And this time I swung her hands.

'Tings nuh run we.'

There was more, though. Weekly the stories trickled in, girls who said they were afraid to tell before because they thought no one would believe them. *One time she wanted me to show her my panty. She wanted us to play spin the bottle with girls only. She asked me if I knew how to kiss.* The most innocuous actions came under microscopic scrutiny; hugs, an incidental shoulder touch, her knees bouncing off theirs in kindergarten Sabbath School class when they were five. It was clear she had been a predator way back then. Prior sleepovers were reinterpreted with fresh eyes. 'Yuh know I didn't think anything of it at the time but now that you mention it she always wanted to sleep in the same bed with Dionne,' I overheard Sister Maxwell tell Mummy.

One Sunday after Pathfinders, Patrick and Howard drowned me out so the lot of us could listen to Annette Standish recall how Camille wanted to share a lollipop with her.

'She licked it first then gave it to me,' she said. Heads shook.

'That doesn't mean anything,' I said.

'I felt badly so I didn't say no.' Annette Standish ignored my protest. 'Her face looked funny when she did it.' I imagined this fourteen-year-old girl crying as she told her mother, hoping to have her fears validated; *yes sweetheart, the girl in the jeans violated you.* The witness records piled higher and higher as girl after girl told the church board their stories.

At Sabbath services no one spoke to Camille. Parents shoved their children to the other side of their bodies as if guarding them from the airborne virus that was Young Sister Peart. Brother Hutchinson cleared his throat when he saw us together and I dropped my head. Carolyn Peralto now sat up front on the right near the piano, her parents on either side of her. She seemed so small, so young; I half expected to see socks and ribbons and bubbles. It was hard to believe she was in upper sixth. I stared at the back of her head, willing her to turn round because I was sure I would convince Camille.

Pastor preached one Sabbath about the unpardonable sin, closing your heart to God for so long that you can't hear His voice any longer.

'Yuh know the phrase "dead man walking"?' he said. 'They say that to prisoners on the way to the gallows. That's what you are when you constantly spurn the Holy Spirit. You walk on this earth dead. Not even God can help you anymore.' Camille squeezed my hand as if to say *take care you don't fall into that trap.* Everyone knew who he was talking to.

The following Sunday afternoon around three o'clock, I lied to Mummy and said I needed to help Dane with Physics. She said, 'Alright, but we need to talk about that girl.' I walked to Camille's house. Everything looked normal now that the crowds no longer kept a vigil in front. The rusted iron gate creaked when I opened it. I knocked on the front door. No answer. I knocked louder again and again. Nothing. We'd planned to meet at three thirty, but I told her I might be late because Mummy didn't want me anywhere near her. I worried that in her anger Camille had left. My watch read three forty-five, I think, well within what we islanders call early. I made one last attempt but this time I shouted her name while knocking. I heard dragging slippers.

One by one the bolts clunked and the door opened, but it wasn't Camille I saw first. Brother McIntosh stood directly behind her and he looked down at me and said, 'Young Brother Archer.'

Brother Ellis, slightly shorter and skinnier, nodded and asked, 'Everything alright, man?'

Brother McIntosh stepped outside, glanced over his shoulder at Camille and said, 'Tell your father I stopped by and I'll see him on Sabbath night.' She stared somewhere beyond my face.

He turned to me once more. 'Young Brother Archer, tell yuh little friend here shi must smile more. Always look suh vex-up vex-up.' I watched them walk away to a car parked four houses down. When I faced her she was smiling behind glistening eyes.

'Why yuh crying? They're going to read you out, don't it? I told you.' I started in on her. 'Why don't you listen to me? Yuh always say I don't listen to you but you don't listen to me either.' Her face hardened; she was finally taking this whole thing seriously. 'So what yuh going to do?'

'Don't worry 'bout it.'

'Don't worry? This is eternal life you're talking about. You going to lose your soul, Camille. I don't want to be alone in heaven.'

'Yuh want to go for a walk?'

'A walk? I don't think you understand...'

'Come wih guh walk, man,' she said but just then her father drove up.

* * *

We met at the mall in New Kingston the next day after school. She wasn't in a talking mood like the last time. I didn't like her like that because her silences hid grim surprises, plans to take down large immovable institutions like church.

'Listen, remember I was telling you last time that we should pretend to be girlfriend and boyfriend like we used to,' I said, 'that way they won't read you out?'

'I have to leave, Matthew,' she said all flat like reciting all sixty-six books of the bible.

'Alright. You want mi to follow yuh?'

'No. I mean I have to leave here; Jamaica.'

'What yuh talking 'bout? Remember, we run tings...' I smiled and shoulder shoved her.

'I have to leave,' she said again, same tone, like déjà vu. We didn't speak for minutes, alternating resting in each other's nook. Then out of the stillness, 'I should have run, Matthew.'

'Run?' And I felt like there was somewhere else I was supposed to be.

'Yeah. I should have run. They were so strong.'

'Who?' I said.

'Them. Brother McIntosh and Brother Ellis!' she said it like who else would she be referring to. 'Brother!' She kissed her teeth.

'What yuh talking 'bout?'

'Antie Merle was wrong. Arm wrestle mi.'

'No man. Hold on, Antie Merle wrong 'bout what?' I said.

'Please. Let's just arm wrestle and don't mek mi win.'

'Camille.'

'Matthew, please. Just for a minute, alright?'

'Okay.' Our right hands linked.

'I said don't make me win.'

'Alright, alright.' It was over in a second, my wrist fully on top of hers.

'Yuh satisfied now?' I said. 'So I was saying. I think we can fix everything. I'll talk to Pastor and we'll clear up this whole foolishness but you have to promise me you're done with Carolyn.' She was quiet. 'Camille, yuh listening?'

'Yesterday when yuh came by…'

'Yeah, what did they say?'

'I should have run, Matthew. Mi shoulda did run like di devil.' And I could feel Sasha breaking through and I began to know where it was I should be. *Not now. Not now*, I said. I'd worked so hard. She was like a worm twisting and curling its way up from that place.

'I didn't see it, Matthew. I just didn't see it. They asked if Daddy was there.' Camille kissed her teeth again. 'I should have seen it. Why wouldn't they know Daddy and Mummy weren't there?'

'What yuh mean?' I said, and swallowed hard, my mouth all dry. I didn't want to hear and I didn't want to know, because I was beginning to understand the world I lived in.

'Antie Merle was wrong. We can't do everything a man can. I couldn't move, Matthew. I couldn't move. I don't know which one grabbed me first. I used to think all those women who said they couldn't fight were weak and stupid. Allowed men to tell them how to be. Yuh know what ah mean? Those stupid weak women, always a talk 'bout man dis and man dat. But I couldn't fight, Matthew. I mean I couldn't move. I couldn't fight. I couldn't scream. I thought I was screaming but I couldn't hear myself. It was like somebody just snatched my sound.'

Don't tell me, I meant to say, *don't say a word*, and I was standing up because I was going to leave; there was violin and piano lessons and Selena who was starting to chat me up.

Sih down, Sasha said.

I can't hear this, I said. *I can't.*

Sih down, she shouted back, like she was using everything to tell me that one last time. So I sat with the tree and the wheel and the hole in the ground.

'I asked God to help me,' Camille said, her head shaking up and down as if I needed convincing. 'I begged God, Matthew. Begged and begged and begged and begged Him. Look at me, I called God *him*.' She was uncontrollable now, her body a volcano of shakes and sobs.

'I'm sorry.' I don't know who I was saying it to. Camille or June Taylor or Sasha.

'Yuh can't tell anybody.' She made me promise.

'I won't.' *Tell me what to do*, I pleaded to Sasha, *tell me what to say*. I didn't care if the world thought me mad. But she was gone back into the darkness and I was alone.

'It was just like that,' Camille said. 'They got me just like that. Just like when yuh wrestled mi. Yuh know when they say that yuh get a bad feeling about something? Well I didn't, Matthew, I didn't get a feeling, nothing. I was happy because I got another letter from Carolyn. She said her parents were still forcing her to say those things. She said she loved me and we were leaving for real this time. We'd go to UWI and then run away to Vancouver. I was really happy. When they came to the door I didn't think anything. It was like Good Afternoon and Good Day and Have a Nice Day, yuh know what ah mean? They said they came to see Daddy and I opened the door so they could come in and they started talking 'bout *when yuh father coming back*? I said *I don't know* and I was walking away, right? Yuh know what ah mean? I was walking away and then that stupid Brother McIntosh seh, *yuh don't have no home trainin'. Yuh don't know seh yuh should offer guests something to drink?*' She said it in his voice, and I was breathing short and I was hoping someone would distract us, that maybe it was suddenly six o'clock, not three and we had to get home right away. There was time, though, loads and loads of time.

'He sat down and smiled and I don't know where Brother Ellis was, I still don't know. But I could feel him, though. Yuh know what ah mean?' She paused, her eyes looking through and past me. Then she closed her eyes and knitted her brow and I could tell she was trying to locate him in her mind, like she needed to read the map's key better.

'Yeah, I know what you mean,' I said because I thought she'd stop there, that she'd said enough and it wasn't too late after all.

'Brother McIntosh was just there looking down on mi like him can control mi. The nerve of him. Him! Control me!' More people turned around to face us; she was shouting now. 'Suh. Yuh. Know. What. I. Said?' She patted her chest with her right hand in time with each word.

I stopped breathing.

'Yuh know what I said? Yuh know what I said? Yuh know what I said?' Camille was out of her seat in her last stand, still patting her chest. 'Is wife yuh lookin'?' And she laughed with a dead face. 'Is wife yuh lookin'? Is wife yuh lookin'? Is wife yuh lookin'?' She was beating up on her chest. I could feel Sasha like a tree pushing up, roots, branches and leaves, and I was ready to let it happen this time. Camille stopped laughing just as suddenly as she started.

'I was looking at him. I didn't know, Matthew. I didn't

understand.' She shook her head and she was crying again. She sat and I reached out to hug her but she said, 'Don't.'

'Okay,' I said.

Wait, Sasha said.

I want to go, I said.

No, wait.

'Yuh know what him seh?' Camille was back but her eyes were gone again. '*Alright, young Sister Peart*. I hate when they say that. I really really hate when they say that. *Young Sister Peart*, like I'm in training. Yuh know what ah mean? His voice was soft. I didn't expect that. So I thought I beat him.'

'You did,' I said. 'Did he really think he could take you on?' And I was glad we were at the end. Then she turned to me and I realised she thought I still wasn't listening. But I was, more than she'd ever know.

'I thought he was going to leave and I started feeling badly about cursing him out, can yuh believe that?' She kissed her teeth. 'Suh I am about to say sorry and I was going to offer him water and he is just standing in front of me and I can't remember where Brother Ellis was. I can't see him, Matthew. I can't see him.' She stopped for a moment and tilted her head as if where Brother Ellis was would fall out onto the bench.

'Then Brother McIntosh look mi up and down and seh, *Yuh nuh look too bad inna yuh shawts, young Sister Peart. Yuh grow up quick.*' She was channelling his voice again, and I knew what was going to happen and I wanted to pee and run and die and I was calling for Sasha and I was telling her, *sorry I pressed you down. Sorry* and I could feel the branches and roots in my throat.

'Then him seh mi must come give him a little kiss, *just a likkle choops right here.*' She pointed to her cheek. 'I told him to fuck off.

That was my first time saying it but it felt right. Yuh know what ah mean? Fuck off. Fuck off. Fuck off. I was laughing at him. Stupid little man that barely finished secondary school. Can't say the word honour without pronouncing the h.' She paused and I was telling myself it was a story, that she told it so well, and then there would be tomorrow and the next day and the next and the beach and the sunshine and no more hole and a wheel and a tree.

'I didn't see it, Matthew. He touched my shoulder and I gave him one good kick in him balls and ah seh, *yuh know the way out.* I was still laughing to myself. I was saying *serve yuh right* and I didn't see it, Matthew. I didn't see it. I don't know which one grabbed me first. All I know is try hard as I might... I tried. I tried. I couldn't move. I couldn't move, Matthew. I couldn't move. The two of them lifted me up. Where was Brother Ellis? I can't see him. I can't remember! He was there, though.' She said it as if I knew, I just needed to say.

'You should tell Pastor.'

'Don't tell anybody. You have to promise mi.'

'What yuh mean don't tell anybody?'

'Promise mi.'

There was an ocean all over her face and I tried to say it was all my fault for what I did to June Taylor. I wanted to tell her it was like the time God made that horrible thing happen to King David's daughter Tamar because David set up Uriah to be killed so he could have his wife. I almost told Camille I should have left the house earlier that day; that Sasha was trying to tell me to *leave now* but I pressed her down and I was trying to think of a good lie to tell Mummy. So I begged God to make it not true, pleaded with God to make Camille say *Ah just joking wid yuh.* She wasn't listening anymore, though, and she buried her face in my chest and she let me hold her.

That following Sabbath the church met for a special business meeting after Sabbath School. I'd never seen the pews so packed; extra fold up chairs lined the aisles. Women fanned themselves as the temperature rose.

When Pastor stood on the podium he barely held the congregation's gaze. Brother and Sister Peart huddled with hunched backs in the front pew. They stole occasional glances back at Camille and me. Their red eyes pleaded for her to join them and for a moment I wondered if she should have given them that one last thing, say sorry about Carolyn and keep her place among God's people.

A few benches behind, Brother McIntosh and Brother Ellis held their hands high in agreement that Camille should be put out from the brethren. I looked around at all the hands metre-stick straight in the air, Brother and Sister Peralto and Carolyn, all of them with no equivocation, Mummy's too. Camille, her arm around my neck comforting me like Sasha used to. And I leaned into her, let myself fall really, for my eyes were red also. Brother Hutchinson cleared his throat and stabbed his finger into my shoulder, but I didn't move.

Then Pastor Logan said, his voice more bass-y than usual, 'Matthew 18:18 Verily I say unto you,' and he looked at Camille, his watery eyes beseeching, *there's still time*, 'whatsoever ye shall bind on earth shall be bound in heaven: and whatsoever ye shall loose on earth shall be loosed in heaven.'

That night I received the last flogging of my life. Mummy tried to hold my arm and swing the belt side to side and over my back but I was too tall. Instead I stood facing her, raised my right arm to line up with my chin, palm up, and took every lick. It was the first time I didn't cry or wince. I took my punishment for what I had done earlier that Sabbath.

After the vote, Camille had walked out without looking back. I'd stood to go after her but Mummy's face told me all I needed to know. I sat in my place, Camille's seat an empty cavern, and I stopped the tears for what good would that do now. The service had ended with a parting prayer and we gathered in the parking lot asking about the week and inviting each other home for lunch. The midday sun dimmed as a stray cloud passed by.

I searched for Camille but she was gone. Brother Peart too. The deaconesses surrounded her mother, offering multiple handkerchiefs. Mummy and two other women greeted each other and made plans for Sunday or next Sabbath.

Everyone looked like they'd just been baptised, buried with Christ, arisen to walk in newness of life. They made the correct decision and God was pleased. And so I saw the mummies calling their children, the daddies already starting cars, and overheard the first warnings that told of beatings to come if *you children don't find your backside in the car right now*. And Brother McIntosh standing beside Pastor Logan and Pastor Logan promising to meet later to play dominoes, and Brother Ellis mentioning something about a West Indies versus India test match on Monday afternoon, then his wife calling after him, 'Wi leaving now, I'll see you at the house.' And Brother Ellis looked like he was pondering whether he should stay or leave right then. And I looked on as Pastor Logan showed Brother McIntosh some text in the bible that made him shake his head. They didn't see me, none of them did.

I looked at my friends, all of them good Adventist young people, everyone destined for marriage with children, not one of them fornicators. We would be going to uni together; medical school, dental school, nursing school, our righteous paths laid bare before us. And Camille on the other end, not in sight. She'd go to uni too, but with whom? She'd be alone and I was back in the darkness again. So there was only one choice in the end. And so I, young Brother Archer, son of Joan – everyone calls her Petal – and Paul Archer, sixth former at Calabar High School, hollow heart where once stood an eleven-year-old girl, and best friend of Camille Peart, took two steps forward and plunged all the weight of my right foot – well sheathed in a black, tough pointy-toed shoe – into Brother McIntosh's left shin. I didn't hear him wail but I know I didn't stop at one or two kicks. Right foot, left foot, right foot, left foot, *one-and-twenty, two-and-twenty, three-and-four-and-five-and-six-and-twenty* and I was thinking of him, this elder who spoke with surety of sound doctrine not watered down with false teaching, *twenty-seveeennn, twenty-eiiiiggghhttt,* this man who knew who inherited what in the sermon on the mount, *twenty-niiinnneee, thriiirrty,* his full body on top of Camille. This man who didn't have the nerve to do it alone and co-opted a deacon. I wondered what scripture he quoted her then, what he whispered in her ear. *Young Sister Peart; and God shall wipe away all tears from their eyes,* his cold tongue on her cheek, *with God all things are possible,* his warm slimy cock trailing along her thigh. *Three-and-thirty* and it is Sasha guiding my fists, *Yuh have fih lick him good or else blackheart man wi get yuh,* she tells me, *Lick him. Lick him.* Feet and fists in chorus and there are hands on me pulling me this way and that but that Sabbath I was stronger than them all. I would complete my task because today I would start to find redemption.

Chapter 22

The rain eases and people are gathering and gawking again. Graeme orders me to stand next to the school building. The digger and police are at least eight yards beyond. Behind me along the covered ground floor walkway there are four classrooms. White aluminium jalousies start mid-torso and rise three feet, making two sets of windows for each classroom. The exterior walls are painted light blue. I peek inside one of the rooms and although it's dark I can tell this is a classroom for younger children. First and second graders. All the benches miniaturised. Teacher has used pink and green chalk to draw the earth. I tell myself I'll bring them a globe when I come back next time, but I'm not sure who it is I'm trying to convince.

I urgently want to find Sasha's classroom. I have to know. I want to see where she sat, who shared a bench with her, what secrets they told each other. Who was in front, on the side, who sat next to the door? Was she a back bencher or did she sit in the middle? She would never sit up front. I want to know the life she had outside of me.

One afternoon I met her at the school gate. We were going to River and it was a secret. I like those kinds of secrets, the ones that tingle your entire body and mould your life. You exist somewhere between iridescent expectancy and bliss.

So I was at the gate waiting because the assistant principal wouldn't let me in and I was willing the bell to ring. It was a time of hand bells, big echoey things that require two hands. Of course, I'd *scull* school that day, (I was on evening shift), pretended I was sick so I could be with her. When it rang she was the first down the stairs, racing towards me and I couldn't contain myself. I had mangoes and June plums and *stangerine* in my knapsack. She ran with exercise book and pencil in her right hand. In brown shoes and brown socks and her kite tail ribbons sailing away. She ran like she was seven years old and her big brother was picking her up for ice cream.

But this place has expanded since last I saw it. Her classroom would have been long demolished, crushed, at the bottom of a landfill where the latest expansion of the housing scheme sits. Another dark place.

I like the gate. That has not changed since then or maybe it has been replaced with the same style of chain link. I can't entirely tell. I want to stand outside and wait because she's going to come running in her brown socks and brown shoes and I want to tell them to stop. The digger, the police, the people. She's coming after all and I no longer need them.

Chapter 23

I find myself vacillating because even though I don't believe it, I want time to heal our sores. Some days it's almost there. Yet the longer I go on I see that the hours, days and years turn those wounds gangrenous, poisons our blood and kills us. We don't smell our rotting sores because we have become so used to them, our grief an in-womb cannibalistic twin. We cover ourselves with bandages and good make-up so no one sees our pain. But those bandages must be swapped for clean ones at some point and the wounds, they too have to be swabbed and disinfected and then it all comes home.

The summer after I completed lower sixth, my family joined the herd of Jamaicans leaving the island for The States. It was 1986. We thought the move temporary; we'd work a few years, pay off our mortgages and return flush with cash ready to reinvest in our Jamaica. Well, best laid plans and all… We settled in America for decades, building new and rich lives. Dying and living, inter-marrying and having children, and saving less than we hoped. We became entangled in Ponzi schemes, immigration frauds and burial societies. We overpaid for houses and played our part as duped consumers in the used car market. Yet we flourished; worked hard with our two and three jobs, pushed our children to excel at school, and created a new generation that out-ambitioned us.

In the years following our emigration I lived my life in summary. I studied, sat my exams, completed my clinicals and graduated with a pharmacy degree. Initially Mummy and I planned on medical school, but one look at the cost sent me to the land of would-be physicians whose disappointment over the stream of rejection letters could only be matched by the vigour with which we attacked the work in pharmacy school. I want to say that something was missing, like pulling into your parking space at work and suddenly realising the stove is on or closing the front door on your way out but the keys are on the other side. I had checked my pockets, though, and they were there, all the keys in a neat little bunch, jingling away.

So my life was on track, tracing its slightly adjusted predestined path. I believed Sasha would never return; she was done talking after she helped me with Brother McIntosh. I tried to explain that I had to leave Jamaica because Brother McIntosh's face and head and back didn't look too good when they finally managed to untether me from him. Sasha wouldn't listen, though. It didn't help that I honoured Camille's request and kept quiet. Not even when Mummy was deep into her flogging or when everyone at church stopped talking to me. Police came round and threatened jail time because I was old enough to know better. Prison. In Jamaica. My sixteen-year-old backside would pay the price.

Mummy stepped in and negotiated and begged Pastor to help. Like Camille, I would no longer be welcomed at church. Daddy spoke to Brother McIntosh, *father to father and man to man*, and a partial lump sum changed hands. Mummy took on the balance with a rigorous monthly payment plan. This was the last straw. She asked only acquiescence and I fell in line.

The years chipped away in silence. I stopped seeing Sasha's face everywhere. The dreams ended and she no longer guided me. It was as if she didn't want to go to America.

Time turned me into a proper man.

I had nineteen bottles by then. I can't remember how I acquired the last thirteen only that I couldn't help myself. I began to wonder if they meant anything anymore. And how long could I keep this up? A decade? Two? Five? I convinced myself there was an end in sight. Now I see it, but back then it was all a blur. I was marking time, doing chores because they simply had to be done. I'd wake, complete my five-mile run, shower, eat breakfast, buy my perfume bottles. Repeat. I've learned to like order, certainty, predictability. This is what these bottles are to me now, things as they should be.

After the state of Florida granted my certification I moved to Hallandale Beach, a city a few miles south of Fort Lauderdale. I signed on with a large pharmacy chain and got a promotion to manager within a year. I bought a two-bedroom condominium within walking distance from work, and I found a new church in Miami filled with ex-pat Jamaicans. I went quietly each Sabbath, head down, and slipped out before service ended so I could avoid talking to anyone.

I couldn't help making friends and acquaintances, however, and eventually I met a nice Adventist woman with whom I was certain I would spend the rest of my life. Our meeting wasn't entirely unexpected and I suspect not without some manoeuvring from my mother. Mummy had been on me all day about attending a social one Saturday night after church and I relented. I was standing in front of the refreshments table unable to determine the lesser of two evils between competing refined sugary drinks and I was about to call it a night.

'Michael Jackson or Prince?' The unfamiliar voice appeared out of nowhere and I sensed she had been watching me for a while.

Still, I wasn't certain she was addressing me so I said, 'Excuse me?'

'Michael Jackson or Prince?' She pointed both her head and ladle to each of the two bowls in front of us.

I heard myself say, 'Is there a third choice?' And immediately I wanted to take all the words back, choose Prince – yes, it was purple grape Kool Aid – and go home. I was thinking of all the work I'd have to put in and a momentary exhaustion overcame me. Then my other brain noticed she was tall with black wavy hair up in a bun. She had grey eyes and proper curves even though I tried not to look.

'Well, are you changing the rules of my game?' She was quick and chirpy even after such a long day.

'So we are playing a game now?' My other brain was all in and my eyes didn't budge.

'Don't look so pleased with yourself, sir.' She matched my stare.

'Archer,' I said, 'My name is Matthew Archer.' I offered my hand and when she gave me hers I turned it palm down, bowed and kissed it. She chuckled and shook her head but she didn't pull her hand away.

'Please don't tell me you just used a James Bond routine on me.' She raised her right eyebrow and it was all I could do to stop from laughing out loud.

I said, 'Oh, I'm sure you'd have it no other way.'

'You are something, Mr. Archer.' Her face turned pink and she walked a pace slower than needed towards her women friends. My eyes followed each and every step. Her posse stood in defence mode, two of them with their backs to me.

'I didn't catch your name,' I said, loud enough for them to hear.

'She's busy,' one of them shouted back. I ignored that one and looked deep into her grey eyes when she turned round to face me. I stood my ground and she took two steps forward and stopped just far enough to still be on her friends' side but close enough to admit defeat. She pursed her lips to arrest a smile.

'961 5811,' I said. 'I find that if you break it up in two parts it's easier.'

'Easier?' she said.

'To remember.'

'Remember what?' The shouter rolled her eyes.

'My number. Two parts: 9-6-1 and 5-8-1-1. I'll talk to you tonight, woman whose name is a mystery.' I walked away before any of them could answer, my shoulders back, a subtle dap in my step. And yes, I was pleased with myself.

I let the phone ring four times and picked up just before the machine. I answered like I wasn't certain who'd be ringing this time of night. I barely had the 'hello' out when she said, 'Phillips, my name is Peta-Gay Phillips,' and we broke down in laughter. I liked that she didn't play games the way I did. More than that, she made it easy for me to drop my act because the *lyrics banton* image was becoming too much.

We covered the basics quickly; she was an ER physician with one year left before she branched out on her own as an anaesthesiologist; went to Immaculate Conception High; emigrated after O levels. Good family with deep Adventist roots. Check. Check. Check. Check. She was the natural bookend of a string of good choices I'd made.

We did Adventist things: handed out tracts and told people about the soon coming Saviour. She wanted slow-going, so we group dated with other serious couples at first. We did pizza nights, played Scrabble and Pictionary, went for walks along the lake, and took in the occasional play. Good clean living. We were engaged one Saturday night a few months later, smack dab in the middle of the church parking lot; a not so modest ring out of a modest pay cheque. Mummy couldn't have been more pleased.

Peta-Gay told me bits and pieces out of the blue, small things about herself, as if taking tiny nibbles of a beautiful cake. She hated healthy food. She didn't like the beach. And, 'I love every Steve Winwood song ever made so go ahead Mr. Archer and say your worst.' One evening she said an un-Adventist thing,

'I always pictured me and my husband in our first dance at the reception. Yuh know. God wouldn't kill us for just one dance, right?'

'Why don't we?' I said and grabbed her hand. 'Our first dance right here, right now.' We were at Mizner Park, our backs on large beach towels. On stage Celia Cruz belted out *Bemba Colora*. I could feel the grass pushing through, massaging, and I suddenly wanted to see the stars.

'No babe. Ah cyaan dance.'

'What? Weh yuh a talk bout? Everybody have riddim.' And I moved her hand in circles with the song.

'Matthew stop,' she said, face flushed, a light chest shove. A mild terror took me just then and I tried to pull my hand away but she wouldn't let me. 'Where yuh think yuh going, Mister?' She leaned in and kissed me and her lips threatened to melt on my tongue.

'I used to dance,' I said.

'Really, Mr. Badventist?' She seemed truly surprised. 'Hmm, mi have nuff tings fi tell Sista Archer bout har big son.' She giggled to herself.

'It was a long time ago,' I said. 'I think…' I meant to say more but these were the good years and Mummy hadn't asked much. 'It doesn't matter,' I continued. 'It really was a long time ago.' And I didn't want to talk about dancing anymore.

I enjoyed the seriousness with which Peta-Gay approached the wedding project. I liked watching her think of colours and flowers and the organist and which groomsman would be matched up with which bridesmaid. She'd meet with Mummy and her mother every weekend and they'd plan. She created a board with several grids and dates and she'd colour in the corresponding grid when that assigned task was completed. I knew she'd be the best doctor, mother, wife. Her mum adored me and her father called me 'old chap' and squeezed my shoulder. She and the mothers had shopping dates and said things like, *girls day out, you boys can't come along*. I felt like a well-cared-for husband.

* * *

We planned our lives with surgical precision. First child in two years; second, a year later because her mother said, 'Time flies fast; best to get it out of the way quickly'; use income from condo to buy the perfect house; children in private school then on to the Ivy Leagues. So this was it. I could ask for nothing more. Only I thought it would feel different. It was like you arrived at your holiday let in St. Lucia to find that everything looked exactly as it did in the brochure. Beautiful, yes, but you hoped to be surprised by something.

I ran into a minor puzzle, however, Peta-Gay's wedding gift. She owned all the things an accomplished doctor would. And I got nothing from our conversations, so I asked her friends on the sly.

Carlene, the one who rolled her eyes at me the first time Peta-Gay and I met, said, 'If you can't figure that out then maybe you don't deserve her.' She was bloody serious too. I used to call her *Arleen* just to wind her up so I sang the chorus from that General Echo song.

'*Arleen a mus' a dream yuh deh dream.*' She mouthed 'fuck you' and I smirked at first before it dawned on me she would tell Peta-Gay. So I doubled my search.

Then one afternoon, Peta-Gay's head in my nook, she revealed another of those nibbles. We were in the living room on her leather sofa and I was thinking she'd never once showed me her bedroom and we'd only kissed and we followed all the rules even though I wanted just a little more; I'd have taken it if she offered, that's the truth, she was all curves and soft. And now her head was in my lap and I'd better do some fanciful shifting; I didn't need any surprises I'd have to explain. A mixed tape played in the background and Steve Winwood finished up *Bring Me a Higher Love* and Aretha Franklin's *Respect* immediately faded in and Peta-Gay was on her feet with one of those tall wooden cooking spoons for her mic, right in time to synchronise:

What yuh want,
Baby I got it.

Peta-Gay could truly sing but she was right about that dancing thing. She was in my face, *just a little bit*, and she made that thumb and index finger signal and I wanted her to keep going and going, long and loud enough for the neighbours to make that courtesy knock. And then she sang, *I'm about to give you all of my money* and I said, 'sing Sister, sing' and she waved me off. She was at the top of her voice when she got to the spelling part:

R-E-S-P-E-C-T
Find out what it means to me
R-E-S-P-E-C-T
Take care, TCB

She collapsed on the sofa out of breath.

I said, 'Well who dat cyan spell *respect*. Watch yah now!' She play-pinched me and I tickled her but she tensed so I stopped for we all know where that leads.

'Speaking of spelling, did I ever tell you I won Spelling Bee when I was ten?' I like that about her, how she spread out her revelations over time and I began to wonder what she'd tell me on our fiftieth anniversary; *I don't love Steve Winwood that much after all* and I chuckled in my head. '1979,' she said. 'How long ago was that? Anyway, I was in *The Gleaner* and everything. I don't even know where that picture is. We must have lost it in the move to America. Who knows? You should have seen me in my Vaz uniform, I was a stick like suh. Mi did skinny bad, yuh knuh?

Look at mi now.' She pointed her index finger to the ceiling. I found my gift to her.

It took me a few days to track down a university library that housed the *Jamaica Gleaner* on microfiche dating back to the 1940s. I paid the non-student fee and headed to the periodicals. I meant to go straight to 1979 but like everyone else I became distracted by other articles, adverts and headlines; fires here and earthquakes there. Bus crashes and robberies that turned into rapes and murders. So I was going backward from the current year because I was missing my Jamaica, and then my eyes caught a glimpse of a tiny entry in January 1998, only a few months into my search. I turned the dial to go forward and I squinted, barely able to make out what it read: *Remains of Girl Found*. It was time to change the bandage.

Chapter 24

I restarted my life then, not a do over, but a reliving of all that had gone before. And so I added more pieces. I was staring at Mummy and Ms. Sheldon in the living room, begging them to keep looking, to ask everyone. It may have been hours or days or weeks after. I can't tell now.

Mummy said, 'She ran away, sweetheart.'

'No that's not true. She wouldn't. We were supposed to…' I began to say, but I stopped because we were *sculling* school, telling the teachers that we were sick and praying they wouldn't tell our mothers. I can't remember why or where we meant to go. It wasn't River or church or to throw stones at the wasp nest at the top of the tamarind tree or peep on Ms. Callahan in her bra and slip. This place was new. I only know that I had planned it, taken my time and plotted out the details.

Mummy and Ms. Sheldon ignored me and went back to talking about big people business. So I said I was going to look for her.

'Just a minute, young man. Yuh think yuh can tell me what yuh going to do in this house?' Mummy said.

I walked off, careful not to sulk, shoulders up like I was being a good boy. I sat in my room, hands in my lap, still as stone, and waited for Sasha. She was taking too long bumbling around out there, lost in the dark. I would make them believe me. I broke into Ms. Sheldon's room, no knocking, no announcing, barged in like a landlady certain that the young teacher was hiding a man under the bed. I gathered Sasha's church shoes, slippers, her one church dress, the yellow halter top and the two *gyanzis*. I dumped them on the floor in front of Mummy and Ms. Sheldon, back and forth I went depositing Sasha's things like a dog anxious to impress its master, trying to tell them that if she ran away she would have taken them.

Mummy told Ms. Sheldon, 'Sorry about this,' and boxed me in front of her and Stephen. 'Pick them up right now,' Mummy said, and I scraped them up one by one and handed them to Ms. Sheldon. I had to smile and say sorry for each item and I understand it better now, crying and smiling. It was Ms. Sheldon's turn to look pleased.

It was seven o'clock later that evening, dark and properly Sabbath. The house smelled like Sabbath lunch, stew peas with salt beef and spinner dumplings and white rice and leftover Friday evening soup. Mummy called us to worship and Ms. Sheldon and Stephen came too. Mummy sat beside Donovan and Donovan sat next to me, three of us on the white settee with the plastic cover. And I remember I wished that Mr. Bentley was there because he would have his own chair and Sasha would have to sit scrunched up next to me. He only came once, though, when Mummy invited him. And it was his idea that Sasha sit beside me. I liked him afterwards for being so kind. Sasha and I held hands and we could barely control our giggles. We wanted to tell each other secrets then but we kept checking our mothers' eyes so we started a knee war instead and she was winning. Mr. Bentley placed a dining chair in front of Sasha and me and he kept adjusting it like he was trying to make room for Stephen and Ms. Sheldon. He stopped when he was straight across from Sasha and Ms. Sheldon went quiet and still. Our knee war ended right then because Ms. Sheldon looked at Sasha, not like she was going to flog her, more like Sasha was this new thing, a new thing that dared break one last girl rule, the biggest girl rule of all. And I didn't know what Ms. Sheldon was going to do. So I tried to look away because maybe she would stop and I saw Mr. Bentley staring at Sasha, different from Ms. Sheldon, though. But he shifted his eyes to Ms. Sheldon with a start, the way I do when Mummy would catch me 'wasting time'.

So I was wishing Mr. Bentley was there that first Sabbath evening Sasha never came home because I could save space for her on the settee. And Ms. Sheldon was on the matching side chair and Stephen on one of the dining chairs he was ordered to take to the living room. He didn't bring the other one like he was supposed to, like a gentleman, so I put it beside him. Ms. Sheldon looked at Mummy and Stephen's head dropped like he thought Ms. Sheldon might box him but he wasn't sure.

Mummy didn't look at me. She said, 'Let's turn to hymn 640.' She'd bought an Adventist hymnal for Ms. Sheldon, black leather bound, and when Mummy gave it to her she looked like this is how church is supposed to be. You sing songs from books with treble clefs and bass clefs and notes. Every song has verses and there are numbers at the top and the names of the writer and the composer.

I am there now. I like how Mummy sings and Ms. Sheldon is pretty good too. Her voice is lower than Mummy's and when they start *Marching to Zion* I always stop and listen because I'm sure that's how heaven will sound. A soprano and an alto in harmony. I imagine they're angels and I forget that Mummy told me two hours ago that if I don't find myself in that bathroom right now 'yuh going to feel it.' And I black out that Ms. Sheldon told Sasha the day before, 'yuh nyam too much.' And so they sing the first verse:

Come we that love the Lord and let our joys be known...

They sound even better than all the other times. Donovan is just learning tenor and he has the right key but it's hard to sing when Mummy's soprano is so sweet, and Ms. Sheldon's alto is so rich, and so I'm the only one that can hear him and he sounds nice.

Sasha can't sing, not a single note, yet she does all the time, everywhere. In the beginning I used to tell her to stop, and sometimes other people would, but she croons along without a care. She doesn't in worship, though. I heard Mummy say to her one day, 'Yuh can't sing, sweetheart, so you just hum along, alright love?' Sasha kissed her teeth and cut her eyes and of course Ms. Sheldon heard about it and ever since she hums softly in worship. We love to sing the choruses from Sasha's church. She taught me *I've found a new life*. I didn't know the tune until I snuck off and went to her church one Sunday.

When we reach the third verse of the hymn, *The hill of Zion yields a thousand sacred sweets*, I wonder if Mummy and Ms. Sheldon are right, if Sasha has

...found a new life.
If anybody ask you, what's the matter with you my friend,
Tell them that you are saved,
Sanctified, Holy Ghost filled, water baptised, Jesus is mine,

I've found a new life.

I have a friend, Graeme, now a detective sergeant, who told me when his grandfather died that he was in heaven. When I mentioned it to Mummy she said, 'We're Adventists, dear, we don't believe in such silliness. We all go to heaven when Jesus comes back again.' But I'm listening to Mummy and Ms. Sheldon, their voices in perfect harmony, and I want Graeme to be right.

We come to the end of the hymn and Sasha's humming, *hmmm, hmmm, hmmm,* a tone-deaf songbird not paying attention. And I think Ms. Sheldon is going to tell her to shut up because it's time for scripture reading. I look at the empty chair, Stephen beside it, head still down, and I'm waiting for the humming to stop at any moment because we all know that a fraction of a second makes the difference between a look and a box. Mummy moves on to Scripture reading and Sasha starts humming *God is not dead but… he's alii-iii-iiivee.* I don't want Sasha to get beat'n again, not for this. So I'm thinking, *stop humming,* and I can't say it out loud because I will be disrupting worship.

So I whisper, 'Stop humming because your mummy is going to box yuh.' I look at Ms. Sheldon, hoping that I will distract her, but she's turning the pages in her light blue bible because Hebrews is somewhere in the New Testament near the end.

The humming drowns out Mummy's voice and Ms. Sheldon's turning pages and I kick out my foot towards the empty chair because Sasha is playing invisible, but you can still feel kicks and thumps because those are the rules. She doesn't scream and kick me back. I won the last game when I made myself small and put my beige sheet over me. I must have looked like a bumpy poorly made bed because she came into my room and searched everywhere but couldn't find me. I wonder if she's gotten better than me but it's not fair because we're not playing invisible now; today we're playing blue car and whoever sees one first gets to punch the other's left arm ten times.

Mummy is asking Ms. Sheldon to read the text and Donovan fidgets. Ms. Sheldon doesn't pronounce the words right and she takes too long. She stumbles at the easiest words like 'evidence' and 'substance'; we're reading Hebrews 11 verse 1. One verse. One stupid verse; fifteen words and it takes her two minutes. And I hear Sasha humming and humming. And Mummy doesn't say anything because Ms. Sheldon 'is a guest at worship, so be nice boys.' She can take as long as she wants. At least it's better than when Mummy asks her to pray but then Mummy turns to Ms. Sheldon and says, 'Would you like to lead us in prayer, Ms. Sheldon?' Ms. Sheldon doesn't even say thank you, she just plunks down on her knees, buries her head in the chair, her bottom facing me. She doesn't know that you don't have to say 'Lord' in the beginning, middle and end of every sentence, that she must pray for our leaders. She says, 'The devil is a liar,' and 'bind him, Lawd, bind him.' She claims a whole bunch of things in the name of Jesus. She prays for Donovan and me too and she prays for her children, 'Lawd, show dem di right way, Lawd. Lawd sanctify dem, Lawd.' And Sasha is humming, and I can't take it anymore, and I tell her, 'Shut up, shut up, shut up.'

Ms. Sheldon cuts her eyes at me when we are all seated, and I know she's wishing that I was her son because she would *show mi something tonight.*

Mummy says, 'I'll deal with you later.'

And I say, 'She was making noise in worship and I was trying to tell her to stop so she won't get in trouble.'

'Ms. Sheldon is a big woman,' Mummy says.

'Not Ms. Sheldon. Sasha, Mummy. She's in the chair and she's humming. Yuh can't hear her because she is invisible. We started this game yesterday, but we're playing blue car today. She got the days mixed up and...'

Mummy's eyes are wide and angry like Boston Beach in Portland. 'You cruel little boy,' she says. 'Cruel.' She forgets about dealing with me later and flogs me right there in front of Ms. Sheldon and Donovan and Stephen and invisible humming Sasha. 'I told you she ran away; yuh know that bad little girl ran away and break her poor mother's heart. That child is nothing but crosses on her mother, nothing but crosses, and you sit in worship and say those cruel things.' Then Sasha stops, like she's sorry she made me get beat'n and I look at the chair and look at it and look at it and blink and blink and she's still invisible.

It is seven forty-five when Mummy's finished with me. I'm to go to bed immediately. She will listen to me pray for forgiveness, ask God to take away my stony heart and mouth full of unkind words. I'm under the sheets alone. Donovan will get to stay up until nine listening to Evie on the record player. He likes her Christmas album and it doesn't matter that it's February or August because that night he's singing *O Holy Night* along with her.

I call for Sasha.

'You can stop being invisible now,' I say. 'I'm not upset that I got beat'n. Just stop it now, alright? Stop it.' I listen for her humming and her singing but she's silent. I think about putting the chair in my room beside the bed on my side and I'll wake in the morning and she'll say, *I win*.

A few days after Friday evening worship the police came; I stood at the end of the hallway and watched and listened. They asked for Ms. Sheldon, three of them; two men and a woman. The men in plain clothes and the woman in her uniform, black skirt with a solid red stripe on each side and a blue and white pin stripe shirt. I loved how the hat's visor barely covered her eyes; I hoped she could see through solid objects. She caught me eavesdropping and walked over.

'What's your name, sweetheart?' she said.

'My name is Matthew Archer.' I said it loud so Ms. Sheldon could hear me and tell Mummy how clever I was.

'So, Matthew, what's your friend's name again?'

'Sasha Knight.' I felt like she was testing me and I was passing. 'She's eleven,' I continued, 'and the last time I saw her...' I don't remember what I said. I think I told her we used to play all the time and I asked her not to tell Mummy or Ms. Sheldon.

'You go where, Matthew?' I realised then I'd said too much so I tried to save things.

'I'm not supposed to tell. It's a secret,' I whispered.

'What kind of secret?'

'The kind you're not supposed to tell.' I took one step back. She smiled.

'I know your mother. She used to go to school with my sister.'

'Yuh know Mummy?'

'Yes and I know she wouldn't want yuh to keep secrets from Police. Hmmm, Matthew?' She wasn't smiling anymore. She smelled of icy-mint sweetie and I was confused. I couldn't speak and she said, 'Cat got your tongue, Matthew Archer?'

'I... I...' I couldn't say more because I was trying to work out how a cat could get my tongue.

She started in on me. 'I don't have all day, yuh hear mi. Suh stop di foolishness right now. Yuh want mi to tell your mother?'

'No,' I mumbled with my head down. I was going to embarrass Mummy and we didn't have timeout and grounding back then. She would tell Mummy I was *facety* and *renk* and Mummy would tell her she was going to handle it and I'd talk then, no doubt. I'd cough up everything and then I'd get another flogging on top of that for what I'd say Sasha and I were supposed to do.

The officer smiled again and held my chin up. 'I know you have something to say to me. We need to find your friend, sweetheart.'

'Yuh going to find her?'

'Of course. Come, tell me right here in this ear. Me and you secret, right?' She tapped her left ear then held out her pinky finger and I did too, and we promised not to tell just like me and Sasha used to. The officer crouched to make her left ear level with my face.

'We go to River,' I whispered. 'Please don't tell Mummy.' My eyes watered but I tried to smile. She gave me a sweetie and wiped my falling tear with her right thumb. She had soft fingers and I knew she would find Sasha.

'That's good, Matthew. What yuh do at River?'

'Swim and talk and lie down.'

'Alright, Matthew. That's where yuh met the little boy?'

'Little boy?'

'Matthew. What did I tell you earlier? I said I don't have time for your foolishness.' She gripped both my arms and squeezed. 'What di both of yuh duh to that little boy?'

'Nothing. What little boy? I don't know him. We don't know anybody.'

'Suh yuh don't know the little boy but you also didn't do anything to him. Which one is it Matthew Archer, hmm? Which one? Yuh can't have it both ways.'

'I mean I don't know any little boy.'

'Suh di both ah yuh didn't do anything to that boy in the canal?' She had eyes that turned you inside out. I didn't want to go to jail or meet the hangman in Spanish Town Square.

'He was dead already,' I shouted. 'We didn't do anything.'

'So now yuh know him. Yuh lied to mi before.'

'Sorry,' I said.

'Well lucky for you I know you didn't do anything, sweetheart, but you mustn't play around with a dead body. What were you thinking? If your mother ever found out...' she said and wiped my face. I tried to figure out how she knew but I was too tired and by then I only wanted to find Sasha.

'Okay,' I said. She hugged me and she felt so warm I didn't want to let go. Then I wondered why she said *you* mustn't play around with a dead body and not *you and Sasha*.

'So where's your friend, love? I need to talk to her too, and then it will all be over.' Her voice was like music.

'Sasha?'

'Yes,' she said. 'Where's Sasha?'

'I don't know.' They were blaming her for orange hair Delroy Kirk. So that's why they were there, to cart off Sasha to prison, lock her up for good and I couldn't lose her twice.

'Shi put yuh up to this, hmm? Shi tell yuh what to do? Shi not really yuh friend if shi asks you to do something wrong. I know you know that. Mrs. Archer trained yuh right suh act like it.'

'You don't understand. She didn't do anything.' I was getting weaker and I cried once more.

'Listen to me, Matthew. Stephen told us about you and her playing around with that boy's body. Yuh si we already know everything so you might as well tell us the rest. Where is she?'

'I can't...'

'This little girl is nothing but trouble, yuh hear mi?' Her voice sharpened. 'Even her mother knows that. Yuh not helping her right now. Suh yuh need to tell mi where shi is.'

'She's in the dark place,' I said, all hurried.

'Dark place?' The officer shook her head.

'I...' I was out of words. She backed away and I stood alone in the hallway. I wanted Mummy but she'd be angry too and say I was making the wrong choices and she was tired of telling me *you are the company you keep*. And so I called out to Sasha. *You're getting me in trouble, tell me what to say* but she didn't answer because she hadn't found her talking voice yet. 'I want to find my friend. She is out there and it's dark, and although she is old enough she doesn't like the dark. And...'

'And what, Matthew?'

'Blackheart man got her.'

'Blackheart man?! Yuh believe in dat foolishness?! Wi don't have time for this.' She walked off and joined the other two officers. I thought it was over. The policemen held glasses of red liquid in their hands and they were laughing with Ms. Sheldon and one of them was saying, 'Don't worry, wi going to find har for yuh and set har straight.'

The policewoman doubled back and this time her face wasn't smiling. She still smelled nice and her voice wasn't sharp and bristly, so when she lifted me up and put me face down across her lap I wasn't thinking it would happen. And when I heard the clinking of the buckle I still didn't believe and when she snapped the belt I was thinking maybe she was just trying to frighten me and we'd all have a good laugh afterwards but it came down on me hard. She was a preacher like Ms. Sheldon.

'Yuh going to learn not to lie. Yuh going learn, yuh hear mi. Where shi is? Where? Answer mi. I said where shi is?' Each whack timed perfectly with every syllable.

'Awright Marcia, yuh cyan stop now,' one of the policemen said. But she kept on and on, 'Ah weh shi deh? Answer mi. Answer mi.' I knew she had a lot more where that came from but I felt someone grab me and stand me up.

'Awright, likkle man. Awright.' The policeman who told her to stop was patting my back and I was bawling and I held on to him and he let me hug him tight. He gave me some cold water; my teeth chattered and my snot and spit poured out like two rivers meeting to distil into the ocean, and he used his kerchief to clean up my face. I begged him not to tell Mummy and I bawled into him some more and he told me, 'Awright man. Awright. Everything goin' be all right.' And he hugged me back.

I want to say that I remember the exact moment I knew Sasha was gone, that the air drained from my lungs, and the skies turned to ash. The day, though, would have been like any other, full of bright sunshine, blooming red hibiscuses and white roses, women coming from market, people going to dance, Mrs. Long across the street firing up the ten-foot speakers for the Friday evening crowd. The truth is days would have passed before I'd have been able to do anything.

After the policewoman beat me, I began to search for Sasha in the house. I checked under my bed, over and over for weeks because I was sure she'd been watching me, waiting for the right moment to sneak back in. I braved the walk to Sydenham and asked the *tegareg* children if they'd seen her. They didn't beat me up that time since they were afraid they'd have to deal with her afterwards. They refused to answer me, though, and walked to another tree. For days I thought she was with them and they wouldn't say, but one afternoon I went to River to find her and they were all there, looking surprised to see me without her.

Today it feels like ages passed by searching for her daily. But that can't be, because children have to go to school, do homework and find new friends to play with. There were seconds, minutes, hours, days, years when I forgot her but then she'd return. And like I said, my life, no, my whole lives, would start over in a cruel Peter Pan loop. I have friends who call me to reminisce over some old memories and I think Sasha was there too. Like when Rory Bowen said, 'Remember when we went to Fort Clarence Beach that time and we didn't have enough money to get in and everybody said it was my fault because I was supposed to bring the funds…' He laughed in the phone. And I said, 'Yes and Sasha was…' and he said, 'Who?' He was right because we met in fourth form, long after she left me.

I rolled around in my bed that first night, my eyes probing the darkness for her. I glanced at the green reflective hands on my desk clock. It read eight and I knew Sasha wasn't with me anymore because she would have been here already, her in their room and me in mine; lying in our beds pretending we could walk through walls and that she could hear me sucking my tongue. I wanted to tell her a secret, but I didn't know what.

She couldn't stand the dark for more than a few minutes. It was black outside and there was only one streetlight in those days a quarter mile down at Old Harbour Road. My ears listened for anything: a scratch, a whisper, one more hum. I was listening and waiting because I wouldn't remember what I'd seen earlier: that thing that made me stand still and want to pee. It couldn't be true, Mummy and Ms. Sheldon said so. It couldn't be true, the policewoman beat me. It couldn't be true because I had to live. It was a cruel prank and everybody knew it except me. The gears on the clock whirred and clicked and the seconds blipped away. Nothing. Empty room. It was eight o'clock. One hour and she was gone.

Chapter 25

I read the first line of the article in *The Gleaner*, a handful of words to cover the snuffing out of a life. *Body of Girl found in Willowdene, Spanish Town*, and it dawned on me what had been bothering me about the title the whole time. It didn't read Body of 'Missing' Girl Found. I willed the millimetre of empty space between 'of' and 'Girl' to be filled. I didn't want to be the only one. Someone else must have missed her. There must have been one other, right? There must have been.

Yet there she was. Sasha, Body of Girl Found. Girl. That's it. No mention of family or anyone to claim her. No inconsolable mother, legs weakened from the horror of it, lying in the dust and bawling. Just add one more word to 'Girl', that's all I ask. How about daughter, sister, schoolmate. Friend.

I realised I should be back in Jamaica to claim her but the article was two months old and I couldn't leave work yet. I forwarded the microfiche machine to the following day and read every headline and byline, the back page, sports, obituaries and errata. Weeks and weeks flew by on the screen and nothing. I printed the article and sent a letter to the author, Mrs. Viola Grey.

I said I was writing from America and I knew the girl she spoke of. I gave her my address and phone number and enclosed ten US dollars to cover any related costs in contacting me. I told her to call me collect anytime. Weeks went by without a reply. I didn't blame her because I'd been warned that post office personnel likely opened envelopes and siphoned off any cash for themselves.

So I called *The Gleaner*. The operator said, 'It's *Miss* Grey actually and she isn't in, may I take a message, sir?'

'Oh, sorry about that. Do you know when Ms. Grey is going to be in? I'm calling from the States.'

The operator said, 'I heard you the first time, sir.' And I knew she wouldn't deliver my message.

I wrote to Spanish Town police station and got nothing from them too. When I called I was transferred to Detective Sergeant Huffington. She made no attempt to mummy me through the whole ordeal. I told her, 'Yes, I'm calling about the girl in the paper.'

'I can't hear yuh.'

'The body you found. I know her.' My left hand cupped the phone while shouting into the receiver.

'Body? Weh yuh a call mi fah? Yuh call the morgue to claim a body. Wha wrong wid yuh?' She hung up before I could clarify. I knew better than to call back, at least not that night. She was the kind of person who made an instant judgement about you and never changed her mind. My only hope was to call the next day and perhaps get another detective.

When I tried in the morning the operator, a different one from the night before, said, 'Oh, yuh want Detective Sergeant Huffington. Call after seven o'clock tonight.'

'Tell her to expect my call. I'm calling from The States.' And as soon as I said it I caught my mistake. I was giving her orders and although she said, 'Yes sir,' she wouldn't utter a word. Worse, she would tell Huffington that *some bwoy seh him a call from America. Talk like him have sup'n up him batty.* And the two of them would laugh.

I still called and Huffington said, 'You di one from last night?'

'Me? No ma'am.'

'Yuh sound like him to me. Well I'm going to tell you what I told the other man. We don't keep dead body here. Spanish Town Morgue; at the hospital.'

'No,' I said, 'you misunderstand, Detective Inspector.'

'Detective Sergeant.'

'Sorry. I'm calling about the body you found four months ago. Surely there's an ongoing investigation?'

'Mr... what yuh say your name was again?'

'Arch... ah mean Cole.'

'If you say so. Well, Mr. Cole. Yuh know how many bodies we found in the last twenty-four hours alone? Six. I can't even tell yuh 'bout a body from last week let alone... two months yuh seh?'

'No. Four months ago in Willowdene. She's a girl. Eleven years old. Maybe. When I saw her last she was eleven. She might be a little older but I know she must be around eleven. She was wearing...' For a second I couldn't remember her uniform. 'Yes, light blue tunic and a white blouse. Her hair plait in three and she would have been wearing yellow ribbons. She left the house that morning around seven o'clock and she was the only one on the road because we didn't go to the same school...' I went on and on but Huffington wasn't answering so I said, 'Hello, yuh still there?'

'How yuh know suh much 'bout dis girl? What she is to yuh?'

'A friend.'

'Friend? You are a big man who friend-up with a little girl. What kind of perversion...?'

'No. No ma'am. I was nine then.'

'Nine? How long ago was this?'

I paused.

'It... It's been a few years.'

'Years? I thought you said this was four months? Wha kinda foolishness dis? Yuh wasting mi time!'

'You don't understand,' I said, and I could hear her rifling through papers. 'Listen, I know that girl. Her name is Sasha Knight. If you just ask around in Cheshire Hills or Horizon Park or Sydenham someone will tell you that she went missing...' I didn't want to say how long but I was already in. '...twenty years ago.'

'Twenty? Horizon Park? You take me for a fool, sir. First you say this girl's body was found in Willowdene four months ago, and now you're talking about Horizon Park and twenty years ago! Don't call mi back here. I don't care if you are calling from America. Because yuh live a farrin doesn't mean seh yuh cyan come rule mi up.' She was gone.

I scrambled to find other contacts I could reach out to. In the meantime, I called the police station a few more times and when Huffington answered I hung up. I tried manipulating my identity and purpose for calling. I'd say I was a reporter with *The Gleaner* or NBC in New York. That last time I claimed I was doing a show on mysterious deaths around the world and, 'I'd like to feature one of your detectives.' I was patched through to the Ministry of Justice. The man said he'd have to get back to me, '...if you leave your phone number and address...' A week later I received a letter from the office of attorneys Greene, Carlisle and Mason kindly reminding me that,

Misrepresenting yourself as an employee of NBC is not only a civil offense but may also lead to criminal charges.

I tracked down my old friend Graeme who had begun working with the Jamaica Defence Force as an IT analyst but was training to be a police officer.

'Can you do anything?' I said.

'Look,' he said, 'word is getting around about you and this thing.'

'It's not a thing!' I snapped a bit. 'Sorry, I didn't mean to shout.'

'I can't help you, Matthew. But as a friend, I think you should get some help.' I sensed he'd tell Mummy. There was no excuse this time. I had a good job and a beautiful fiancée who would not stand by and watch me make a mess.

I tried the hospital several times and they refused to connect me to the morgue. I'd exhausted every lead. Peta-Gay was a patient fiancée and although she had the wedding and her work and shopping with the mothers, she had a limit I didn't care to test. Then it all became clear; I would simply have to go. So I boarded a plane to Jamaica, back to a wide black hole, and I could hear Sasha humming again, *Can you hear the drums Fernando?* She sounded happy, like we were going to River.

Chapter 26

One of the policemen stands guard at the gate. For a moment I wonder if he's keeping people out or holding Sasha and me in. I walk towards him and all eyes are on me; the children in their uniforms, the housewives, the bank tellers and nurses who should be on their way to work, they all fix their gaze. I'm a curiosity, no, a danger. They instinctively shuffle back as I approach them and the policeman swings round to face me. It's contagious, this madness I bring. His palms are up. I'm not allowed to proceed any further.

I scan the crowd, unsure what or who I'm trying to find. I listen. It's all mismatched, this. It's out of place. They throw furtive glances. They whisper. They laugh. They shout.

The sun has burned off the last of the cloud cover and the mist is all but gone. A man with a wooden cart is crying out for empty soda bottles. Our eyes lock. He's sweating already, foreshadowing a hot day. It won't rain after all. The earlier drizzle was a tease. We don't know each other, yet we understand that something has shifted. We are on the cusp. I smile and everyone stops talking all at once like when we used to be in class and the whole room goes silent and we'd say, *angel pass through*.

Chapter 27

Star apples. It's what I miss most when I think of Jamaica these days. Purple ones and green ones. Round. It's a silly thing, really. You split it open and it's fleshy with a creamy white liquid at the edges. It tastes like jellied sugar. Their smooth oblong black pits tempt me to swallow them whole but not before rubbing them against the sides of my tongue. 'A tree ah guh grow inside a yuh,' Sasha used to say. I believed her until I learned about my stomach and hydrochloric acid and intestines in Mr. Beach's first form Integrated Science class. When I was a child I never figured out how to eat star apples without leaving my mouth sticky like ineffective glue. I'd press my lips together and open them, pushing against the viscidity. Over and over, never tiring of it.

I returned to Jamaica expecting its gestures, moods and mores to be intact, a still image of my youth. Worse, that it would devolve in my absence. But Jamaica had survived all those years. Toll roads were being built. New and better supermarkets anchored streets and replaced buildings once left to decay. When I rang up Nana she asked me why I hadn't emailed her. Nana, fully eighty years old living on a farm with her chickens and pigs. I felt a certain resentment because I wanted to believe we'd made the right decision to leave, that our homes would die without us.

There was something else. I wished a gloom to hang over the place, for them to be sorry they'd forgotten Sasha and I secretly hoped that a plague had decimated every town and city. Instead I found a bustling airport and traffic jams, young men playing scrimmage football on patchy fields, boys and girls in the same uniforms I recalled heading to and from school.

At the last minute Daddy agreed to pick me up from the airport. He pulled up in a brand new BMW M3. The aftermarket sound system was crisp, clean and loud even though it was eight o'clock in the morning. He turned the music down, shook his head and said, 'Yuh brother seh dis ting faas.' I hopped in and within a second we were on the bumper of a JUTA bus. 'Nevva guh pass third gear since I get dis ting.' He kissed his teeth and I knew then Donovan had talked him out of buying his usual Mercedes. He introduced the girl in the back seat several minutes after we started our journey.

'Sandrina, dis my big son.' I felt my head smiling. I caught a glimpse of her when I half turned round, and she cut her eyes at me because Daddy told her to go in the back seat to make room. I didn't say 'no that's fine.'

Like everyone else I told him I was meeting friends for a last fun trip before I took the marriage plunge. We both pretended he didn't know I was lying.

'Ah cyan tek yuh roun' if yuh want,' he said when we got to Red Hills Road. Sandrina's insistent knee dug deep into the backrest of my seat, piercing my lower spine.

Before I could say anything she said, 'We have an appointment, Paulie, remember?' Her tone compliant, suggestive, respectful. An unpleasant word crossed my mind but I bit my tongue. Daddy didn't answer. She said something about how long it took to plan the whole thing and she kept with it until we got to the house in Stony Hill where she reached over and adjusted his collar.

We sat in front of the house with the engine running. His old Mercedes took up the left side of the car port. The house had grown since last I saw it; he'd been busy adding floors and wings over the years. Sandrina was still talking, multiplying the ever-growing list of reasons why they couldn't cancel their trip, when he said, 'Keep it. Map inside the glove compartment,' and handed me the keys to the BMW. He paused and looked at me. I opened my mouth to tell him the whole thing but he squeezed my shoulder and said, 'Try mek it before night. Sandrina, come awn.'

I drove with the opened map on the passenger seat and headed to Heathfield. I couldn't help feeling that Sasha was behind the mountain walls along the river road, under the tar my wheels rolled on, and on every minibus and executive taxi. I wished, then, I'd taken Daddy up on his offer.

I would be staying with Nana after she said, 'I don't believe yuh. Come to Jamaica and cyaan put yuh eye on your grandmother.' The hotel grudgingly refunded half my deposit. The tributary road to the house had changed little since I was a child and I smiled at the exercise in dodging crater sized potholes. I could see the mirage of her place a half a mile away as I slowly passed a bicyclist struggling up the hill. The tyres resisted the incline but the man persisted, his skinny legs and sweat soaked back joining the effort. He had a light pink sack on the handlebars, one of those old flour bags repurposed. Its weight made his ascent more difficult. I had a sudden desperate need to know what he carried as if he was hiding something that rightfully belonged to me. I stopped and waited for him to catch up then pulled alongside him on the empty road, only metres from Nana's house.

'What yuh selling?' I asked. He studied his sack then looked at me and the car, his face puzzled, his eyes certain that he could never have anything I'd desire. I drove even closer, almost touching him. The bicycle tyres wobbled and I was sure now more than ever that he was concealing the contents of his sack. I drove past him by a metre then turned the car to block his path. I opened the door to cross examine him but he was already pedalling ferociously in the opposite direction down the hill.

'Matthew? Is that you, sweetheart?' Nana was at the gate. In the quiet of the rural midday her voice was a bullhorn. My eyes searched the spot where I cornered the bicyclist, but I couldn't recall why I tried to stop him in the first place. I swallowed hard and whispered to myself, 'Keep it together, Matthew.'

The star apple tree was still there, its branches a canopy stretching well over the front concrete fence, green leaves speaking of health and youth. My stomach rumbled. But there was no fruit.

'Long time since ah get a single one from dat tree,' Nana said. She mumbled something about cursing it and laughed. 'Lena, bring di bag dem,' she called to the girl leaning on the broom.

Nana isn't like other grandmothers. She'll take the medications I send from America, boasting to her friends of her doting grandson. I came across her top left kitchen cabinet and she had kept every one of the empty bottles, dozens of them, in order of month and year.

After I settled in she introduced the girl as her part time days worker. I was happy to see Nana in good health, but I would have preferred to be on my own because now I had to traverse a bit of a minefield to avoid her finding out my real purpose there. And she'd tell Mummy the first chance she got but not before properly upbraiding me. I had a week and a half at most, and I needed to start my days early if I was to accomplish anything.

My room was the same one I used when I visited the last two weeks of summer every year as a child. The same bed and mattress and more likely than not, the same pillow. It was so flat it served as a coaster for my head. Nana took a good look at me.

'Yuh put on weight,' she said, and Lena chuckled. She shot Lena a sharp glance and the girl found herself in another room.

I didn't have a plan or any real direction as such. I began at Nana's because the house was close enough to Sasha's people. I say that, but I was guessing, building a sand castle on the words of a child spoken in haste and hope. We had traipsed off to the new part of Cheshire Hills housing scheme one afternoon, Sasha and I. She'd put her right arm round my neck so tight that although we were supposed to be walking side by side my body was slightly ahead of hers. It was as if I was her smaller conjoined twin. Bright white marl stretched on for acres and the best part, large concrete pipes dotted the landscape like baled hay.

We were warned not to play in the construction zone and Cheshire Hills children obeyed their parents. They frightened us with the tale of a Sydenham boy who was hiding in one of the pipes and when the tractor scooped it up he drained out and landed straight on his head. When Mummy told me she clapped her hands together and said, 'Smash!' I imagined the boy's brains oozing out like thick cornmeal porridge.

So Sasha hugged my neck tight as we walked and when we were in one of the big concrete pipes, our backs taking the shape of the long curve, she told me, 'Daddy live inna Whitecastle near yuh granny.'

'Can I meet him?' I said.

'Yeah. Him a guh come fi mi and wi a guh ah Cuba. Him taller dan di Ackee tree.' Her eyes shone bright when she raised her hand as high as the inside of the pipe.

'Cuba?' I said. I was thinking that Mummy hated that country because Fidel Castro was influencing the current prime minister and he was 'going to bring communism to Jamaica and destroy our way of life.'

'And him have a big bike and him cyan ride faas and dilly dally tru all di cyar dem.' Her hands stretched out in front of her, fists balled up like she was gripping the handles. 'Vroom vroom. Mi tell him 'bout yuh.'

'Mummy doesn't like Cuba,' I said.

'Yuh cyan come,' she said as if she didn't hear me, and I put my arm around her.

Of course I had to one-up her so I said my father brought us ice cream and Jello every Saturday night after church. I told her that he wore nice colognes but sometimes he smelled like beer and that one day he was going to show me how to drink it. There wasn't much else to say then so I allowed myself to be inserted into her fantasy of her motorcycle riding dad. I imagined us on the bike, blaring exhaust rattling the neighbourhood, she in his lap and I in hers, wind blinding us as we sped down Old Harbour Road. I didn't really care if we went to Cuba but I figured he would take us anywhere we asked him to.

* * *

So now years later I was at Nana's, only a few miles from Whitecastle. Dada had been gone two years now and she never let me forget that I missed his funeral. She still had his old piano he couldn't play. His last unopened pack of Matterhorn cigarettes she kept on the dresser and instructed Lena not to move it. Lena showed up every day sweeping and dusting all the things Nana pointed out to her. Nana went over the same list every morning and Lena stood there and *yes Mrs. Johnsoned* her. When she wasn't looking, Lena smiled and shook her head as if to say, *well it's your money, you can spend it any way you like.*

Lena asked if I was from America and I could tell she already knew the answer; not that Nana would have told, more like Lena overheard her saying things. She said her sister lived in Florida too, 'North Miami.' I asked her the same question and she said, 'Linstead, but most of my family is from Whitecastle.' I couldn't believe it. I prayed that night, thanked God for all His mercies and blessings, for sending this girl with a broom and feather duster who would guide me to the open door.

The next afternoon she asked if I could give her a ride home. And so I followed God's direction and made our way to Linstead where she told me to keep going. We headed north to Whitecastle. We crossed a bridge just wide enough for one car. Below, a creek splashed over beige rocks. Further in the distance, a crèche of women, most of them with babies, took advantage of the break in the rain and pulled their clean clothes from the river and laid them in aluminium wash pans. Twin hills of green trees on either side contained the river and the women like a well-marked highway. The water wandered left and the highway of trees followed it.

We headed up. 'Turn left,' Lena said, and we began an even steeper ascent that threatened to shove Daddy's brand new car down the hill. I held the gear and floored the gas but the back end began to fish tail so I eased up. Behind me a taxi driver pressed his horn. Lena stuck her head out of the window and shouted, 'Hey bwoy yuh cyaaan wait?' He slowed and the distance between us increased. The road narrowed as we inched higher. Several times I pulled dangerously close to the hill's edge to let vehicles going the opposite direction pass.

We drowned in green everywhere; deeper and darker the shade became the further we climbed. 'Turn right ya suh,' she said, and we were down a gravel road. On each side were small cinder block houses in varying colours with low zinc roofs, concrete fences and tiny painted iron gates. Various fruit trees overshadowed front yards.

'Right here. Mi have a surprise fi yuh,' Lena said.

The house was like all the others. Lena stooped, grabbed a large pebble, and knocked on the iron gate.

'Who there?' a woman's voice returned.

'Lena.'

'Lena?' the woman's voice cracked.

'Missah Palmer granddaughter.'

'Oh.' The woman shaded her eyes with her right hand even though it was overcast. 'Yuh get big. Last time I see yuh, yuh was likkle suh. Come een.' Lena led the way down a red tiled path with crotons on either side. The woman opened an artfully crafted wrought iron door and invited us to sit. Two chairs faced the garden and the road while potted plants took up every free space on the parapet wall. Lena pointed me to one of the chairs.

I said, 'No. You sit please.'

She smiled. The woman looked at Lena and Lena said, 'Sorry Mrs. Knight. Dis is Mr. Archer. Mrs. Johnson's grandson.'

'Yuh sure dear? Him look too big.'

'No ma'am, Mrs. Johnson in Heathfield. Di lady that marry to the man dat used to run di orange juice factory.'

'Ooooh yes,' Mrs. Knight said. In the light on the veranda she looked much older than her voice. She was Nana's height, barely five feet. She had slanted eyes and she wore a floral patterned white duster. She squinted at both of us as if she knew it best to wear her glasses but after so many years couldn't bring herself to put them on. She lit a mosquito destroyer; its smoke swirled up and as it reached the parapet wall the wind spread it around.

''im here 'bout somebody name Marsha,' Lena said.

I exhaled hard and said, 'Sasha actually.'

'Don't think I know any Sasha,' Mrs. Knight said.

'Her name is Sasha Knight and she told me her father is from Whitecastle.'

'Lots of Knights round here, sweetheart.'

'She would have been thirty-one or thirty-two by now,' I said.

'Sorry my dear but—'

'Her mother...' I cut Mrs. Knight off before she could dismiss me out of hand. She sat deep in the chair and I knew I was about to lose her. 'I'm so sorry Mrs. Knight, what were you saying?' She nodded as if my apology redeemed the good thoughts she held for Nana.

'That was it, dear. Don't know any Sasha.'

I told her I loved her plants and she gave me a history of each of the roses to the left, the crotons down the tiled walk path, and even the grand breadfruit tree that overhung the fence.

'I was wondering,' I said when I thought we were through, 'if you might know her mother then.'

'Let mi hear the name.'

'Ms. Sheldon. I don't know her first name.'

Mrs. Knight stood and boxed me. 'Yuh bring gossip and susu susu in mi house. You don't know mi from Adam and this is what yuh duh?'

'I don't understand, Mrs. Knight.' I rubbed my left cheek. 'I need to find anyone that knows Sasha. She went missing some years...'

'Is what dat wutliss gyal tell yuh? Shi sen yuh round here to get money from mi? Yuh involved in her samfi business?'

'What samfi business? Sasha never would...' I tried to salvage things.

'Sheldon and har t'iefing self. That woman is full of lies. Shi told you wi have money, is that it?'

'No Mrs. Knight, you don't understand. I knew Sasha as a child. I can't find her.' I tried to say more but she rushed us off the veranda.

'Get out. Get out both of yuh. And you, Lena. You're another one. Ah not surprised yuh mix up in this. Yuh mother should know better but yuh was always a troublemekka.'

We drove without words down the hill, the silence making my head swirl.

A bit of madness took me just then. I began to think the Knights conspired to remove Sasha from her rightful place in the family. The grandfather, Mrs. Knight's husband, must have left an inheritance for his favourite grandchild that displaced the other ungrateful children. Mrs. Knight herself got nothing and the house she now propped herself up in rightfully belonged to Sasha. So someone in the family, or maybe a hired assassin, tracked down Sasha that morning, abducted and killed her, then dumped her body in Willowdene.

But why? The house wasn't much to write home about. Then I thought Sasha's father loved her more than his legitimate children. They overheard the promises made to Sasha, that he'd whisk her off to Cuba, so she had to go.

Or maybe Sasha was a real Knight and the others, Mrs. Knight and her family, were all imposters. They had to silence the one piece of evidence. I was full of theories, all of them equally ridiculous.

I ran the scenarios over and over all the way down, rubbing my cheek the entire time; that woman had a healthy swing.

Lena asked if I could take her to work because it was too late for her to go home and change.

'I thought you worked for Nana,' I said.

'Mi other job ah di grocery store.'

The next morning Lena brought me news of Mrs. Knight, stories she gleaned from her mother. Mrs. Knight had four sons; two lived in Canada, one in New Zealand and the last remained by her side, first caring for his father and now her. Randal Knight, Lena's mother said, owned a bar in Whitecastle's town square.

The next day I was headed to Spanish Town Hospital morgue to see the coroner. I would check out Randal Knight another time. Nana caught me as I pulled the door lever. She handed Lena a piece of paper and asked if she could tag along to pick up a few items.

We drove along the river road, the sheer mountains on the left rising several hundred feet, and the Rio Cobre on the right. Beyond the river were more mountains. Single file we drove in, skirting the edge of the hill and the river bank. The heavy morning mist was a blanket covering our windshields and it reduced visibility to a few feet.

'Yuh must really did like har,' Lena said when we entered Flat Bridge, her voice, like God, calling me to life. Until then I had driven with an empty head. The green water underneath flowed towards Linstead as if warning, *you should turn back now.* I considered Lena's declaration for a moment before I said, 'Yes,' and we were quiet again.

At the hospital a red and white candy cane pole held us at bay.

'I'm here to see the coroner,' I said to the guard. I glanced at Lena and her hands tightened in her lap when he spoke.

'What's your name, sir?' the guard said.

'Archer.'

He scrolled through the papers on his clipboard. 'I don't see any Archer here. Pull up and turn around right there, sir.' He pointed to the u-turn ahead. A few yards up the paved driveway the low-slung building was a lightly planted tree in the zoysia landscape. Directional arrows pointed visitors to each department. The morgue required a right turn.

'Can you put me on the list, then?' I said.

'Who yuh here to claim?'

'Okay, it's complicated. I know her as Sasha Knight but…' He dropped the clip board and pen. 'She's an unclaimed body from a few months back. Remember the story in *The Gleaner* about the body in…'

'We don't have anything like that here. Please turn around right there, sir.'

'Maybe there was an inquest. If you just…'

'Right there, sir.' He was done talking. Behind me a convoy

of cars blasted their horns. I thought of making a dash for it as soon as he lifted the pole. I could make it before he had time to radio his partners and then they would have to respond. And I doubted the hospital had more than two security guards. But then I glimpsed the revolver on his hip that I was sure he would have no hesitation about emptying in my back, so I complied.

'Babylon,' Lena mumbled as we pulled away.

'Yeah,' I said and joined the traffic heading east. I had come this far and only a handful of steps stood between me and an answer. A few days before, I'd searched court records and there was nothing. No inquest. No cause of death; 'inconclusive'. I would have taken that. I couldn't go on. I called several times the next day but no one picked up. So that morning Lena and I drove towards Kingston, no destination, no place to be. There was a good and proper life to get back to but I couldn't see it then.

'I don't know what to do,' I said.

Lena looked at her watch. 'Mi cyan tell yuh a secret?'

I didn't answer.

'Mi nevva guh beach yet, yuh knuh.'

'What? You've never been to the beach in your life? Ever?'

'No.'

'I don't know how that's possible. You live on an island...' She turned quiet as I judged her. 'It doesn't matter.' We passed Greendale and the police training grounds at Twickenham Park and the big roundabout with Jose Marti High School at the far end. Central Village was next. As we approached the turn for Portmore I looked at Lena and she relaxed into the seat. I realised then she would have been just fine if I drove off into eternity. I made a right towards the causeway and traced out the direction to Hellshire Beach.

Sasha and I were supposed to go. I saved up money to buy festival and fish and we'd swim all day. I tried to recall how far along we were in the plan when she left with blackheart man. Maybe if we were really close it would change all this, like 'almost' was good enough.

Lena's eyes were all sparkles when I parked. We were the only ones there on a Tuesday morning and she trudged through the sand with her sandals in her hand.

'Mi sih dat in a movie one time,' she said.

'Saw what?'

'Dis lady a walk pon di beach with har slippers in har hand. Shi did look nice yuh knuh. Har hair just a blow inna di wind.' Lena's hair wasn't long enough to do that but she pretended it was, running her fingers through and turning her face to the breeze. She walked close to the water's edge and when the waves came ashore she skipped away. On and on she went.

I couldn't move. I watched her spinning like a child in her first father–daughter dance. Lena in her pink jeans and white shirt, twirling herself.

When she came back she said, 'Why yuh don't laugh? From a meet yuh, yuh nevva laugh yet. Not one time.'

I didn't want to talk.

'She was your little friend, don't?'

'Yuh mean Sasha? Yeah.'

Lena walked ahead of me for a few minutes. I looked out to sea. The sun stood high to my left.

'Alright, mek mi tell yuh a joke,' she said. I didn't hear her return.

'No, that's not necessary.'

But she started to tell it anyway; a racial one.

'A Chiney man and a Nayga man guh inna one bar. Di Chiney man seh…' She was laughing before she got the whole thing out. 'How it guh again? Lawd, yuh mek mi figget.' She punched my chest.

'We should go,' I said.

Lena wore beads in her hair like Venus and Serena Williams. White beads and pink jeans and white sandals, and a button-down white shirt she tucked in. She was leaning on her broom at the entrance to the room Nana reserved for her on the rare nights she slept over. She had asked me about Sasha again. I told her I thought I was going mad, that maybe everyone was right all along.

'I have most of it here.' I pointed to my head. 'There's something else, I think, but I can't remember.'

Lena said life is hard, that I must laugh sometimes. She told me, 'I believe you.' She asked me to tell her more, everything. So she dropped the broom and we sat hip to hip on the stoop at the back door. She held my hand in hers. I cried.

The next night we went to see Randal Knight at his bar. The place was a wooden shack painted in red, green and gold stripes with three steps leading up to the entrance. Inside was dark. A single naked light bulb suspended from the ceiling with a long chain attached. A jukebox stood guard in one corner and a pinball machine in the other.

I joined the two customers at the counter quietly contemplating their drinks then introduced myself to the bartender. I assumed him to be Randal Knight. He wore one of those Michael Manley type bush jackets. He faced me just long enough to say, 'Mama tell mi 'bout yuh,' and resumed returning the used bottles to their correct slots. He was skinnier and shorter than I'd imagined. His hair was cropped low. He had dark skin with even darker pits on his face. He wiped the counter after each drink he served. I searched his face for familiar lines and angles, something that would give him away as Sasha's father. I tried to recall if I saw a motorcycle on the road anywhere near the bar.

'So you know why I'm here then?' I said. He didn't look up that time and he never said another word to me. He just served drinks and wiped the counter. Lena busied herself with the jukebox, browsing the limited selection of 1970s favourites.

Fifteen minutes later, my blank mind studying the bubbles in my kola champagne, one of the customers said, 'Over there.' His finger pointed to Randal Knight's back as he headed to a door behind the counter. I looked at Lena sipping the drink I bought her. She smiled as if extending her approval. I followed Randal Knight through a hallway and out into the black evening.

Crickets sang. A barking call and response began between neighbourhood dogs. Beyond the back door I could barely make out a structure. In the moonlight phantom bodies flitted about. The night air was cool and bracing, and I closed my eyes for a moment to enjoy the sensation as it swept over my body. Then I stepped on something sharp and felt myself fall.

It's strange when someone punches you and you're not expecting it. You don't feel the pain at first, it's shock that overcomes you, disorientation. The world is not as it should be. I felt another and another in quick succession. Someone, the same man from the counter I presumed, helped me to my feet. I walked slowly, slightly doubled over. I retook my place in the bar and I diluted the salt taste in my mouth with saliva. The man placed a glass of

Irish Cream in front of me and said, 'Don't worry 'bout it,' when I tried to pay him. So I sat on a stool and looked at Randal Knight, Sasha's father I'd hoped, this man who sucker punched me at the back of his bar because I upset his mother, and I realised there was nothing else. I was out of everything.

Lena said I should buy her another drink, rum and milk, and I was so happy someone believed me, that maybe I wasn't going mad after all, that I bought her the drink. And another. And another. I bought her five drinks, three rum and milks, and two Irish Creams and I let her unzip my trousers when I got to her house. She let me unhook her bra. We sat on her bed in the single room she rented from a Mrs. Dailey.

'Shi Adventist like you,' Lena said, my cock resting lightly on her fingers and my hand around her waist. She set my back flat on the bed and stood over me, her legs on either side of my pelvis. And when she turned to face me I could hear those beads; *swish, swish, clink, clink*.

I was thinking it was nice to be happy again, just for one moment, so good to hear a girl ask me if I was alright. I recalled how I'd met her earlier that night at the grocery store where she worked part time. She said nine but at nine fifteen I was still sitting in my car watching shoppers pop in and out. I walked in and she was at the cash register, a green apron slung over her shirt and trousers. She was rude to all the customers but her queue was the fullest because she was the fastest and people don't care about nice when they can get out quick.

She sat there scooting bottles and tins and sacks of rice over the scanner. Every item made a beep and I remembered a stupid little rhyme we sang when we were in high school every time we walked by a store. Paul Bennett, Arun Singh and I used to buy

Bustamante candy at the pharmacy on Beckford Street in Spanish Town. It was Arun and Paul who started the whole thing. We'd gather by the exit door and sing it loud enough so the cashiers could hear us:

Cashier, cashier,
Come 'ere come 'ere,
Di ting between yuh leg have a whole heap a hair

The cashiers would tell us to, 'guh suck out yuh mumma,' and Paul and Arun would laugh. I was thinking all this when Lena stooped down towards my pelvis, low like how women pee when there is no toilet around and they're in the woods or at the back of Shoppers' Fair. In one go she went, *no hesitation no concentration, names of girls* – God I loved that game. I was thinking I shouldn't be here; I need to go home now; there's nothing left for me in this place, that Sasha was gone forever. Lower and lower Lena stooped until I could feel the cartilage inside her grip and hold me in place. I stopped thinking about home then. I wondered if I would always be stuck here, if I could never leave Jamaica alone. Lena, whose last name I realised I didn't know, who was no girl after all, but a proper woman; I keep getting that wrong. Lena *cashier, cashier,* who couldn't go any lower, right? Lower and lower, and I could feel her warm buttocks slapping my hip bone. I was thinking I liked how I could see the light bulb above the headboard reflected in my glistening cock. *Swish. Swish.* The beads sounded like hundreds of them singing at once, each clamouring to be heard.

I was thinking about what Peta-Gay was doing just then. How it would be a beautiful wedding and we'd have pretty children, two at least; with any luck, hazel or grey eyed children; how everyone at church would be happy for us. Not one bit of envy. And Lena was going and going, up and down, sliding away, not a waiver, not a stumble. I was thinking what good aim she had, how steady those legs, how strong those muscles. And I was wondering if she would slip but she hit the target every time. I was thinking I could die here now and I wouldn't have to explain. But I wouldn't die and I'd have to tell Peta-Gay because Sasha would make me. And I was thinking I hate you, Sasha. I hate you because you should have told me you wouldn't come back.

So Lena rode and rode, grabbing my cock with every rise and loosening with each descent. I thought now would be the time to tell her when I was about to break. She was riding harder and faster than I could have ever imagined from her skinny frame and I was ready to bust open but she was saying, 'Not yet Fuckah, don't even t'ink 'bout it.' I wanted to hold back like when you know you are going to have the best crap of your life if you could just squeeze it in a little longer. I was almost there but she said, 'Mi nuh ready yet.' I was almost there and she said, 'Aye, Daddy, aye,' and that whole incestuous reference should have turned off the spigot, but it wanted to open up even more. *Now. Tell her now*, my mind screamed, because later would be too late and then you'd have to lie. Later, you couldn't admit that you were the lone twenty-nine-year-old Jamaican man virgin.

The next night I didn't buy her a drink. She brought me one instead.

'Mi know yuh Seven-day, suh mi mek some peanut punch fi yuh.' She poured it in a cup, it came out thick and rich, *plop plop*, and I was barely finished before the waist of my trousers made a ring around my ankles. 'Mi love fi sih it grow,' she said. She was looking at me and caressing my balls with cold fingers that grew warm the longer she rubbed. I should have stopped. That's what we all say with our 20/20 vision when life gets complicated. But I was seeing perfectly then, and when I saw Lena again the night after, when I snuck her in after Nana had fallen asleep and when she put her tongue on it and I recoiled because Jamaican women were not to do such things, that's what all the dance hall artists say; that's what all my friends say, *only dutty gyal duh dem tings*, I was seeing perfectly. But I was on the mountaintop and when she opened her legs wide, wide as the Sahara and moist as the Rio Cobre and salty like Hellshire Beach, I realised all those dance hall artists and all my friends who said, *dem man eat undah table*, were a bunch of hypocrites because I knew they all did it too.

So I took my turn at the table to taste good, potable, salt water for the first time. I felt like I could swallow di ting between har leg with a whole heap a hair. Swallow and swallow. I liked how she shoved it deeper into my mouth as if cramming it in; *yes, more can fit, you simply have to adjust like so*. She was on my mouth, my cock, my legs, my face, my back. Days later I could still smell her on me and it was good; very, very good.

As I said, I should have stopped then but I was angry and alone, so I spent my remaining nights in bed, wrapped in Lena's arms and I didn't want her to let go. I was departing Jamaica light and heavy, leaving Sasha again for good, finally putting this place behind me, all the people who would tell me nothing and ask for *anything yuh cyan duh Mistah. Send mi a cyar stereo. Send mi a pair a Nikes. Send mi a bokkle ah Drakkar Noir. Send mi a Polo shirt* and they meant Ralph Lauren, not that generic shit at K-Mart.

'Yuh a guh write to mi?' Lena said right before I drove off to meet Daddy at the airport. I told her yes and I meant it. I really did. But distance gives you clarity and it was time to get back to my good choices and marry Peta-Gay.

Chapter 28

There are more children at the gate waiting. They queue properly to avoid the belt if the principal drives up and they are disorderly. She will swing indiscriminately, catching backs, shoulders, legs and bottoms. The girls self-segregate and play their clapping games. I want to play too. It's a chorus,

Reeedim.

Concentration.

Names of... Boys. A.

Anthony, the first girl sings. They cannot miss a beat.

Andrew, the second.

Adam, the third.

Alan, the fourth. They exhaust the A's.

B. They sing together,

Brian, Bruce... ahm, the third girl misses the beat as the name escapes her. She's out. Sasha and Andrene would go on for hours, it seemed, beating out the other girls in the neighbourhood. Andrene would have said *Byron, Bentley, Baron, Ben* and Sasha would challenge that last one because, 'Ben short fi Benjamin,' and we'd all agreed before.

Sasha taught me but I was never fast enough. It didn't matter to her, we'd still play. Sometimes when I missed her hand, hers would land on my nose. I'd laugh and say, 'You're picking my nose naught.' And she'd slap me and run away and I'd chase her.

The principal is here. Two boys pull the gate back. They're full of goodness. They adore order. They love authority. She eyes the girls playing and she stops and opens her door. The other children make way for her, fingers on lips. No one warns the girls but the one facing the gate stops and joins the line. It's too late for the others. One whack each and then tears. The queue is quiet.

Sasha would have hated it here. She never said, though; nothing of school, of the games she learned, of the friends she made, broke up with and befriended. None of them knocked on our gate and asked after her when she was gone. I wonder now if they knew but wouldn't, or couldn't, tell.

It's not only children at the gate now. The curious have spread towards them. Women in yard clothes with hands on hips. Some of them pointing. They know something I don't. The grapevine goes from Graeme to the digger operator to the woman he's chatting up then the others by the gate. The ground undulates beneath me. I stand still.

Chapter 29

Twenty-one bottles. Niagara Falls on holiday with Daddy and his fourth wife and my three-year-old half-sister, and I made a wrong turn. I was in a gift shop and I overpaid and I didn't care and I was only supposed to get key chains but I saw the peach bottle and it was in Canadian dollars and I remember I was trying to do the conversion but I didn't know the exchange rate that day. I bought it because I have accepted there will be no end. My first will and testament said I was to be buried with them but then I was sure Peta-Gay would understand. Even better, she'd continue my journey and it would pass to our children and grandchildren on and on far into forever. Only I hadn't told her yet.

I came back to a change in plans. Her parents begged Peta-Gay and me to move in with them. *We'll renovate, we've hired an architect, the house will be yours, no mortgage, more than enough space, the grandchildren will be close by, please allow us to do this for you.* There was only one answer.

And then there was Lena.

The letters started a week after I got home. Sagas of her life. They'd come every other day in a white envelope with red and blue perimeter edges with the words *Par Avion* scribbled in the bottom right-hand corner. Then the phone calls. Lena surprised me. I expected her to ring with hands open; *yuh cyan send dis fi mi*; *yuh cyan send dat fi mi*. She used her own money at a telephone box.

When I answered she always asked, 'Yuh miss mi, baby? Mi cyaan stop t'ink 'bout yuh.' She said she was coming to visit me one day and I said okay.

Every Friday evening just before Sabbath, after she picked up her pay cheques from Nana and the grocery store, she'd buy her phone card and call me. She told me about her day and her week, of the grocery store and *di facety custommah dem*. She was ambition on fire. She said she wanted to buy a house. She said she wanted to start a business but she didn't know what yet. Her friend who came to Miami every other week bought name brand clothes and shoes and nice smelling lotions and diapers and she was making a mint.

I said, 'Yuh mean to tell me that your friend is a higgla?' And she got quiet, so I apologised because I was judging again. I told her she should do it. I said I would help.

Eventually I let the machine take the calls and I ignored the letters. I resumed the life I'd put on pause when I went to Jamaica and I felt wholly rejuvenated. We'd postponed the wedding a couple of months because the Phillips' were unhappy with the reception hall and other minor details; I didn't quite follow. But things were back on track. I dedicated myself to the few remaining wedding tasks. I decided to rent rather than purchase a new suit. I took the organist off Peta-Gay's hands and finalised arrangements for the cake. Everything was in place. Brother Phillips even joked that all I needed to do was show up.

* * *

Then I received two letters on the same day a couple of weeks out from the wedding. The first crushed me. It was from Ms. Viola Grey, the journalist at *The Gleaner*. Her letter was to the point. She apologised for her delayed reply, thanked me for the funds to cover mailing costs, then said:

I followed up on the body of that girl in Willowdene. Turns out it was a boy. Some mix up in the press release. The parents have claimed him. He fell out of a tree on the abandoned property three years ago. It seemed there was no need to print a resolution at the time. I hope you find that girl Sasha Knight you mentioned. I took the liberty to check the name and I found no death certificate or police record so she might well be fine. Yours Sincerely…

I made some nasty and hasty remarks about Jamaican ineptness and bad governance and sloppy police work. I remember using the words 'for fuck's sake' several times. My night would have ended there, my mind filled with Sasha and the futility of my search so far and how I was ready to accept it once more. I thought of the wedding and how Peta-Gay would share my journey, that there could be new life after all and a cautious smile bubbled in me. Then I opened the second envelope without thinking.

Dear Matthew, it began. I rolled my eyes because I recognised the handwriting as Lena's: *I miss you very much. I thought you were going to write but Mrs. Johnson says that you are a busy man. I want to talk to you again. I miss your voice. You sound so sexy, Baby…*

'Oh Christ,' I said to the room. In frustration I tossed the letter in the garbage can and as I turned away I glimpsed the word at the very end of the second page, the first letter un-capitalised: *baby.*

Chapter 30

fished it out from the gravy and read the curry-stained pages in their entirety, over and over again. This wasn't the first time she'd mentioned it. It was part of a dialogue she assumed or wished we'd had.

She quoted a number of declarations from her mother that basically boiled down to: *Mummy says don't worry about the baby.* She had mentioned the mother a few times back when I was taking her calls but it was all background noise to me. I opened the living room side table drawer and the other sealed envelopes spilled out. Backward I read.

May 4. *The doctor says I shouldn't work so hard. What do you think, Baby?*

May 1. *I am supposed to get the vitamins from the pharmacy but Mummy says she going to boil this herb and if I drink it...*

April 28. April 25. On and on till finally I got to March 15. *I tried to call you, Baby, but I know you are busy with the wedding. You didn't think I know about that? Well Mrs. Johnson told me. I don't want to spoil your life, Baby. It wasn't on spite, I promise you but I missed my monthly and I started to feel throw up like. I don't want to bother you and I don't want to spoil your life. I said that already. Sorry, Baby. It's true, though. I just don't know what to do, Baby. Just call me please. I want to talk to you. Not even Mummy know yet. Call me.*

She ended with a line of exes and hearts. There was an oil stain next to *Your Sweetest Love* and when I put it to my nose it smelled of every flower ever created. I remember thinking, *she missed her monthly.* Then, *who the hell still calls it monthly?* I emailed Nana to get Lena's phone number. Two days later Nana called me collect.

'Matthew, I don't know what you said to this girl but she wants to talk to yuh. Talking 'bout some emergency but shi can't tell mi.'

'Alright let me talk to her,' I said.

'What yuh involved in?' Nana said.

'Nothing Nana. I was helping her with school work and the test coming up soon.'

'Well that's no reason for her to come in here and order me around. Put her straight for mi.'

'Alright Nana. I promise it won't be a problem. Yuh can put her on?'

'Hi, baby,' Lena said.

'Is Nana in the room?'

'No. Shi on di veranda. Yuh miss mi?'

'Well... yeah. Sorry I haven't been able to talk but yuh know... work and everything.'

'I miss you too, baby. Mi sistah send mi dis nice crib.' It was as if we'd been speaking every day for a year and she was catching me up on the last hour.

'Shhh. Why yuh talking suh loud? Listen Lena...'

'Yuh get mi letta dem yet?' She was breathing into the phone like we were old lovers parted by the winds of war.

'Yeah.'

'Weh yuh t'ink?'

'Think about what?' I said.

'Di picture?'

'I haven't opened all of them yet. Look, about this baby business. We need to think clearly here…'

'Open dem.'

'What?'

'Open di letta dem. Mi have a surprise fi yuh, baby.'

'Lena, it's kinda late right now…'

'Open dem nuh, baby?' She was all breathy and I admit I got, well, you know.

'Alright. Hang up and let mi call yuh back. This is collect.' When the phone rang she answered as if we hadn't been speaking a few seconds ago.

'Hello, baby.'

'Lena. This thing with, yuh know, the thing.'

'Yuh open di letta dem yet?' I covered the receiver and breathed out hard then grabbed the letters from the drawer and spread them out in front of me. One envelope had something harder in it, an item less pliable than writing paper. I moved the letter out of the way and there she was, pictured in a white two-piece bikini at some beach. And yes she looked good. Leggy with sunglasses and a wide brim hat. The good life fit her.

'Yuh like it? Mi tek it fi yuh. Mi guh beach all di time now sake a you.' She was still breathing hard with a laugh in her voice. I imagined her biting her nails as if secretly talking with her sixteen-year-old boyfriend that lived one town over, their fascist parents standing in the way of true love.

'Mi have another surprise fi yuh, baby,' she said. 'Mi get a visa todeh. Mi a come up tomorrow. Mi sistah a guh pick mi up. When yuh going come visit mi?'

'I... I... I'm in the middle of some important work right now.' I was stammering for real. 'Listen Lena, what have you said to Nana?' I tried redirecting her.

'Nothing yet, baby. Hold on let mi tell har right now.'

'Lena wait,' I screamed. She laughed.

'Yuh frighten, don't it?' And she laughed again. 'Mi a joke wid yuh. A lie mi a tell, mi nuh get nuh visa. Suh when yuh a come visit mi? Miss Kitty ah get anxious.'

Miss Kitty. She named her vagina! It startled me at first but she was the one who started to talk during our sessions. She taught me to say 'pussy' and 'whore' and 'cunt', to slap her backside, *slap it nuh*? Even after her I couldn't say the words without shame and then that woman at Niagara pushed me even further. So I was worried I was hurting Lena but she would cock her head and say, 'When yuh done mi nuh supposed to cyan sih down.' I slapped soft at first every time, testing her tolerance. She scolded me. 'Ah weh yuh a duh back deh? Slap di sup'n nuh man. Slap it like yuh mean it. Yuh nuh serious.' Sometimes I had to stop and regroup; I was on the brink. Then I'd start again and she'd say, 'Call mi a whore.' And I'd say, 'What?' And she'd shout, 'Say it. Mi soon cum.' And I'd say it, squeamish and tepid, the face of every woman I'd known flashing across my eyes, heads shaking side to side. 'Yuh soun' like gyal pickney,' Lena said. And so I called her a whore with bass in my voice and I called her a 'cunt' and a 'slut' with bass in my voice, and I called her Miss Kitty, 'pussy', with bass in my voice. And she'd box me, and shove me, and thump my chest. Of course I was hard again.

'Alright. Yeah. Listen to mi, Lena. We need to think about

what's best for the child, okay? And right now none of us is in a position to take on this kind of responsibility.'

'Hold on. Yuh granny coming back.'

'Okay, don't tell Nana anything. Don't say anything to anybody. Alright? I'll call you next week Wednesday at seven. Your landlady has a phone?' She recited the number and I promised to call and this time I did because she was the type to tell Nana everything. And she'd paint me up pretty badly too. She was some *gyal pon di side* I just threw away. And when that belly started getting big and she was in her tight up jeans and stretchy blouse, there was no denying that. This was the part that my *downtown-gyal-yuh-must-give-a-woman-di-wuk*-father hadn't warned me about: her writing you the letter. *Yuh going to mine yuh baby*? There was shame here, on Mummy's head, in Nana's eyes and Lena would tell Nana that we did it in the bedroom next to hers, at least five times, how I told her that, 'Nana can't hear anything, love, don't worry.' All true, but nevertheless...

I called at six fifty-nine and ten seconds. I'd hoped she wasn't there or had changed her mind. Lena answered on the first ring.

'Hello?' I heard songs in her voice, the flowers of spring in the 'lo'. 'I'm carrying your child' it said. I had worked all day with my head in another place. On my way home I mentally rechecked each milligram of every script. I tried to remember if I warned Mrs. Von Heimberg that lidocaine should be used topically. And if I didn't, she would blame the Jews in her building anyway. 'Nasty little things you know,' she'd always say and squeeze my hand.

Lena said Mrs. Dailey was at prayer meeting.

'Shi Adventist like you.'

I didn't bother telling her she'd told me all this before.

'Listen Lena, about this thing. We need to be serious and think about the life this child will have. I'm all the way in America and you...'

'Yuh going sen' fi mi?' She wasn't joking. Not one bit. This whole business was shifting, sliding, drifting from me.

'Lena. I don't think you understand, Sweetheart. I'm engaged, okay love? The wedding's in a couple of weeks.'

'Yuh gettin' married? Why yuh nevva tell mi?' And she laughed, and I laughed a little too.

'Lena!'

'Mi love weddin'. Mi have a nice likkle dress with a split all di way up, baby. Wait till yuh si mi inna it. Mi sen' yuh a picture yuh hear?' She went on and on about the dress.

'Lena, you don't understand. Just listen for one second.'

'Shi pretty?'

'What? Yeah I guess so. That's not the point, love. We need to consider every option here. We have to be open-minded.'

'I know, baby. Mi cyan wait. After di weddin' just tell di church girl seh yuh wid me now.' She was going through with it and I could tell she had visions of love child and us every month when I went to Jamaica on 'business', we three on the beach, at the mall, on a walk through Bog Walk.

We hung up and I sank into the settee, formulating the words for Peta-Gay because there was no way out now. I should've told Mummy first and maybe I should have called Daddy but I owed Peta-Gay this one thing. I'd see her on Sabbath mornings in her black pinstripe suit or a floral summer dress delivering the health segment in Sabbath School. And Dr. Phillips, soon to be Dr. Phillips-Archer because her father insisted her name be hyphenated, *who was I to argue; I am only the pharmacist after all,* was smiling at me because the wedding was in a week.

Through unearned confidence I was sure if I had one more talk with Lena there was a sliver of hope, that she'd come to her senses and do the right thing. I had the cash and there was plenty to cover the procedure and keep her rested for weeks if necessary.

Five days before the wedding Lena showed up at my condo, waiting by the door, two bags in her hand. She wasn't joking about that visa after all. She had been sitting on the steps for two hours.

'No I don't mind, not at all,' I said. I thought how lucky that Peta-Gay wasn't with me.

Lena said, 'Yuh miss mi, baby?'

For three days we went on. I'd go to work in the mornings and her sister would pick her up for more shopping, then at nights we were in bed. On the Friday morning, two days before the wedding, she sat up with her back against the headboard. I was towelling off from my shower when she said, 'Nuh marry har.'

'What yuh mean?' I said.

'Ah joke mi a mek.' She hit me with the pillow. 'Mek mi show yuh sup'n.' She was off the bed and in the bathroom in one bounce. She returned in a tight, short, beige dress, sequined to the hilt. It was hard to tell there was fabric underneath. She spun round and round. A split ran from mid-thigh close to her pelvis.

'Mi look sexy, don't?' she said. I lay back down on the bed staring at her, legs all strong. Yes, she did.

'Lena. You can't come to the wedding.'

'Yuh nuh like di dress?'

'Yes, I do. But…'

'Come here, baby.' She crawled into bed, slipped her tongue in my left ear, and pulled me on top of her.

'Lena. Yuh can't come to the wedding. I don't want to talk about it anymore, alright?' I pushed her away lightly.

'Mi naah guh seh nutten. Sorry, let me say it speaky-spokey like yuh church girl. I won't say anything dahhhling.' And I couldn't help laughing with her. 'Mi just waaan fi guh. Mi tell yuh already seh mi love weddin'. Shi don't have to know, baby. Tell di church girl seh mi a yuh cousin.' She stood again and modelled the dress for me and I understood there was no saying no to her.

Later that night, when it was fully Sabbath, I looked at Lena in my bed, her back to me, her arms bare, the blanket up to her hip. I reached out to touch her because I was beginning to think she was all a dream, but then I could smell the cocoa butter she used on her stomach and that's the giveaway isn't it, you can't smell when you're dreaming. The clock on the nightstand read 23:20 and I reminded myself there was really no need to have it in military time after all. Lena had asked what 21:08 meant when she was painting her toes earlier and it took so much effort to explain it and I said, 'It's after nine, I'll fix it.'

We slept together after that, the scent of the polish still fresh in the room.

'I love you, baby,' she said when it was over, her head on my chest. She'd grown past the beads and her hair was properly creamed. I said nothing. She played with my chest hairs, her fingers circling and circling.

'Yuh love mi?' she asked, her voice all soft and needy. She may have been crying; I felt something wet on my chest. I didn't know what to say so I lay there and asked her about how things were going with the business. I told her she was clever and she should think about going back to school. She leaned in and kissed me and said, 'Yuh don't need di church girl.' She was sulking and I was afraid that she was right, but not in the way she thought.

For an instant I wanted Sasha there in the room, she would know what to say, she always did and Lena was no match for her. The thought left me and I knew I had to face the thing I had done. What did I really think would happen here? That Lena would realise nineteen was too young an age to bring a child into the world? Most of her friends had been mothers since fifteen. That I would leave stability for chaos? She'd watched all the romance comedies and of course that would happen. That she'd have enough sense to realise I was ten years older and living in another world and Peta-Gay Phillips was a whole other level?

So I rolled over as still as possible and I called Peta-Gay when I thought Lena had fallen asleep proper.

'We have to talk,' I said, all whispery.

'I know,' Peta-Gay said, and I could hear it in her voice, all flat and monotone. It was over and I would show up that Sabbath afternoon for my dressing down. And it would be public and classy, the only way Dr. Peta-Gay Phillips could pull off, and I would take it.

Chapter 31

I dropped Lena off at her sister's before making it to church. She kissed me with purpose before saying, 'Call mi latah.'

I watched her walking away, her white jeans pasted to her skin and I was certain this was the last time I'd see her because that's how God handled things, didn't He? Remove the obstacle in the way of your miracle, and so I trudged on in renewed faith.

After church, Peta-Gay invited me to her parents' home for lunch. When we stepped through the door her entire family was there: uncles, aunts and cousins from both parents' sides. And Mummy. I excused myself to use the toilet; I was convinced I could smell Lena on me. I put my fingers to my nose. I took a quick whiff of my armpits. I even smelled my wrists. I tried to recall how vigorously I'd scrubbed down there and whether I used the mint-scented moisturiser Lena gifted me the day before. I wasn't satisfied but it would have to do because if I stayed any longer I'd definitely raise suspicions. I washed my face thoroughly, practised a smile, and took my time walking back to the living room.

Brother Phillips slapped my back as soon as I rounded the corner. He cleared his throat and the house went dead.

'God saw fit not to bless me with a son. Instead He did one better; He gave me the light of my life. Our Peta-Gay.' His glistening eyes smiled at his wife and he squeezed my shoulder. 'And God knew I couldn't raise a son as devoted and loving as yours.' He looked at Mummy and she was all teeth. 'So we welcome you to our family, Matthew, and we are glad to add our daughter to yours, Joan. Come up here Peta-Gay. Hear, hear!' Glasses of sparkling non-alcoholic apple-cider raised and clinked. Smiles and applause everywhere. Peta-Gay and I stood on either side of him with his arms around us and he was full on crying now. It triggered an explosion of tears all over the house and I was thinking we should just get married right then and there in the dining room.

I desperately wanted one more smell test but it was too late; the family had already descended on us with hugs. I said my *thank yous*, even though I sensed Lena at my heels nipping at my tendons, and I still couldn't quite shake her aroma. It should have terrified me more than it did but I liked the feeling of being marked, the warning scent to ward off all other women; *this one's mine, find your own*. And the truth is I didn't want to share Lena's smell with anyone so I wanted the family off of me. Brother Phillips cleared his throat once more and everyone began to retake their seats, but Sister Phillips walked close by and I overheard her say, 'Mark, save some for the reception.'

Peta-Gay whispered something in my ear just then that I didn't catch because one of the boy cousins, dressed in his little man suit, bow tie and all, was shaking my hand with his whole body. She made a face like I gave her the wrong answer to a very easy exam question. She turned to her parents.

'May I borrow my husband-to-be for two minutes?' She

awaited their approval before she put her arm through mine and led us to the front door.

We walked, quiet, to the lake. I searched for the right pause because lengthy silences don't make for good segues.

'I finally have you to myself,' I said when we were a couple of blocks away from the house but she didn't answer. She gripped my arm tight, so much that she almost pinched me. I matched her gait although she seemed so much faster than usual. I brushed it off as wedding jitters. I love how easy she could be, like doing the homework your teacher and all your friends said was really hard but was effortless for you. That was Peta-Gay; she didn't require work, no guessing. She was as you saw her.

I made a mistake with her once. Other than kissing we'd kept ourselves, in Mummy's words, circumspect. One evening, the week after I came back from Jamaica and Lena, I was rubbing Peta-Gay's knees in the car and her legs were opening and I was at mid-thigh, both her arms around my neck, and the bottom of the steering wheel was digging into my left hip.

I said, 'Tell mi what yuh want,' all throaty and full of certainty. I caught myself before I could say more but her legs were already closed tight. My left hand grazed her bra's wire when I pulled back.

'I don't want to spoil it,' she said. 'It should be special, love. We'll have plenty of time afterwards.' She paused and I realised too late that she was waiting on me to say I agree. 'I want it too but God will bless us for waiting,' she continued. It sounded like she was delivering her lines in a poorly written and acted Christian public service announcement for abstinence. I almost chuckled.

And so we walked that Sabbath afternoon hand in hand, old

fashioned and blessed by God. We were five blocks from the lake and I suddenly wanted to run. Her parents' neighbourhood was not so different from Cheshire Hills with its cookie cutter pastiche Mediterranean beige houses and terracotta tile roofs. The long fingers of her right hand rested warm against my biceps, and her head pressed against my shoulder, and a smile settled in my abdomen. I heard a scratching and tapping against wood and I knew what was coming and my belly was a choir of laughter.

You're back, I said. *I thought you left me for good this time.*

And Sasha said, *How come yuh suh fool*? I meant to be angry because I had so many questions. Like why she left me when I was back in Jamaica, but it didn't matter now because she was right on time.

If only I could see the water it would be perfect. I imagined myself re-baptised and Peta-Gay and Sasha watching from the shore, my white baptismal gown puffing up. Lena and the baby seemed so far away. Better, they'd fit squarely into God's plan for Peta-Gay and Sasha and me.

We sat at the first empty bench.

At its widest point the lake is a hundred feet. Behind us a paved run/walk path traced the circumference. Across the water a father tried to calm a toddler whose ice cream fell from his cone into the dirt for all the ants to consume. Farther down a couple, not unlike us, held hands as they walked. There was a flurry of activity by the boat ramp as kayakers and canoers readied themselves to row. A family of Muscovy ducks entered the water. One of the ducklings stood at the edge and watched its family wade away. It danced from leg to leg in indecision. The family was a quarter of the way across when it stepped in and paddled towards them. Peta-Gay stood and pulled a plastic-wrapped slice of bread from her purse and bit by bit she scattered it in the lake. The ducks spread out and feasted.

Sasha and I found a chick once. She mistook it for a duckling even though I told her it wasn't. We took it to River and tried to make it paddle. It flapped its unformed wings furiously as soon as we let it go. No matter how hard we tried it refused to take to water. Sasha said we should make a boat so we scrounged for tree barks and empty milk cartons. We found a quart sized orange juice box and cut it in half lengthwise and checked its seaworthiness. Satisfied, we put the chick in and we swam to the middle of the river. The little boat bobbed and weaved and the chick eventually balanced itself. We treaded water alongside it, pleased with our ingenuity.

'Wi have fi find im modda,' Sasha said. We made big plans to traverse the banks of the river to locate its mummy. But then we started to argue over which way we should go and which side we should be on and we didn't notice that the chick had fallen in. We dove deep as far as we could but it was nowhere to be found. We cried with each other that night; we wanted to send it off to heaven the right way.

I must have been full on laughing then because Sasha was telling me *yuh like girl too much* and when I looked up Peta-Gay was smiling back. Peta-Gay sat next to me: her posture perfect with hands together in the middle of her lap. For several minutes we looked on, silent, at the lake and the people and the ducks. I was still grinning when Peta-Gay said,

'Yuh ready?'

'Yeah. You?'

She played with her fingernails but she wasn't looking at her hands. I enjoyed the precarious stillness between us. I stared at her. Long black hair, naturally curly, but blown out straight that day, skin between olive and milk. She looked like a proper woman, curves and all, like bearing children would fit neatly into an otherwise uneventful day. And I could see them both, Sasha and her filling out my life. So I loved Peta-Gay as hard as I could, like loving something so perfect there can be no other thing to do. She didn't answer my question.

Sasha said, *Tell har*. Sometimes I wish she'd preface her commands with beautiful words before ordering me to do the hard thing.

Peta-Gay said, 'Matthew.'

I waited for more but that was it.

'Listen,' I said.

Mi seh fi tell har. Ah weh yuh a wait pon? Sasha insisted.

'I've been meaning to tell you…' I started.

'Am I a good woman?' Peta-Gay said. She looked like she was speaking to the lake.

'What?'

'I think I'm a good woman. I try. Don't I?'

'I don't understand.'

'It's a simple question, Matthew. Am I a good woman?' Her voice biting.

'Of course you are. Why would you even think otherwise?'

I could hear Sasha inhaling and I told her *I'm going to do it, just give me a minute*. For what's the best ice breaker when you have to explain to your fiancée yuh have a gyal pon di side, that she was marrying a *baby-faada*. Peta-Gay bit her bottom lip and I began to wonder if she'd known from the very beginning; what mistakes did I make, what were the giveaways.

'What did I tell you when we started getting serious?' Her voice was back to normal again, but I knew it was preparation for the crescendo. *Tell har. Tell har. Tell har.* And Sasha was right, I just needed to get it all out.

'I... There's this girl... I mean woman, I met in Jamaica.' Like saying woman instead of girl gave it the appropriate veneer. 'It just happened. She's pregnant. Her name is Lena.' I should have practised it before. I heard myself say, 'It didn't mean anything,' and I shook my head at the words so many men before me relied on as a palliative. The truth is, that was the best I could do. They were both silent and I didn't understand what that meant.

'Who's Sasha?' Peta-Gay said to the lake. She bawled before I could say. I didn't mean to laugh but it was going to be so much easier than I'd imagined; if she didn't blink at pregnant, then Sasha would be a cinch.

'Oh, Sasha?' My voice was all joy and Sasha was happy too.

'Yuh think I wouldn't know? Really Matthew? Is that what you think?' Peta-Gay said.

'What? No. No. Yuh don't understand.'

'Yuh listening, Matthew? Yuh listening to anything I've said? Am I good woman?' We were at the crescendo. 'I gave you my heart. Yuh hearing mi? I gave you everything.' She stopped herself and dabbed her eyes because women like her and Mummy do not share their pain publicly. And I don't know why her crying surprised me.

'No, no. It's not what you think. I mean, yeah, you're a good woman.' I kept answering her words and not the meaning behind them. 'Look, it's so much better. Oh you just don't know.' And I was laughing and holding her hand, but she didn't want to hear anything.

'Yuh think I wouldn't know? All those times yuh fell asleep and you were calling out her name. You really think I wouldn't know? I can't share you, Matthew. Yuh hear mi? I can't.'

'Hold on, Peta-Gay. Please. Okay, I'm not saying it right. Look, she's my…' and as usual I was trying to find the words for Sasha and me.

'Of course yuh can't even say who she is. Stupid me.' And she shook her head and laugh-cried. 'Carlene warned mi.' Carlene the little fucker-*Arleen a mus' a dream yuh deh dream-Carlene; Yuh don't deserve her-Carlene*. And there'd be more from her for sure. *And Carlene tell mi seh Jamaican man nuh good. And Carlene seh Jamaican man cyaan control dem self. And Carlene seh… And Carlene seh…* I was a series of prophecies fulfilled. Nevertheless, I couldn't stop laughing even though I was losing the plot and that made Peta-Gay bawl more and more. She took off walking back to the house and I followed her. She upped her pace to a run and I jogged slowly behind her, the way your friend who is faster than you lets you have the lead because they know they'll catch you anyway. I wasn't afraid anymore. We were at her house in a minute and she blocked the front door. Brother Phillips opened it and stood behind her.

'We're best friends,' I said, slightly out of breath, a cheerleader warming up the crowd for a close match against their arch-rival. 'Yes, that's it. Sasha's my best friend.' I nodded in affirmation and smiled. 'I know I should have said before. I'm sorry. It wasn't the right time. It's just… look, it doesn't matter. Now you know, alright? Now yuh know.' All the aunts and uncles and nieces and nephews and cousins pushed their way through the front door. And Mummy too. She looked cross. She'd sacrificed much to network her way into the Phillips' circle and she'd taken care of the Brother McIntosh business so the least I could do was obey. Was that too much to ask? And she'd tell me later that night, 'Suh yuh just like yuh father after all,' and hang up.

I wanted Peta-Gay to myself and I understand now what she needed me to say; tell her Sasha was over and done, you never have to worry about her again and the wedding would be on. We'd endure a bit of gossip but all that would die down when they saw our first child. Peta-Gay stood her ground with the family and Mummy so I was boxed in; I looked on both sides of me as if the wrong person might be eavesdropping and I said it for all the world to hear. 'We'll find her. Me and you, together. Yeah, me and you.'

'Find her? What?!'

I braced myself for a slap that never came. I couldn't understand why she was so angry.

'Is this a joke to yuh, Matthew? Is this a joke?'

Sister Phillips stood in front of her daughter, so I made my plea to her instead.

'Sister Phillips, you understand, don't you? Tell her. Please. She's talking to me again. I can hear her. She won't leave this time. She'll show us the way.' I avoided Mummy's eyes. And Sister Phillips shook her head. I walked around her and took Peta-Gay's hands before Brother Phillips could stop me.

Then Sasha said, *Yuh sure bout dah gyal yah, mi nuh like how shi talk.*

And I said, 'Don't call her that.'

And Peta-Gay said, 'What?' Because I must have said that part out loud. So Sasha walked over and held Peta-Gay's hand and looked up at her, held her hand like she was her mummy and they're going to Tom Redcam library to get her favourite book and afterwards they'd eat ice cream at Crazy Jim's. And they'd wait for me.

I took one step back, the second anchor in a salsa dance and Peta-Gay was with me. I said to Sasha, *I told you, we're coming for you.* Sasha was smiling but then she suddenly turned serious. Peta-Gay was looking back at Brother and Sister Phillips, and all the family, and Mummy: all their cross faces. Sasha let go of her hand and her mouth was full of air and she was leaving again and I said, 'Sasha wait.' And Peta-Gay screamed, 'Yuh calling mi her name?!' And Mummy had to hold Peta-Gay up because she was about to fall over.

'I'm not saying it right. Listen, please. Please, Peta-Gay. She was just holding your hand. Didn't you feel it? Look at mi, Peta-Gay. Please. Let's run. We can get married tonight. Don't worry about Lena. Don't you see? God worked it all out. We can leave tonight.' We were only a metre at most from my car and her body steadied and eased. Just two more steps and I said, 'Me, you and Sasha. We cyan run from blackheart man.' And I saw light in her eyes but the light was water and I couldn't understand why she was still crying because I told her the whole thing. I begged her to come but she stood there bawling. The family had their hands on her and I wanted to fight them all and I begged Sasha to help me like she did with Brother McIntosh but she said, *mi tell yuh 'bout har* and she was gone again.

Chapter 32

I thought I broke one of the bottles; the tenth one. That same night when Peta-Gay wouldn't come with me. I was standing in front of the linen closet counting them over and over. A sharp line, perfectly straight, etched diagonally from the top right corner to the bottom left. It refracted the liquid and made the perfume seem like there were two bottles in one. It disturbed me. I felt like I'd carried them all these years only to drop them as I reached the end. All of them crashing down, splinters everywhere, and then I wondered if they were spoiled, rotting, foul. It never occurred to me that there must have been expiration dates that had long since passed and here I sat hauling these things like a pregnant woman refusing to give birth to the still child inside her. I looked at the used ones June Taylor sprayed all over herself and for the thousandth time asked why I couldn't bring myself to replace them. I began to hate her and love her, and I was sorry all over again. I scrutinised this scratched bottle and stepped away for a minute. I felt it all untangling and I willed myself to keep it together for one more hour, day, year.

There would be no wedding of course. Mummy stopped talking

to me because of Lena and the baby but mostly for holding on to di foolishness. Daddy called several times but I let the machine take it.

'Yuh alright, man? Just making sure everything copasetic,' he said each time and I knew Mummy told. Whatever she said about me must have been serious enough to risk having one of his girlfriends answer his phone.

I meant to call him back, but I was thinking Peta-Gay and all of them took Sasha away from me and he should have been there because I knew he'd have my back.

'If yuh need anything just call mi…' he said in one of the messages. He paused and ended with, 'Sometimes life complicated… Just call mi when yuh ready, alright?' I almost picked up then, but it was too late. This was the beginning of my final descent.

Chapter 33

It wasn't long after the wedding disaster that Lena started calling me again. This time round I answered every time. She said her *Hi babys* and *Yuh miss mi's*, and I let her talk. She mentioned some overly complicated plan to go to Canada that involved me investing in a fast food franchise (I wasn't really listening), and how it was getting more and more difficult to get around now that she was big. Every other week she changed friends because the ones before turned out to be liars or jealous. She asked me about my days. I said fine or okay or good, and she was glad to go back to her stories of backstabbing former friends and 'bad mind people'.

We got on well for a few weeks before we began to argue. She said I was using her up and 'if yuh t'ink yuh goin just throw mi weh yuh have anodda ting comin.' She'd apologise and in the next sentence tell me that I still loved 'di church girl'. And right after, she'd remind me that I was the one who wanted to get rid of our child. I told her she didn't understand.

'I was only suggesting that we explore all options,' I said.

Then we argued over the name of the child. I'll take the blame for this one because I could have been more reasonable. There were things, though, she couldn't understand, events that lined up just so.

'Name the baby after yuh dead frien'?' Lena said when I told her *Sasha*. It was the first time I pitched the name. Not exactly pitched, more like insisted.

'Lost, not dead. I told you before.'

She stopped calling for a while after that. She was punishing me because she claimed I raised my voice at her. As I said, there were things she couldn't understand. Like when I began to suspect that the child that grew inside her was Sasha. I called Lena every weekend after that. I insisted on the most minor of updates. Is your hair still brittle? How much did you eat today? She was always throwing up so I even demanded she measure her emesis.

She told me of her weekly visits to a local clinic. I pictured packed waiting rooms and a queue stretching outside and around the building, the sole overworked doctor in an underfunded and undersupplied surgery barely keeping up. There would be days when Lena couldn't be seen because there were too many others that needed his attention. So I checked around for the best gynaecologists and found Dr. Beverly Silva at Medical Associates in St. Andrew. I set up Lena's appointments and paid the doctor directly. I even secured the taxi ride from Whitecastle.

I sent Lena bags of vitamins and supplements only to be informed she was selling the things as part of her *higgla* business. I doubled down. I flew to Jamaica one weekend and watched her take the pills myself. She changed towards me then. No *I miss you, baby* or anything. She refused to let me touch her stomach so I could feel Sasha kicking. I eyed her taut belly and I saw Sasha spinning around, calling out to me. I almost touched it once but her mother stepped between us and asked me to leave. It didn't help that her mother's boyfriend was standing off to the corner peeling an orange with a pocket knife and staring me down the whole time.

When I returned to America, I showered Lena with kindness. I sent her blankets and sheets, the high thread count kind, and lotions. And not just her. I gave her mother and sisters shoes and towels. Pens and pencils for their children and grandchildren. I sold the double bed in the guest room and set to work filling Sasha's bedroom with onesies, bibs, crayons, markers, teddy bears, a stuffed Big Bird, and a Cookie Monster, gargantuan packs of nappies, wet wipes, baby powder, baby oil, dresses and one of those high-end Victorian prams with the horse-drawn carriage wheels. And so I held out in anticipation for the one happiness I had left. I waited for Sasha to come.

My days were filled with stupid grinning at work. Still, I kept my joy close to my chest. I wanted to hold her, feel her weight and the wriggling body as she tried to find the most comfortable position. I dreamed of fishing, hiking and camping together. I researched the best ballet schools, the latest learning aids and the top pre-K programmes. I purchased every Mozart concerto and symphony to mould my Sasha's developing brain. I checked out all of Dr. Brazleton's books from the public library. I would make it right this time. She wouldn't have to wash anybody's clothes or peel yellow yam or sweep out the house. She could play and sing and nobody would stop her.

And what did I receive for my hard work and care? Constant complaints. Lena claimed that I was trying to control her. She said she knew what she was doing, that, 'Yuh betta watch it or else.'

I took the threat to mean she'd keep Sasha away from me.

I signed up for an international calling plan so we could speak every night. That would show her. My interrogations intensified. Did she see Dr. Silva at regular intervals? Was she taking the other supplements I recommended? Was she eating fruit and vegetables? Was she getting enough fresh air? 'Are you taking the tablets?' 'Have you been walking?' 'Yuh staying away from smokers, right?' 'Yuh not drinking, right?' 'Yuh wearing the slippers I sent yuh?' 'Yuh using the mosquito net?'

Her reply was always the same. 'Yuh cyan do it yuhself.' After which she exploded in laughter.

I failed to see the humour in any of it but I'd learned to walk a bit of a tightrope with her. She parsed every word and tone for what I assumed were any indications that I'd leave her in the lurch with a fatherless child.

With two months to go I was tempted to tell Lena what a precious thing she carried because I feared she'd harm herself in some way, not intentionally, only through her carelessness. However, I balked at the thought of burdening her with the weight of the child's significance to me. In the meantime I told Sasha I was going to get her out of that dark place. *It won't be long now*, I said, *you'll have your new body soon*. She didn't answer, though, but I didn't mind.

So I bit my bottom lip and held my tongue when Lena annoyed me. And then I stepped in it. Big. I suggested, perhaps more forcefully in tone than my actual words intended, that maybe the child should be in my care when she was born.

'She?' Lena said, 'Wha mek yuh t'ink is a girl?'

I had just completed a double shift after one of my staff called in sick.

'Trust mi, it's a girl,' I said. 'I still don't know why you can't simply ask the doctor. Oh and by the way I spoke with Dr. Silva and she says you haven't been to see her in a month.'

'Mi nuh like har.'

'Why don't you like her? She's the best in Jamaica. You don't have to pay anything. I told you already that it's all taken care of.'

'Mi seh. Mi. Nuh. Like. Har.'

'Alright then.' I paused. 'Yuh know I was thinking that with your situation the baby might be better off with me.' Of course I didn't quite say it like that. I began with a polemic on fathers who abandon their children and devolved rather quickly into a slight on her fitness as a parent. She called me a pussyhole and I said, 'You're proving my point.'

'Sorry lovey, I meant to call you a fucking pussyhole. And yes mistah man I can be speaky-spokey like yuh church girl.'

We didn't talk for a week.

The closer we got to the time the more I believed she knew the baby was Sasha and she'd use that to blackmail me, hold her hostage to gain my love. On one call I asked if she'd decided where she was having the baby. By then she'd moved to Kingston so one of her sisters could help when it came time to deliver.

'Mi naaah worry 'bout dat. Nuff hospital 'bout di place,' she said.

I was horrified. What kind of medical care would she get at KPH's Jubilee Hospital? I could see her then, swollen belly, on a gurney in the hallway waiting patiently on the one and only OBGYN slated to deliver twenty other babies that night. Would Lena remember to bring her own toilet paper? I should be there, I thought. I believed her competency in bed was inversely proportional to her ability to handle the complications of birthing a child. Sure her mother would be there but if that mother was anything like Lena – and I was convinced she was – she'd show up in jeans and tell her daughter everything is alright before heading off to get her hair or nails done. They couldn't be trusted, the lot of them. I kept my head, though.

I called a few friends I still had in Jamaica and asked them to look in on her, discreetly of course. 'She's a girl I'm helping get back on her feet,' I said. I pre-arranged with Nuttall Hospital to handle the birth because I refused to have Sasha delivered at Jubilee.

Then one morning a few days before Lena was due, she rang me at work and said, 'Call mi back, the phone card soon finish. Call mi!'

I dropped everything and hurried home.

'Hi, baby,' she said when she picked up. She was breathy, not sexy breathy, though. 'Dem carrying mi now. Sorry, baby. Mi really sorry.' She began to moan, a long monotone drone. I wanted to tell her I was sorry too, that I took back every harassing word, that maybe Sasha can be her middle name even though I didn't mean it.

I booked the first flight to Jamaica that night. My thoughts swam of Sasha swirling around and calling out to me. All the rental cars were sold out so I had to take a taxi to Jubilee. I ran in and left my bags on the seat.

'Maternity ward,' I shouted at the receptionist.

Without looking up she said, 'This is a maternity hospital, sir.'

I gave her my name then Lena's. She pointed to her left.

I ran with everything, my hands growing heavier with each step, as if birthing Sasha myself. When I saw the attending nurse she said, 'Sorry, we tried our best, but we could only save one.'

'What yuh mean?' I asked but she wouldn't say more. Young

women with nice round firm bellies filled the hallway. Some were sitting and others walking with what looked to be friends, sisters, mothers or grandmothers. I was the only man there and they gave me angry looks. The nurse guided me to the room. There were two beds side by side surrounded by families. The scent of an aggressive cleanser burned my nostrils. Right by the second bed, its curtains drawn, Lena's mother and sister sat with red eyes. I held them both and told them sorry. I said it over and over and they sobbed into me. I told them everything was going to be alright, that I'd take care of her.

'I give you my word. Can I see her?' I said. I should have been more solemn but I was going to see Sasha again and although I was trying not to be too happy, to laugh on the world, I couldn't hold back the smile.

So Lena's mother pulled back the curtain and Lena was still there, so I stormed out and called the nurse. I took her to the room and asked why she wasn't covered. The nurse looked like I was trying to abduct her but I didn't care.

'Cover her up,' I demanded. 'Yuh just making it worse for us.' Then I felt a hand in mine, roughish with cold fingers.

'Hi, baby. Mi sorry. Mi sorry. Mi sorry.' Lena was alive and I was thinking it was a miracle, that someone's prayers were answered. God was smiling on us. Lena was still saying sorry and she was crying like she wanted to bawl but she didn't have any more water left.

'Yuh forgive mi?' she said. And I understood it all then. The red eyes, the miracle that wasn't a miracle, *We could only save one.* They had chosen for me, her mother, her sister and KP fucking H!

I fell to the floor, laid flat. Lena's people encircled me and patted my head and rubbed my chest. They told me I'd be alright. But

I wouldn't move and the hospital sent two men to haul me away. They made me stand and they helped me into the hall and I saw all the taut bellies from before, all of them with Sasha swimming around. I grabbed the first woman, a child really, young and thin and terrified. I touched her belly.

'Sasha?' I said. 'Sasha?' And the men pulled me off, and I went to the next woman and the next and I called out to all the bellies there, 'Sasha, answer me. Sasha. Sasha. Sasha.'

Chapter 34

There are two boys at the gate, the same ones who opened it for the principal's car earlier, first and second graders it looks like, holding each other's hands like their mummy must have told them to. After they close the gate, they re-join the queue like the good children they are, watching the principal's car like it's their duty. They look like they can't wait to come in. I want to tell them to go back home, that there's sorrow here, that this lot has a black cloth over it. Mostly I want to tell them that this is my place and my time. I don't want to share it.

I hear the steady coughing of the digger's muffler. I see police lights. I smell orange peel. Graeme is mouthing something to me.

'What is it?' I say and cup my right ear.

'Just waiting on some paperwork,' he says.

'I thought everything was a go,' I say.

'Don't worry, man. Just a little paperwork, that's all.' He walks away.

I'm looking at the top edges of the orange sun on its way to cover Jamaica. I need something to happen, someone to start doing. We've been here over an hour and we've managed to cordon off the back half of the parking lot. I feel like running and jumping. *Wait*, she says. *Ah soon come.* And I smile. It's finally happening.

Chapter 35

Mummy came for me the day after my implosion. They said I'd frightened everyone, that I wouldn't let go of the girl's belly. I don't recall which one. It took them an hour to unhitch me from her. I thought I'd let her go. I told them I didn't mean to. 'You don't understand, it's Sasha, though.' And they nodded and said, 'Yes sir.' 'Is that so, sir?' 'Could you step this way please, sir?'

There was no avoiding hospital this time. I gave the nurses my arm and they pumped liquid in, good calming mind deadening goo. Weeks passed as I sat in a room, my head cloudy, Mummy coming day after day when the patients gathered in the room designated for communal family visits.

I don't remember everything that happened there, only that we patients kept to a rigorous schedule. I was ordered to do this or that and I did it because the orderlies who kept a keen eye on us took great pleasure in restraining the uncooperative.

When they let me out I saw my therapist every week, on time like I'd promised because I didn't want to go back to that mausoleum. I told her about Sasha.

'She isn't real,' I said all meek and earnest. 'I'm sorry I made her up.'

'Now Matthew, remember we talked about the steps in the grieving process?' Dr. Miller said. I nodded. 'What number is denial?'

'One,' I mumbled, my head down.

'It's okay to go back for a while if you like.'

'No, no. You're right. She is real. She ran away. She is... was... eleven.' I paused and said it again with certainty this time. 'She is real. She ran away. She was eleven.'

'Exactly. Now Matthew...' I knew what she was about to ask and I dug deep. 'Is she talking to you now?' Dr. Miller held my gaze. I promised Mummy, swore on my life, that I'd say if I was hearing Sasha. I thought of that cold mad prison they called a retreat, and I couldn't go back because Sasha didn't like it there. And I wanted to stay in the office with the big smiling lady and the warm lights and the candle on the ledge. She needed to know the medication was working.

'No. She isn't.' I mustered every strength I had to sound convincing.

'That's right, Matthew. That's right. You did that because your mind needed a way to deal with a terrible trauma.'

'Yes, Dr. Miller.'

'And what was the trauma, Matthew?'

'Sasha...' I couldn't say it.

'Matthew?'

'I...'

'Your childhood friend running away and leaving you. Remember?' I lowered my eyes. 'If you want to get better you will have to accept it. And you get better by making new friends. Right?' Dr. Miller looked serious and tender at the same time.

So I took my pills like I agreed to and I returned to work.

My colleagues asked me about the 'accident', and I said I was fine now. Of course Mummy checked in with me weekly for the first few months. Every Friday evening just before Sabbath she let herself in and more often than not she found me on the settee staring at nothing. She brought me food for the following week and hired a cleaning company. Slowly, though, over the next two years I gradually morphed into normalcy. Mummy's visits reduced to once per month then once a quarter then she returned my key.

And so I plodded on. I had a series of brief affairs, each subsequent one increasing in insignificance. I floated through life comfortable in my daily routines. I was promoted twice. I joined a gym to bulk up my thin arms and legs. I co-wrote a paper for the annual convention of the Florida Pharmacy Association on the death of independent pharmacies in rural towns. A few people asked polite questions.

The baby things languished in Sasha's room for months before I donated them to my brother. He was on his third by then. I was neither happy nor sad and I suppose that suited me just fine.

After Mummy stopped checking in so often, I secretly hired a portrait artist, Jace, no last name, simply Jace, to do a few paintings of Sasha. I kept them in a climate-controlled storage unit a half a mile from my condo. But none of the renditions were quite right. The eyes were too brown, the lips too thin, her smile too much like a grin. The yellow should have been lighter or darker or it was too orangey.

We were on number forty when Jace said, 'I can't do this any longer. This child is beginning to take over my life.' I paid him and we parted ways. I couldn't stand to look at them, so I destroyed the lot.

I joined a local theatre group and volunteered as a stage hand. Occasionally I landed a one-line speaking role.

I cycled. I swam. I read.

I remodelled the condo, room by room, until I completed the entire thing.

'Minimalism,' the architect said, 'requires a disciplined mind.' I filled the space with white ash floors and white cabinets and no accessories. I overpaid for everything, but it looked magazine worthy.

Then I discovered gardening. I filled in a small patch of land at the back of my ground floor unit. At first I planted varying perennials, Blue Speedwells, Russian Sages and Jewels of Ospar. The disallowed dogs treated them like prey so eventually I ditched them. My next-door neighbour, an environmental fundamentalist, put me on to native grasses, but they grew at a phenomenal rate and I quickly lost control.

Through pure serendipity I happened upon a book on Japanese gardens at a garage sale. So I replaced the plantings with a rock and gravel landscape that fit my newly redesigned apartment. I raked the gravel every morning and evening. Sometimes I'd shape it into an animal or a slice of bread just to be silly. I liked the crunchy sound it made when I walked on it and I'd spend hours using the rake to comb and re-comb so I could hear it.

One afternoon I got into a tiff with my neighbour directly above me. She took to experimenting with her green thumb on her balcony and had been quite liberal with her use of potting soil. Bits of the black dirt fell through the railing and on to my gravel garden. I lodged a complaint with the condo board, but the president said that it seemed like a problem best handled informally between neighbours. I chose to ignore my neighbour and began the daily chore of shovelling the black dirt away and topping off my white gravel, raking it into perfect concentric circles.

I went away one weekend on a training session and when I returned there was a trapezoid mountain of black potting soil in the middle of my garden. I was going to head straight up and give her a proper talking to. However, as I stood there, more dirt came down on the mountain like a light drizzle. I stood hypnotised.

I shouted up at her, 'Pour the whole bag. I'll pay for it.'

It came down in larger clumps, like shovels of brown sugar, building up and up. It wasn't enough. I bought three more bags and emptied them on the mountain. It was five feet high when we were done. A week later I received a 'this is just a gentle reminder' letter about the state of my garden from the condo board.

One evening I came home and the mountain was gone. Only a messy rice-looking collage of black dirt mixed with white gravel remained. A hole drilled deep inside my heart and I cried for hours. There was an image that twirled around in my chest that I couldn't quite realise. It was like being on the cusp of the perfect high that never materialises.

I tried and failed to shake the sensation. I sketched the image over and over on blank sheets of artist paper. I lacked the talent so I used a drawing software to replicate it on my computer. Nothing worked. Evening after evening I'd stare at the spot where once stood the black dirt mountain. I walked around to explore it from varying angles. It was no use. I needed the soil again. I elicited my upstairs neighbour once more and in her dementia she was all too happy to help. She rained it down from her balcony.

'More,' I said. 'More.' All night we went.

We were at five feet again and I said, 'Stop.' I walked around. The feeling that I was close returned.

She looked over the balcony and said, 'It's not finished.' Then she emptied the next four bags and some of it fell on me, cool black potting soil, and I had it.

'More,' I said. 'Pour more on me.' And it came down in a storm. I danced in the black dirt rain. I spun and spun because I saw the whole thing then, well most of it; the Macca tree, all the wheels and tyres rolling and turning when Mr. Davis used to ride up and down North Avenue; the bicycle man with the sack whose contents I had to get to; the pink blanket protecting the woman-not-a-girl in my room that day I fainted. So I danced and laughed and cried. Five and a half feet, six feet, six and a half feet, and I couldn't stop laughing. I couldn't stop crying. I was taking my medicine like I promised and I couldn't stop.

'Thank you,' I said. 'Thank you.'

My neighbour came down. 'Did I do it right?' she said.

'Yes. Yes. Yes,' I said. 'You've done it right. Don't you see?' I retrieved a blanket from the linen closet and placed it in her hands. I pointed to the black dirt mountain, the car tyres in the parking lot, the oak trees, and then the blanket. Once. Twice. Thrice. 'See?' I said. 'See?' And she nodded like she understood. I rolled the dirt around in my hands and made little dumplings and crushed them into soil again. I let it sift through my fingers. 'Don't you see? I found her. I finally truly found her.' And I was laughing and weeping.

Chapter 36

They say you can never go home again. But I wonder if we ever leave. We carry bits of it everywhere we go and it takes little to bring us back: an accent, a smell, a note in a song. We come home because we've left someone behind and they won't allow you to. They scream and holler. They hitch themselves to your back for a *jackey ride* and you take them to Beijing, Sydney, Nigeria. Heaven.

So here I am today in a parking lot big enough to hold fifty cars that's mostly used by children playing *stucky* at recess. I have come here to lose Sasha forever because I must live. There's no hiding now, no stuffing it into a tight rubber band ball. There's no one to fear here, no police to paddle me, not Mummy, not anyone. *Ah cyaan get beat'n from nuhbody.* I can hear decades' worth of bells ringing because lunch time is over. The good students skip back to class on cue but the less mindful don't hear it and the vice principal's belt is out. I think now how much they've trampled on her in those twenty-four years of thirty-minute recesses and little feet. Twenty-four years of boys and girls screaming, 'cree'. Twenty-four years' worth of bloody noses because somebody didn't follow the rules or someone hits too hard.

I think of all the cars with their transmission fluid and oil leaks seeping into the ground, changing the dirt, distorting its character. Has she changed too? We're almost at the edge of the building and someone says, 'Yuh too close to the foundation.' I hadn't thought of that. The digger operator, his name is Denton, scoops out the first layer without answering, and I realise it isn't asphalt but marl with a thin layer of tar. He swings the digger scoop right, trying to find a spot. It looks like ice cream searching for a cone. On and on it scrapes away, the hole growing wider and deeper.

The children are steadily making their way to school; clusters of three and four. A group of girls, five wide, arm in arm, stride in rhythm, their legs kicking up and out Rockettes style. They sing as they move along, 'Anybody in wih way, wih kick dem down.' One boy walks too slowly with his back to them and it's too late when he feels their legs on his bottom. He stops to fight but they are too many and the digger is proving more fascinating than revenge. A teacher guides them to class.

In five minutes the campus has gone quiet as children get to the business of homework collection. The sun's out and it's warming quickly. The small crowd is now within the gates. Their eyes follow the digger. They are here because, despite what the sign says, public works do not require five police officers standing guard.

I watch the crowd draw closer and closer, leaning on the tape, almost snapping it. They whisper their suspicions to each other. I tell Detective Sergeant Graeme, because that's what he wishes to be called in front of the men, that I worry about the damage the digger will do. He says I need to stop fussing. He has made up his mind about all this. He doesn't believe me, and I know he's going to tell Mummy even though I've sworn him to secrecy. Regardless of my agreement to pay off the Saab he got on hire purchase a year ago; or the five thousand US dollars I gave Denton, his brother-in-law, to bring his digger and the five hundred dollars each I have shelled out for the other police. I should have come by myself with pick axe and shovel and scaled the fence one Saturday night. I would have been gentler and quieter with none of these gawking faces. She is a spectacle to them.

'Wait,' Graeme says to Denton. He motions to two men with spades. I move with them, but he puts his hand on my chest. I can only see the top half of the men. Grains of dirt jump out in even wedges. They stop and one of them calls Graeme over. He tells me to stay where I am, but I don't. That woman from before shouts, 'Nutten but dirt and dry up bone, Lawd, dirt and dry up bone.' I see a piece of cloth, once pink, blackened with red dirt. I see the strings at the edges and I jump.

Twenty-four bottles. That's what I have on me. I bought this last one yesterday morning at the same Ammar's store as the first one. There are newer and nicer faces at the counter. I tell the young woman, 'It's over. I'm home and it's finally over.'

She smiles all gracious and hands me my credit card and says, 'Next,' before I can continue. The bottle is green like spring, full of hope, green like grass. And the tree is growing, leaves spreading. And now the hole in the ground and the wheel...

I look on that great big hole and I understand it. All the scattered pieces have fallen into place; the picture is whole. I can no longer avoid it. I have become untangled. If I am to have peace, if Sasha is to have peace, I have to bring it all back, the thing I would not remember. I must face the end.

That morning we were to meet, Sasha and I. 'Scull school,' is what she said. I devised the plot to trick our parents into thinking we were where they supposed us to be. I don't believe we had any detailed plan beyond our meeting. Only that we would run far, far away. She would leave that morning and go to school and pretend she was sick. They'd send her home but she would walk around the neighbourhood until I could get back. Meanwhile, I left with Mr. Carpenter. He dropped me off at the usual spot a few blocks away from my school. I watched him follow the turn in the road on Hanover Street and I waved down a taxi. At the terminal I took a second taxi back home.

Sasha was supposed to meet me at the gate because Ms. Sheldon was the only one in her family with the key to the house. When the driver dropped me in front Sasha wasn't there. He asked if I wasn't going to school, so I told him I was sick. He shook his head and drove off. I became angry because Sasha was taking too long. I warned her not to walk too far, that I would be there soon. But she was always late. I waited at the gate for a minute but I didn't want any of the adults to see me or they'd tell, so I made my way inside.

I put the key in the lock but it wouldn't turn. I thought I'd broken it and I was fretting about how I was going to tell Mummy all this, to explain why I was in the house at eight thirty in the morning when I should have been submitting my Maths homework to Mrs. Williams. I was causing Mummy to spend money again, *nothing but a money pit, eat too much food, growing too fast, every six months buying a new pair of shoes*. And I was beginning to change my mind because we shouldn't run away after all.

I pushed down on the handle and prayed. The door opened

wide. Dust particles floated in the streaming sunlight. With relief my key slid out. Someone had left the door unlocked and if Mummy found out there would be hell to pay. I planned to secure it on my way out. I meant to pop in a minute, use the toilet, and look out for Sasha from the kitchen window. The place was dark like I expected, all the curtains drawn and windows closed. I shut the door because of the flies. Outside, to the right, beside the crotons, there was the unfinished trench Mr. Bailey was digging. His wheelbarrow and shovel leaned against the fence in the front yard. Mummy was going to tell him to move it again. 'Put it in the back yard,' she'd say. There was no need for the whole world to know she was having work done.

I heard voices in the house, a man and a woman, arguing.

'A weh yuh a guh duh?' the man said. I knew that voice. It was Ms. Sheldon's boyfriend Mr. Bentley. Someone answered and I was going to call out, 'Sasha,' but the voice wasn't hers.

'Guh get the wheelbarrow a di gate,' the woman said. I didn't recognise that person.

'Jesas, Jesas, Jesas, a weh yuh get mi into, woman? What kinda a shit yuh get mi into?' Ms. Sheldon's boyfriend said.

'Bobby. Mi seh guh get di wheelbarrow.'

I ran to the kitchen to hide. We were being robbed and they would kill me if they knew I was there. And Mummy would blame me. *Serve yuh right*, she'd say. *Why weren't you in school like yuh supposed to be, hmmm*? So I was waiting there, still, in the kitchen, with pee stretching my bladder. Silent like we were playing the quiet game now. Fingers on lips, fingers on lips.

I was in my khaki shirt and short trousers and brown shoes and socks under the chopping table in the corner by the fridge. I wasn't fooling anyone because the knapsack wasn't big enough to mask me, but I covered myself anyway. I crouched foetal-like waiting for them to leave.

The woman was telling Ms. Sheldon's boyfriend, 'Bring it up more. Yes, right deh suh.'

They were dragging something along the floor, something soft and heavy because I could hear Ms. Sheldon's boyfriend say, 'Bwoy dis heavy.' And I realised afterwards that he wasn't saying *bwoy dis heavy* he was saying, 'bwoy shi heavy.' Bwoy Ms. Sheldon was heavy and he couldn't manage her.

And I can hear that woman's voice, 'Put yuh back inna it. Awright shi inside now.' And they closed the door and I heard the click-click of the key locking. I didn't want to look but I had to make sure they were gone; I was hoping Sasha didn't come now, since they would kill her too.

Stay Sasha, stay, I was thinking, *don't move I'll be outside soon.* Then I thought they'd be back to complete the robbery; the TV and the record player were still in their corner and I was sure Mummy's window air con unit would fetch a mint. I kept on willing Sasha to stay. I shouldn't have been worried since she was always savvier than me; she understood danger, its shapes and forms, its faces and rhythms. So I waited on forever to pass before I stood in the kitchen and looked through the window.

They were still there in the front yard with the wheelbarrow and Ms. Sheldon's pink blanket covering her. They were struggling because the tyre wasn't fully inflated and the wheelbarrow wobbled left and right. I watched the tyre spin and stop as they tried to work out how they'd get out the gate and up the road. That tyre with its rim full of caked-on dried cement. I felt an urge to tell them, to shout, *You're not doing it right. Mr. Bailey showed me how. You have to back up first, run a little, then you can slow down.* The woman opened the gate and Ms. Sheldon's boyfriend, his shirt stuck to his back from sweating so much, made it through and turned left. The woman looked straight at me, right straight at me and our eyes made four; I was looking at her and she was looking at me and my mouth was dry, and Ms. Sheldon was looking straight at me, but not at me because she closed the gate like it was nothing.

I waited a minute then opened the door, then the gate. I was thinking how Ms. Sheldon could change her voice, that she must have seen me and she was going to come back. There was no doubt about it. But we both couldn't tell because I should have been in school and she shouldn't have been stealing.

So I watched them walk along. They looked like a man following his wife to work, a husband so caring, so loving, that he cannot stand the thought of never being in her presence. I was yards behind them, walking close to the fences and gates in Cheshire Hills. There were white walls and white gates, yellow walls and black gates, pale blue walls and gates in the process of being hung. I walked past the empty houses with parents and children already at work and school, past the folly house at the corner of Main and Winchester, the unfinished concrete structure fighting back weeds and roots and Macca trees.

Ms. Sheldon's boyfriend tried to look back a few times, but she punched his arm and he kept his head straight. We walked past Sasha's school and I was wondering if she was upset because I'd left the house. But I had to know what they were doing with our things. I saw a little house shop and I was in new territory, a place whose roads I had never traversed. On my left was a yard with a little boy riding his tricycle round and round in the driveway and he paused at the gate and smiled with me, but I put my fingers to my lips and he kept on pedalling. The streets were vacant like my neighbourhood. An old truck laden with bags of concrete and rebar drove by me. I hid behind it until it overtook Ms. Sheldon and Mr. Bentley and the wheelbarrow that no longer wobbled. It rolled along smooth on that half-inflated tyre. Then they turned right like this was the place they'd planned on all along. He struggled to get the wheelbarrow up a small mound of compacted dirt. The breeze that dried his sweat tamed and he was dripping again. In a moment he was over the mound and I had to run to catch up.

When I reached the property, it was a forest of Macca trees and that other tree that looks like tamarind. The place was big and they were way ahead at a spot that seemed right to Ms. Sheldon. They whispered but they didn't need to because no one could hear except me. She handed him a shovel and I wondered where she found it because she didn't have it in her hand when I saw her leave. He dug like he willingly offered his body to some greater force, like he'd come this far and now that he was committed he was going to do the best job he could. He dug up nice neat chunks of dirt; down, twist, dump. Down, twist, dump.

I was standing behind a Macca tree, its prickles scraping and scratching my legs and arms. Standing in my shoes and socks and holding that pee in. I watched Ms. Sheldon watch her boyfriend dig a hole. Spoonsful of red dirt laying the foundation for a small mountain. *There was a little tree, all in the wood, the prettiest little tree that you ever did see*. Down and down he went, and I hid there. *The tree in a hole and the hole in the ground*. I hid with the scrapes turning into welts that morphed into cuts that made droplets of blood run down my legs and arms. *And the green grass grows all around, all around. The green grass grows all around*. More and more red dirt; it was coming fast and steady, like red curry powder geysering out of the ground.

Ms. Sheldon's boyfriend grew shorter and shorter the deeper he went. Macca trees everywhere. *And a hole in the ground.* I can see it all in front of me now. I am hiding, always hiding. Ms. Sheldon's boyfriend unwraps the pink blanket. And he picks up that body, that body in her uniform and her shoes that Mummy gave her that don't fit right. And her brown socks. He lifts her like chopping wood, like he's taking her to make a good roaring fire that you roast yellow yam and fish on at a social one Saturday night after church when your friend is caught with a girl and she will be forever dead to God. He lifts her like she's five pounds, he could just sit on her and watch her squirm; he doesn't know how strong he is, and he's sorry because he didn't mean to. He lifts her like she's a girl who has seen the world and knows there's a better way but she can't fix it so she turns on the boy that's visiting for the summer. Lifts her like the woman you are sleeping with for fun, only fun, gyal pon di side, one juk and done, and she has lost the thing you most cherish. Lifts her like when you find out life is hard for a girl chile, and she has to be quiet, really, really quiet because no one will listen when she talks.

I left Sasha here. That's the truth of it. I must have ruffled a leaf or stepped on a stone because Ms. Sheldon's eyes arrowed in my direction and I ran all the way home and I didn't stop there; I went all the way to Old Harbour Road and into the first taxi I saw.

Last night before I came here, I dreamed of the evening Sasha never came home. Mummy had sent me to bed and I waited till everyone fell asleep and crawled out. I was shadowing Sasha from the sky, retracing the wheelbarrow and its almost flat tyre. Then I lose her in the blackness. It must be dark where she is too. There's no other way to imagine it: dark, wet, grimy, the stench of thousand-year-old moss. She's calling for help. No, not help, she must know that no one can hear her. But that's what she's doing, calling, her voice growing hoarser with every passing minute. *I'm coming* is what I want to tell her, *just wait for me, I am coming* but I have no sound, just like Camille that day.

I'm supposed to understand that it's Friday evening, Sabbath night, and I should be ready. Mummy won't let me go find her. Something has fallen on Sasha, a pebble, a rock, a grain of sand. No, not sand. I can't seem to get it right. There's no sand in this part of Jamaica. Fruits and vegetables can grow here. It rains every afternoon at two and ends at four. There are no brown patches in the lawns and the yellow, green, red fruits grow bright and beautiful, the Lord God made them all. Yes, lawns and flowers in the front yards and vegetable and fruit beds in the back, every house in every grid.

There are twenty-four grids. I found that out last year. Twenty-four years ago when we lived here, the grids were not all filled in with houses and husbands and wives and little children learning ABCs and *Mary Had a Little Lamb*; with teenage boys wanking furiously to Linda Lovelace and teenage girls dreaming of Andy Gibb. Back then, they were only carving out the lines, making mock sketches of the rest of Cheshire Hills.

She's underneath one of them, picking her way through red dirt. There's something cold on her cheek. She flicks it off and screams. Decades later she hears a buzzing coming towards her. She tries to punch the earth above, but she can feel the dirt piling on her. All the work she did before, all of it for nothing. The buzzing sound is playing a game with her. *How far you are, how far you are, how far you are, how far.* Then it gets closer, *How near you are, how near you are, how near you are, how near.* Then far away again.

The earth is in her eyes, her nose, her mouth. She must crawl back from where she came, back into the wetness and the stench of moss. She must move quickly or she won't find any more air. She digs her fingers in and pushes herself. Down and down she goes. Too fast, she's going too fast but she doesn't care because she can breathe again. Her back suddenly feels the sharp edge of a steel ladder. There's no time to wince before she's falling into the tunnel once more. Splayed on her backside, the cold water drowns her legs.

She wants to stand but her right foot won't let her. She sits for a minute and cries. She's calling, 'Mama, Mama, Mama.' She must get out of the water. A while back, she cannot tell when, she thought she heard a train, but it was a rush of water that rose to the tips of her nostrils. She tried to follow the water but her legs came loose and she swallowed a gallon. Her burning lungs forced her to reach out for something and her fingers caught the bottom rung of the steel ladder. She pulled herself up and up and that was how she reached the dirt. She coughed for an hour and she swore she'd never be caught in the water again. Yet here she is. There is no train this time. She knows she must find another way.

She pushes herself to stand. She reaches out with her right hand, nothing. She takes one step, two, three, before she feels cool concrete. It's rough. Step by step she follows along, her hands and legs guiding the way. Bubbles of gas roar through her stomach. She's hungry and feels so far away from home. We are not far away, though, only three grids to the east. She cannot know where east is. That's not how she understands the world. It's not how any of us understands our world. We make a left at the big Julie mango tree and cross Mr. Parchment's field and then go down James Street. No north, south, east, west. Her new world, the one she has been dragged into, is the same.

I walk a few metres to find her. I am calling out her name.

'Sasha stop playing around. You're being stupid.' It's getting dark now. It's properly Sabbath and Mummy wants me back home. I'll get a beating if I'm not there in five minutes, but I'm twenty minutes away in the construction zone. I stop just beyond the edge of a patch of grass and see a stick in between the two Macca trees. I get it and begin to dig. Red dirt flies in every direction. 'Sasha. Sasha. Sasha.' My stick takes me one centimetre down. The ground is too hard. Underneath she's calling my name, 'Matthew. Matthew. Matthew.' But that can't be true because no child calls after their friend when they're in trouble. I was right before. She's calling after her mother because she still trusts her. It's her mother who takes her to church. It's her mother who will make her get baptised so she can go to heaven.

She follows the concrete until she feels a cool breeze. The farther she walks the fresher it smells. Home, she must be thinking, I'm finally home. And I'm there waiting in the cool breeze. I have June plums and jacks and marbles. Come sit with me. *Long time gyal mi nevva see you, come let mi hold your hand.*

The breeze feels good. She thinks she smells curry chicken and yellow yam and boiled banana. She thinks she hears her mother calling after her. 'Yes Mama,' she says. 'Ah soon come.' She begins to run, ignoring the singeing pain in her right leg. Left foot, right foot, give a dog a bone; grandma, grandma sick in bed, send for the doctor, the doctor said; Reedim; what can you do, Puncienella likkle fella. She is running and laughing. She is going to skip tomorrow morning – jump rope with Simone, *one, two, three antie lulu* – and play one-and-twenty with the girls at school on Monday at recess. She will flick my ear and hide my pencil case. She is going to play Brown Girl in the Ring. *Show mi yuh motion,* she's singing out loud now and she sounds good for once. Me and her singing. *Show mi yuh motion,* and then she's falling. *Show mi yuh motion, Traah, la, la, la, laaa.*

I know now what happened that morning just before I came. I know because Sasha has cupped her hands over my ear and whispered it, her warm breath forcing a giggle out of me at the start. I know because she takes me there, her hand in mine and my hand in hers. I want to pee; I can hold it, though. It's her turn now. She says I must say it all, *'don't leave out nutten, yuh hear,'* the whole thing in one go or it will choke me, coming out like vomit and I'll make a mess. We walk up the driveway path. She points to the Ackee tree. Our crocus bag fort is there, untouched. Then we are in my room. I hold her hand tight now and I try to step back.

'I don't want to see,' I say. 'Please. I want to go home.' She keeps walking slightly ahead of me, her hair ribbon coming undone, and she doesn't answer. We are both barefoot and I tell her, 'We can just go now.' She still doesn't answer.

We stand and watch ourselves. She's wearing her school uniform and we're arguing over whether she should change.

'They're going to ask us why we're not in school,' I say.

'Nuhbody nuh care 'bout dat,' she says. We are running away this morning, going to Belize to be with Daddy because he said he was coming for me and when I told her she looked sad. She said,

'Belize fool like.' And I was beginning to understand that I didn't want to go without her so I said, 'Do you want to come?' And she said, 'Mi like Belize,' even though she called it stupid and fuh-fool earlier. And I didn't care. So we were going to Belize since I called Daddy collect from Andrene Carpenter's house and I asked him if Sasha can come. He laughed like always and said, 'Yuh have a little girlfriend.' I hated him for it but I wanted to go. And I had kept all the precious things in my life because we would sleep on the beach and in the rain forest and we'd feed the monkeys and live in a tree house.

And we think we have all day so we flick each other's ears and play trip. The grip is almost full when we hear the key in the door and our hearts stop. We could have left earlier but I insisted that she didn't have enough things. And I was telling her more about Belize and I was saying, 'I told Daddy you're coming with me and he says he can't wait to meet you.' We would go to Montego Bay and wait for his boat. He told me he'd be at Walter Fletcher beach and I begged her to just stay under the bed with me and then we could go and no one would know. Daddy said he'd be there the next day and I had our bus fare in my tin and I had my bank book with all the money I'd saved from Nana and Dada's Christmas and birthday presents. And money from the time I helped Mrs. Anglin graft her crotons. And money from Daddy just because. I had five years of savings because I was a good boy and it felt like I had all the money in the world. So we are hiding under my bed and we are whispering when Ms. Sheldon comes into my room and we stop dead.

'Likkle girl,' Ms. Sheldon says once, not loud, not shouting. Maybe she isn't as angry as I think she is. Maybe she'll overlook us. And I wonder how she knows to come to my room first. I feel a coolness on my hand. I look down and see that Sasha has let go and I'm still trying to tell her to just wait here, quiet, and Ms. Sheldon won't know.

'Stay,' I whisper.

Sasha shoves me and says, 'Shi goin find out, eediot.'

She's right, it's the first place parents look when they're trying to find you and they better not find you before you say. You better give yourself up and Sasha was doing right. I reach for her hand and I hit air because she's already on her way out.

Then I say, 'We can go afterwards, yuh hear?'

And she says, 'How come yuh suh fool?' She laughs loud so Ms. Sheldon can hear her.

I try to say something but I have no come back. She's cleverer than me that way, the right words in the right places. I want to tell her just then, who she really is to me but I don't know how to say it. Because who blurts out *you're my bestest friend* from under the bed even though you know you won't get to say it again?

'Mama, mi under the bed,' she says, and then crawls out. She smells funny. I know that scent. She always smells like that after Mr. Bentley leaves. And Sasha always wants to play afterwards. Ms. Sheldon is quiet when Sasha stands in front of her in my room. It's what Ms. Sheldon must have smelled on Mr. Bentley that morning; her daughter on him. And that's what she sees, Sasha *on* him. And I can see Sasha's shoes and I can see Ms. Sheldon's slippers. Two pairs of feet in a stand-off. *Run*, I say. *Please run.*

Sasha came back before me that morning like we'd planned, only Mr. Bentley wasn't supposed to be there. 'I don't want to see this part,' I say. Don't make me look. Beg yuh.' And she doesn't speak and we are in their room. I say, 'don't' and she lets me go.

So she came back earlier that morning. The small bumps on her chest weren't as small as the first time I saw her and he was looking at those bumps and I realise now that's what he was looking at in worship that Sabbath evening. Looking at them, his eyes thinking of Ms. Sheldon and her breasts on the brink of making their way southwards, of these new breasts, small bumps not so small anymore.

And I hold on to Sasha real tight and she shows me the whole thing and the cat has got my tongue and I feel warm liquid roll down my legs. Mr. Bentley leaves when he is done, doesn't say a word to Sasha, and I hear the door and it's me and Sasha's smiling and I feel happiness from her and we start to pack. Ms. Sheldon comes home and she can see it in his eyes, how sparkly and bright, hear it in his voice, all satisfied, smell it on him.

Run, I say again. *Run*. And Sasha takes off but it's too late. Ms. Sheldon pulls her hair and drags her to their room. And Mr. Bentley stands there innocent, like that night when he watched Sasha get flogged for sitting on his lap. Ms. Sheldon doesn't have time to get a switch, instead she punches Sasha, punches her like a man and Sasha falls and hits her head on Mummy's shiny terrazzo floor. I'm seeing it all and I stand still. I meant to stay under the bed and wait for her but I didn't. I looked. That is the truth. I looked and I should have said.

Ms. Sheldon didn't stop at one punch. She emptied it all on Sasha, blow after blow. And I was still standing there. And Sasha wouldn't fight. Ms. Sheldon is the only person she doesn't fight. She will take the thumps and the slaps and the punches. She will take them because Mummy knows best. This would be the last flogging and Sasha was going to learn not to be a slut. So Ms. Sheldon is punching away. Thump. Thump. Thump. Thump.

Thump. Thump. Thump. She is an artist, a carpenter, a prophet, and she is shaping that face into an angel.

The crowd beyond the tape has thickened.

'A girl!' I hear a woman say.

'Nutten but dry up bone, chile,' the woman from before keeps saying.

I ask Graeme to push them back, tell them what police always say, *nothing to see here*, but this is Jamaica. They are here to take in the whole business, Sasha opened wide to the world, but I stand in front of the hole because she will not be on display. She's someone's bestest bestest friend. The prettiest little girl that you ever did see. Beyond the crowd, the old woman at my rental car is walking away. That walk hasn't changed and I try to tell Graeme. I tap him and I hit him.

'It's her,' I say. 'It's her.'

And Graeme says, 'It looks that way. Sorry man.'

But he's not looking at my outstretched finger, at the old woman disappearing behind the crowd. I try to say her name, *Ms. Sheldon*, and nothing comes out. I want to run after her, make a citizen's arrest, but she's moving too fast, and if I go I'll miss Sasha and Graeme will take her and she will be gone forever. And that woman won't stop shouting, 'nutten but dirt and dry up bone, nutten but dirt and dry up bone.' And I know they all believe her, that there is nothing left, her uniform, shoes, ribbons, socks, that they have rotted to dust after twenty-four years but Sasha has preserved it all for me. So I turn back to the hole and it's the fine blackened string from the edges of the blanket I see first, the blanket that Ms. Sheldon's boyfriend must have left behind after I ran, and I feel better because at least Sasha is warm. They're not careful with her and I beg Graeme to take his time, but they're pulling her out like an unruly root and I push Graeme and the two plain clothes policemen with him. I shove them hard and jump in and I hold the edges of the blanket. It feels like old thick wet cartridge paper. I don't want to look but I must see. There are her shoes still laced up and loose brown socks. Her uniform isn't tight anymore. I am on my knees and I am covering her. Someone has broken through the police tape and I hear the thud of baton on skin.

Sasha is smiling wide and deep and big and I smile back. She has beautiful teeth. I hand her a June plum.

'Okay, I'll eat it first,' I say and I bite in. Juice drains down my chin and falls on the hem of her tunic. 'I'll help you wash it later,' I say.

'I knew you'd come for me,' she says all speakey-spokey.

'Don't say it like that.'

'Alright fuh-fool bwoy. Mi did know seh yuh woulda come fi mi,' she says it right this time. I'm in the hole with her. I'm here and it's getting dark, and she cannot be afraid again. I lie down in this hole, my new home. I tell Graeme he can go now. They can all go home. His mouth is wide open and he just stands there. I don't understand.

I point to Sasha and say, 'You are too skinny.' I laugh then I get serious. I can feel my bones and muscles shrink. I am nine again. I hold her bony right hand and I tell her, 'Blackheart man won't get you. All of them are gone forever, yuh hear? I'm here now. We don't have to run anymore. We can buy grater cake and sugar bun and patty and bulla and cheese,' I say.

'Wih cyan guh beach?' she says.

'Yes of course we can go. And River too. And guess what?'

'What?' she says.

'Guess nuh?'

'Why yuh love fi mek mi guess? Just tell mi, stupid.'

'No, yuh have to guess.' Before she answers I give her the other June plum, and I spill the jacks and marbles from my right pocket. I have a stuffed empty orange juice box so we can play dandy shandy later. I have an ABBA CD and I tell her it's just like a record but smaller. I have a case of yellow pencils, ten pencil sharpeners so we can draw; and the marble she gave me. I have everything we need because I'm not leaving, not again, not ever.

'We can stay here,' I say. I open the bag I'm carrying. I sing Happy Birthday. 'I forgot to give you this when you turned twelve.' All the bottles for all the years; all the letters and cards. They are with me. And I hand them to her one by one. I tell her I bought this one at Ammar's and the other one in Montego Bay. And this one when I went to Niagara Falls.

'You'll like it. It's the biggest river I've ever seen. Maybe we can swim in it one day.'

'How come yuh suh fool?' she says, and I laugh and laugh.

'You're the stupid one,' I say. 'Look at you in this stupid hole in the ground. Look at you. Tomorrow we can go to River and then church and yuh cyan show mi how to get inna spirit again.' And the hole is growing deeper and deeper, down we go, this hole in the ground, down we go into the sunshine and the breeze and the sky. And she puts her arm around me and I put my arm around her. And we are laughing and laughing in this hole in the ground and the green grass grew all around and around. And the green grass grew all around.

Acknowledgements

There are so many persons who have touched this work along the journey but I'll start with my local coffee shop, West Pecan Coffee in my home town of Pflugerville, Texas, whose beans kept me awake during those revisions.

I will be forever grateful to Clare Allan, my tutor at City University who told me, 'I love this little girl'. My dissertation advisor Jeremy Page who helped me sharpen my voice. Lisa Jennings and Ehigbor Shultz, both of whom gave me tireless feedback.

A special thanks to my uni mate Ashley Hickson-Lovence for pointing me in the right direction.

Shae Davies for fishing out the first few pages of this work from the submissions. It means more to me than words can express.

To copyeditor Deborah Blake who painstakingly converted my American English to 'proper' English. Thanks for cleaning up all the commas; you do understand I'm never going to get that right. ☺

Jason Morgan and Crystal Mahey-Morgan of OWN IT! who took the greatest of leaps; I am beyond joyful.

ACKNOWLEDGEMENTS

And lastly... to Mr. Anthony Perry, my beloved second and third forms English teacher at Calabar High School; you gave me licence to imagine. Here Sir!!

#SashaKnight

About the Author

Sean Godfrey was born in Jamaica and left the island at sixteen to join his mother in America. He has held various jobs including cashier, lab assistant and janitor. When he is not writing he works as a librarian in his home state of Texas, USA.

JAMAICAN STREET MURALS

In Jamaica, street art mural culture is a way for the working classes to celebrate and commemorate notable individuals within a community. The art may be painted on walls, or the side of a shop, or a local rum shack. The subjects may be celebrated musicians, sport stars or other notable personalities, either still living or who have passed away and who have come from the local community. They act as a beacon of inspiration to locals often having helped to benefit the community in some way by their talents or good works. This includes community leaders, called 'Dons' by some and 'gangsters' by others. The murals have been controversial to some within Jamaican society including the government, who feel that people involved in crime should not be celebrated or glorified by street art. This has led to the government cracking down and starting to paint over or whitewash the artwork of individuals who they believe are criminals.

Who is or isn't seen as a criminal is subjective, just as who may be seen as notable or worthy enough to be depicted is. What is clear, though, is the need for people in Jamaica to depict *their* heroes and heroines, and not wait for government agencies to decide who should be celebrated or have statues erected in their honour.

Street mural art has become an important way of life in Jamaica and this has inspired the cover for Sasha Knight.

ABOUT OWN IT!

A storytelling lifestyle brand, publishing and producing powerful stories across books, music, art and film. Whether publishing, representing, or adapting for Film and TV, at the heart of everything we do is a desire to share, empower, celebrate, and inspire. OWN IT! release, represents and adapts original and authentic stories.

WWW.OWNIT.LONDON

@OWNITLDN
OWN_IT_LDN
@OWNITLDN